Mari Jungstedt lives in Stockholm with her husband and two children. This is her third novel set on the island of Gotland. The previous two, *Unseen* and *Unspoken*, are also published by Corgi Books.

Also by Mari Jungstedt

Unseen
Unspoken

and published by Corgi Books

UNKNOWN

Mari Jungstedt

English translation by
Tiina Nunnally

CORGI BOOKS

TRANSWORLD PUBLISHERS
61–63 Uxbridge Road, London W5 5SA
A Random House Group Company
www.rbooks.co.uk

UNKNOWN
A CORGI BOOK: 9780552158893

First published in the USA in 2008 by St. Martin's Minotaur
as *The Inner Circle: A Mystery*

First published in Great Britain
in 2009 by Doubleday
an imprint of Transworld Publishers
Corgi edition published 2010

A CIP catalogue record for this book
is available from the British Library.

Addresses for Random House Group Ltd companies outside the UK
can be found at: www.randomhouse.co.uk
The Random House Group Ltd Reg. No. 954009

The Random House Group Limited supports The Forest Stewardship
Council (FSC), the leading international forest certification organisation.
All our titles that are printed on Greenpeace approved FSC certified paper
carry the FSC logo. Our paper procurement policy can be found at
www.rbooks.co.uk/environment

Typeset in 11/14pt Giovanni by
Falcon Oast Graphic Art Ltd.

Printed in the UK by CPI Cox & Wyman, Reading, RG1 8EX.

2 4 6 8 10 9 7 5 3 1

To my beloved children, Rebecka Jungstedt
and Sebastian Jungstedt,
who are the apples of my eye

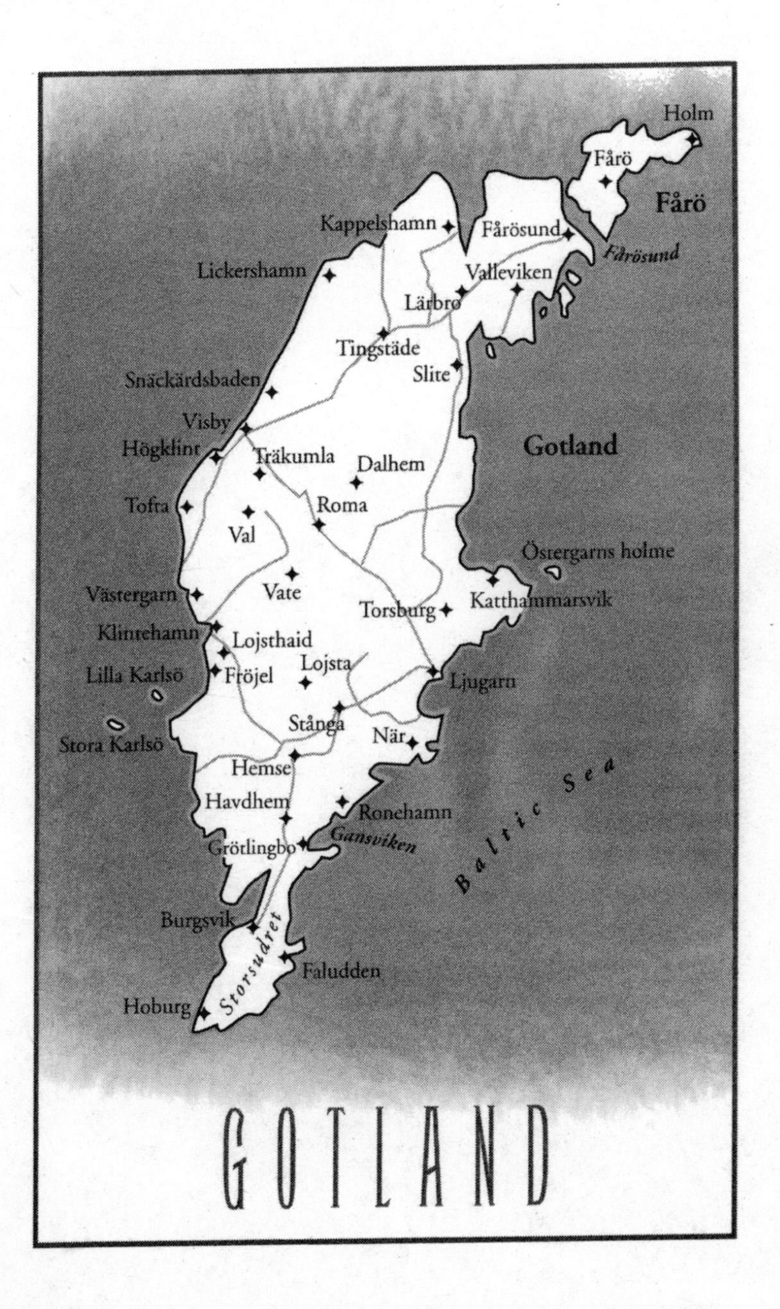
Holm
Fårö
Fårö
Kappelshamn
Fårösund
Fårösund
Lickershamn
Valleviken
Lärbro
Tingstäde
Slite
Snäckärdsbaden
Visby
Högklint
Gotland
Träkumla
Dalhem
Tofta
Roma
Val
Östergarns holme
Västergarn
Vate
Katthammarsvik
Torsburg
Klintehamn
Lojsthaid
Lojsta
Lilla Karlsö
Fröjel
Ljugarn
Stånga
Stora Karlsö
När
Hemse
Baltic Sea
Havdhem
Ronehamn
Gansviken
Grötlingbo
Burgsvik
Storsudret
Faludden
Hoburg
GOTLAND

PROLOGUE
VERNAL EQUINOX, SATURDAY, MARCH 20

From a distance only a faint light was visible. Igors Bleidelis spied it in his binoculars as the Estonian freighter passed the jetty on its way out of Visby Harbor. He was standing on deck on the port side. Dusk had settled over the desolate harbor, and the glaring lights of the ferry terminal were coming on.

The boat was moving away from the medieval city with its tall merchant houses, the ring wall twenty feet high, and the cathedral, whose black tower rose up toward the sky. The buildings surrounding the harbor seemed deserted; the windows were like black, unseeing eyes in their facades. Only a few fishing boats were rocking uneasily at the wharf.

Almost all the restaurants were closed at this time of year. Not a soul was on the streets. He saw only a solitary car waiting for the ferry down by the harbor. The city was as dead in the winter as it was lively in the summer.

Bleidelis shivered in his oilskins. His nose was

running. The air was cold and raw, and the wind was blowing, as always. A craving for nicotine had driven him out on deck. Behind the funnel he found some degree of shelter, and he dug out the crumpled pack from his breast pocket. After several attempts he managed to light his cigarette. The wind was icy on his face, and the chill air ruthlessly slipped inside his collar.

He yearned for a warm bed, he yearned to sink into his wife's soft embrace. He had been away from home for ten days, but it felt longer.

He raised the binoculars to survey the coastline. The steep cliffs dropped straight down to the sea. Beyond the harbor on this side there were only a few houses. He let the binoculars pan across the rock face. From where he was standing, the island seemed barren and inhospitable.

Darkness fell quickly. He tossed his cigarette butt overboard and was just about to return belowdecks when the light suddenly grew stronger. Flames appeared on a cliff jutting out into the sea.

He stopped and raised his binoculars once again, adjusting the focus as best he could. High up on the cliff a fire was blazing against the dark sky. Like a Walpurgis Night bonfire, but in March. He glimpsed the shadowy figures of people around the fire; they seemed to be holding burning torches in their hands. Their silhouettes were moving rhythmically, according to a set pattern. Someone held up an object and hurled it into the flames. That was all he could make out from such a distance. The next moment the freighter had moved past, and the light disappeared from his horizon.

Bleidelis lowered his binoculars and cast one last look at the rocky cliff before he opened the door to the cabin and went in out of the cold.

MONDAY, JUNE 28

Below Fröjel Church the fields of rapeseed and other crops spread out like yellow and green carpets all the way down to the sea. In one corner of the fields a motley bunch of people was digging. Occasionally a head would stick up above the tall grass whenever someone straightened up to stretch out an aching back or change position: a white cap, a straw hat, a pirate's bandanna, long hair that a woman twisted into a coil and held on top of her head for a moment in an attempt to find some relief before she let the tresses fall back over her shoulders. Beyond the bowed backs the shimmering waters of the Baltic were visible as an auspicious blue backdrop. Bumblebees and wasps buzzed among the bright red poppies; the oats rippled gently back and forth as a light breeze drifted past. Otherwise the air was practically motionless. A high-pressure system from Russia had moved in over Gotland and had remained parked there for a week.

Twenty or so archaeology students were methodically excavating what had once been a Viking

Age harbor a thousand years in the past. It was hard work that required patience.

Martina Flochten from the Netherlands was squatting down in a pit, scraping at stones and earth with a trowel. She was using the small tool eagerly but cautiously so as not to damage any potential finds. Now and then she would pluck out a stone and toss it into the black plastic bucket beside her.

Now the fun part had started. After a couple of weeks of fruitless digging, she had finally been rewarded for all her efforts a few days ago. She had found several silver coins and some glass beads. The feeling she got from holding objects that no human being had touched since the ninth or tenth century was just as strong for her every time. It started her imagination going, thinking about how the people in this place had once lived. What woman had worn these beads? Who was she, and what thoughts had passed through her mind?

Martina was one of the foreign participants in the course. Almost half the students came from other countries. There were two Americans, a British woman, a Frenchman, a Canadian whose family had originally come from India, a couple of Germans, and an Australian named Steven. This was part of his around-the-world journey; Steven was traveling to sites of archaeological interest all over the globe. His father was apparently quite wealthy, so Steven could do whatever he pleased. Martina was studying archaeology at the university in Rotterdam, and that's where she had heard about the courses in archaeological fieldwork that were offered by the college in Visby. The course was worth ten college credits, which would be accepted toward her Dutch degree. Martina was also half Swedish: Her mother was from Gotland. Although the family had lived in the Netherlands for Martina's whole life, they often came to the island on vacation, even after her mother died in a car accident three years ago. Having the chance to stay on Gotland for a longer period of time and devote herself to the most interesting work she could imagine was an opportunity she hadn't wanted to miss.

So far the training had been beyond her expectations. The participants got along well together. Most of them were her own age, about twenty, although some were older. Bruce, one of the Americans, was in his fifties and kept mostly to himself. He had told them that he worked as a computer technician, but archaeology was what interested him most. And Martina guessed that the British woman was about forty; she seemed rather odd.

Martina enjoyed this mixture of the Swedish and the international. The mood of the group was raucous but cordial. Laughter often echoed over the area as the team members joked about each other's digging techniques and varying degrees of success in making finds. So far poor Katja from Göteborg hadn't dug up anything but animal bones, which were plentiful. Her pit seemed to hold nothing else; even so, the job had to be done. So there she sat, day after day, sweating hard without finding anything of interest. Martina hoped that Katja would soon be allowed to try another pit.

The excavation course had started off with a couple of weeks devoted to theory in classrooms at the college in Visby. After that came eight weeks on a dig in Fröjel on Gotland's west coast. Since Martina was so interested in the Viking Age, nothing could have suited her better. This entire area had probably been inhabited during that period. Various digs had produced finds from the early Viking Age of the ninth century all the way up to the end of the era around 1100. The section of the excavation site where the students were now working included a harbor, a settlement, and several burial grounds. It had also most likely been an important trading center, considering all the weights and silver coins that had been dug up.

Suddenly Steven gave a shout from where he was crouching down in the next pit. Everyone went rushing over to him. He was in the process of uncovering the skeleton of a man, and he had found part of what he suspected was a circular brooch made of bronze lying near the man's throat. Staffan Mellgren, the excavation leader, cautiously climbed down into the pit and reached for a small brush that was in a bucket along with other tools. Carefully he began brushing away the dirt, and after several minutes he had uncovered the entire brooch. All the students stood gathered around the pit, watching with fascination as bit by bit the well-preserved brooch came into view. The leader's enthusiasm was infectious.

"Amazing!" he shouted. "It's all in one piece. The pin is intact, and take a look at the ornamentation."

Mellgren switched to using an even smaller brush, and with light strokes he swept away the rest of the dirt. He used the handle of the brush to point at the upper portion of the circular brooch.

"What you see here was used to hold the inner shift in place—the thinner garment that he wore next to his skin. If we're in luck, he'll also have a larger circular brooch at his shoulder. It's just a matter of continuing to work."

He gave a nod of encouragement to Steven, who looked both happy and proud.

"Proceed with caution, and don't stand too close to the skeleton. There might be more."

The others returned to their work with renewed zeal. The thought that they, too, might find something noteworthy had energized them. Martina kept on digging. After a while it was time to empty the bucket. She went over to one of the big wooden sieves that were lined up along the edge of the excavation site. Carefully she poured the contents of her bucket into the sieve, which consisted of a rectangular wooden box with a fine-meshed steel screen in the bottom. It was sitting on top of an iron bar, which made it possible to roll the box back and forth. She grabbed hold of the wooden handles on either side and began shaking the box vigorously to sift out the dirt and sand. It was hard work, and after a few minutes, she was soaked with sweat. After she had strained out the worst of the dirt, she meticulously studied what was left in the sieve so as not to miss anything of value. First she found an animal bone and then another. There was also a tiny metal object, probably a nail.

Nothing could be thrown out; everything had to be carefully preserved and documented since no one would be allowed to dig there after them. Once a site had been excavated, it was considered "disturbed" forever after; that was why archaeologists had such a big responsibility to preserve everything that might reveal how human beings had lived in that particular area.

Martina had to take a break for a few minutes. She was thirsty and went to get her knapsack with her water bottle. She sat down on an upended wooden box, massaging her shoulders as best she could and watching the others as she caught her breath. Her teammates were focused on their work, kneeling, squatting, or lying on their stomachs alongside pits, tenaciously searching through the dark soil.

She felt Mark's eyes on her but pretended not to notice. Her feelings were engaged elsewhere, and she didn't want to encourage him. They were good friends, which was enough as far as she was concerned.

Jonas, a likable guy from Skåne who wore an earring and a pirate's bandanna on his head, saw that she was giving herself a massage.

"Are your shoulders sore? Do you want me to rub them?"

"Sure, thanks," said Martina in clumsy Swedish. She knew a little of her late mother's peculiar language, and she wanted to get some practice, even though she and everyone around her spoke fluent English.

Jonas was one of her best friends in the group; they got on well together. She appreciated his offer, even though she sensed that it wasn't purely out of concern for her well-being. The attention that certain men in the group paid to her was nice, but not something she especially encouraged.

WEDNESDAY, JUNE 30

He drove the red pickup along the dirt road, sending up clouds of dust. It was very early, about 2:00 A.M. The first rays of the sun were just making their way above the horizon. The whole countryside was asleep, including the cows, who lay close together with their eyes shut in the pastures he drove past. The only movement was a rabbit or two bounding across the fields. He smoked as he listened to the all-night radio station. It had been a long time since he had felt so content.

The narrow dirt road was wide enough for only one car at a time. Here and there it widened so that it was possible to pass cars coming from the opposite direction; the passing zones were marked by blue road signs with a big white *M*. Not that it was really necessary. No cars ever came from the other direction on this road. Their farm lay at the very end; it was impossible to go any farther. When he was a boy it was not something he thought much about. He probably just assumed that everyone lived more or less the same way. It was the reality that he knew, what he had grown accustomed to.

Every time his childhood home appeared from around the last bend in the road, a touch of that old panicky feeling would arise, as if on command. He felt a pressure in his chest, his muscles tightened, and his breathing grew strained. But the symptoms quickly subsided. He was surprised that it never got any better. After all these years, his body still seemed to react on its own, without any coaxing from him.

The farm consisted of a house that had once been quite magnificent, made of wood and painted yellow; the paint was now peeling off. On one side stood a low, dilapidated barn and on the other a small hay-barn. The remains of a manure heap in the back recalled the time when they'd had animals on the farm. The surrounding pastures were now empty; the last of the livestock had been sold after the death of his parents a year ago.

He parked behind the hay-barn—a precaution that wasn't really necessary, but it was an old habit. He opened the tailgate, took out the sack, and walked briskly across the yard. The barn door creaked, and the air inside smelled musty. Thick layers of cobwebs hung from the ceiling, along with sticky ribbons covered with the black dots of long-dead flies.

The old freezer stood in its customary place, even though it hadn't been used in a long time. Several days earlier he had plugged it in to make sure that it still worked.

Cold air struck him as he opened the lid. The sack fit inside easily. Quickly he closed the lid and then carefully wiped off the exterior of the freezer with soap and a wet rag. It had probably never been this clean before. Then he picked up the bundle of clothes and the rag and put them in a plastic bag.

Behind the barn he dug a deep hole in the ground and stuffed the bag into it. Carefully he filled up the hole, placing some straw and branches on top. Nothing aboveground gave away his hiding place.

All that was left was the truck. He brought out a hose and spent over an hour cleaning it up, both inside and out. Finally he took off the phony license plate and replaced it with the real one. No one could claim that he wasn't thorough.

Then he went inside to make breakfast.

A fresh mist slowly floated over the meadows still damp from the night, weaving its way between the grass and stalks of grain. It caressed the clumps of reeds where a couple of swans were meticulously grooming their white plumage. Several terns were squawking over the bay, and rowboats rocked serenely at their moorings a short distance out in the water. The rotting gray fishing boats at the shore were no longer in use.

It was an uncommonly beautiful morning—one of those summer mornings that would be summoned up as a memory when winter drew its silent dark coat over the island of Gotland.

Twelve-year-old Agnes was awake earlier than usual. It wasn't even eight thirty when she woke her little sister, Sofie. In her sleep-muddled state she was easily persuaded to go for a dip before breakfast. Their grandmother was sitting on the steps, having her coffee and reading the paper. She waved to them as the girls pedaled off with their towels in the bike baskets. The dirt road ran parallel to the beach, a few hundred yards higher up. They had to bike about half a mile before they could turn off to reach the section that was good for swimming.

Agnes stayed ahead of her sister, even though they could have ridden side by side. The traffic on this road was practically nonexistent, even at the height of the summer. Agnes always wanted to be slightly ahead. She had plucked a blade of grass from the roadside and was sucking on it; she liked the taste of the fresh sap.

The dirt road first wound its way through the woods, and then the landscape opened before them. Fields and pastures stretched out side by side down toward the water, which was visible almost the whole time. Several farms were located along the road, with horses, cows, and sheep grazing. At the last whitewashed farm building on the road, they biked past a large pasture before they turned off to go down to the beach. The horses—three Gotland ponies and a Norwegian fjording—were outside day and night at this time of year, along with the shaggy Gotland sheep. The rams were splendid with their twisting horns like pretzels on each side of their head. Sometimes the farmer allowed the girls to ride the ponies. He had a daughter who was a few years older, and if she felt like it she would let them come along for a ride. Agnes and Sofie visited their grandmother and grandfather often. They spent large parts of their summer vacation here in Petesviken in southwestern Gotland while their parents stayed home in Visby to work.

"Wait a minute. Let's say hi to the horses," Agnes suggested as she stopped at the fence.

She clicked her tongue and whistled, which had an immediate effect. The animals stopped grazing, raised their heads, and came trotting over to the girls.

The biggest ram started bleating. Then another and another, until they all joined in. The animals crowded around the gate, hoping for a treat. The girls patted all of them as best they could. They didn't dare venture inside the fence when they were alone.

"Where's Pontus?"

Agnes surveyed the pasture. There were only three horses. Their favorite pony, a black-and-white dappled gelding, was missing.

"Maybe he's over in the trees."

Sofie pointed to the narrow grove of trees that stretched like a dark green ribbon down the middle of the pasture.

The girls shouted and then waited a few minutes, but the pony didn't appear.

"Forget about it," said Sofie. "Let's go swimming."

"How strange that he doesn't come." Agnes frowned, looking worried. He was always so affectionate. Her eyes swept over the hillside, past the water trough, the salt licks, and the trees farther down the slope.

"Oh well, never mind about him. He's probably lying down somewhere asleep." Sofie poked her sister in the side. "You're the one who wanted to go swimming. Come on." She got on her bike.

"There's something wrong. We should at least be able to see where Pontus is."

"They've probably taken him inside. Maybe Veronica is planning to go out riding."

"But what if he's lying down somewhere and he's sick and can't get up! He could have broken his leg or something. We have to go and see."

"Don't be silly. We'll say hi to him on our way back."

Even though the ponies were gentle and small in size, Sofie had respect for them and wasn't eager to go into the pasture. The fjording was big and powerful and didn't seem trustworthy; he had kicked her once. The sheep were also a little scary with those big horns of theirs.

Agnes paid no attention to her sister's protests. She opened the gate and went into the pasture.

"Well, I, at least, have no intention of forgetting about Pontus," she snapped angrily.

Sofie groaned loudly, to show her disapproval. Reluctantly she hopped off her bike and followed.

"You'll have to go first," she muttered.

Agnes clapped her hands and yelled to shoo off the animals, and they bounded off in all directions. Sofie kept close to her big sister and looked around uneasily. The tall grass tickled and scratched at their legs. They didn't say a word to each other. The pony was nowhere in sight.

When they reached the grove of trees without having found anything unusual, Agnes climbed up on the fence on the other side of the pasture to get a better view.

"Look," she cried, pointing.

Farther off, at the edge of the trees, she could see Pontus lying on his side. He seemed to be asleep. Overhead a flock of crows cawed and screeched.

"There he is. He's sleeping like a log!"

Eagerly she ran toward the horse.

"Then it's all right. There's nothing wrong. We don't need to go any farther, do we?" Sofie objected.

Their view was partially blocked. The horse didn't move a muscle.

The only sound was the noisy screeching of the crows. Agnes, leading the way, had time to think that it was odd to see so many crows. When she got closer she stopped so abruptly that her sister ran right into her.

Pontus was lying there on the grass, and his coat gleamed in the sun. The sight would have reassured them if it weren't for one thing. The place where his head was supposed to be was now empty. His neck had been severed. All they saw was a big bloody hole and the flies that were swarming in a black cloud around the fleshy opening.

Behind her Agnes heard a thud as her sister fell headlong to the ground.

Detective Superintendent Anders Knutas discovered to his dismay that patches of sweat had already started to appear under his armpits by the time he parked his run-down Mercedes at police headquarters. It was one of those rare days in the year when it became painfully obvious that the old car had no air-conditioning. Now his wife, Lina, would once again have grist for the mill when she lobbied for purchasing a new car.

Under normal circumstances it would never occur to him to drive to work. His house was located just outside the South Gate, only half a mile from his office. Knutas had worked in the Visby police department for twenty-five years, and he could easily count the days when he had not walked to work. Sometimes he would stop at the Solberga Pool and go inside to swim a mile or more. This summer was no exception. In August he would celebrate his fiftieth birthday, and over the past few years he had noticed the difference the minute he stopped exercising. He'd been more or less thin all his life, and that wasn't something he wanted to change. It just required a little more effort nowadays. Swimming kept him in shape and helped him to think. The more complicated the case he was working on, the more often he paid a visit to the swimming pool. He hadn't been there in quite a while. He wasn't sure whether that was good or bad.

On this last day in June his family was planning to drive up to their summer house in Lickershamn to mow and water the grass. Knutas was intending to leave work early and pick up his wife at the hospital when she was done with her shift at the maternity ward. Contrary to all expectations, their twins, Petra and Nils, who would soon turn thirteen, had agreed to come along, even if they weren't thrilled about it. Lately they usually preferred to spend their time with friends.

Cool air struck Knutas as he stepped through the front door. Silence reigned in the hallway of the criminal investigation division. Summer vacations had started, and it was noticeable.

Knutas's closest colleague, Detective Inspector Karin Jacobsson, was sitting in her office talking on the phone when he walked past. Knutas and Jacobsson had worked together for fifteen years, and they knew each other well on a professional level. When it came to their private lives, Jacobsson was much more reticent.

She was thirty-eight and single, or at least Knutas had never heard her talk about any boyfriend. She lived alone with her white cockatoo in an apartment in Visby, and she devoted most of her free time to playing soccer. Right now she was sitting there waving her arms around and speaking in a loud and furious voice. She was petite, with dark hair. She had warm, lively brown eyes and a big gap between her front teeth. Her mood could change dramatically, and she didn't make much of an effort to rein in her hot temper. She was a splash of color and a bundle of energy, and her sweeping gestures were in sharp contrast to the less than uplifting backdrop of closed blinds and gray-painted bookshelves.

Knutas sank down on the chair in his office and started going through the mail from the past few days that was still untouched. Among the anonymous official letters he found a colorful postcard from Greece. The picture showed a typical Greek meal: grilled chicken on a spit with a bowl of tsatziki and a bottle of wine on a round café table. In the background was a glimpse of sunset, and light was glinting off one of the two wineglasses on the blue-painted tabletop.

The message said: "Not exactly the same thing as grilled lamb's head with mashed turnips—what do you say, Knutie? On Naxos for two weeks, taking it easy. Hope you're well, and maybe we'll have a chance to meet again soon. Martin."

Knutas couldn't help smiling. How typical for Martin Kihlgård to send a postcard with a picture of food on it. The inspector from the National Criminal Police was the biggest glutton Knutas had ever met. He was always eating. They had worked together several times on various homicide cases when Knutas had asked for reinforcements from the NCP.

His thoughts were interrupted by a knock on the door. The next moment the door was opened by his colleague Thomas Wittberg, who was more than twenty years his junior. Wittberg refused to cut his thick blond hair, in spite of constant kidding from everyone at work. The tight white T-shirt accentuated his suntanned torso, which was subjected to regular sessions in the gym at police headquarters. Wittberg had real charm, and he knew how to use it on vacationing women as soon as the season got started. The young detective liked to joke that his goal was to meet women from every region of Sweden, from Samiland in the north to Skåne in the south. Knutas didn't doubt for a moment that his colleague would succeed. As far as he knew, Wittberg had never had a relationship that had lasted more than a few weeks. Every summer different women would call him at work, and some would even show up unannounced to see him.

On the job he had also made good use of his popularity with the ladies. It had helped the police to make progress in quite a few investigations. Thomas Wittberg had quickly been promoted from a cop on the beat to the violent crimes division and then to police detective, and for the past two years he had been a regular member of Knutas's core group. Right now his intense blue eyes testified to the fact that something special had happened.

"You've got to hear this," he said as he dropped onto Knutas's visitor's chair holding a sheet of paper in his hand. Knutas noticed that it was covered with Wittberg's illegible notes.

"A decapitated horse was found in a pasture outside Petesviken. Two little girls discovered it this morning."

"Good Lord."

"Around nine o'clock the girls were biking to the beach for a morning swim when they noticed that one of the horses was missing. They found it lying farther off in the pasture with its head cut off."

"Are you sure they didn't just imagine the whole thing?"

"Their grandfather and the owner of the farm went back with them to have a look. They just called in the report."

"What sort of horse is it? And who owns it?"

"An ordinary pony. The owner is a farmer named Jörgen Larsson. He has four horses that his family keeps for riding. The other three were in the pasture."

"And they weren't harmed in any way?"

"Apparently not."

Knutas shook his head. "That sounds very strange."

"There's one more thing," said Wittberg.

"What's that?"

"The head wasn't simply cut off. It's missing. The

farmer has searched everywhere for it, but he couldn't find it. It's not anywhere near the body, at any rate."

"You mean that the perp took the head away?"

"So it seems."

"Did you talk to the farmer yourself?"

"No, I got the information from a patrolman."

"I hope he doesn't go rummaging around in the pasture, disturbing all the evidence," Knutas muttered as he reached for his jacket. "Let's get going."

Several minutes later Knutas, Wittberg, and the crime-scene tech Erik Sohlman were sitting in a police car heading south. Sohlman was one of the officers that Knutas valued most, along with Jacobsson. Both of his favorite colleagues shared a temperamental nature and an interest in soccer, but unlike Jacobsson, Sohlman was married and had two small children.

"What a strange thing," said the technician. He brushed his curly red hair back from his forehead. "I wonder whether it's some mentally ill person who likes to hurt animals, or whether there's something else behind it."

Knutas muttered something inaudible in reply.

"Do you remember that trotting horse that bolted during a race at Skrubbs and ran off the track?" Wittberg leaned forward from where he was sitting in the backseat. "The driver fell out of the sulky and the horse took off. I seem to recall that we searched for a week."

"Oh, right. The one that was later found dead in the woods in Follingbo," Knutas interjected. "The sulky had gotten stuck between two trees, and the horse died of dehydration."

"My God," said Sohlman with a shudder. "That was not a pretty sight."

They continued in silence along the coast road, past Klintehamn and Fröjel and the little village of Sproge with its lovely white church. Then they turned off on a dirt road, a long straightaway heading toward the sea with short pine and spruce trees on both sides. They soon reached Petesviken. Several farms stood in a row, with a view of the sea. In the pastures livestock was grazing. It looked as harmonious and peaceful as could be.

At Jörgen Larsson's property a truck was parked on the gravel in front of the house, along with a newer-model Opel. Several cages for rabbits had been set up on the lawn, and the officers were met by a beagle happily wagging his tail. A man wearing blue overalls and a cap came out on the front porch just as their car turned into the yard. The man took off his cap in the old-fashioned way of greeting as he said hello to the three officers.

"Jörgen Larsson. We might as well go right out there. This sure is a nasty business. I can't believe it happened. My daughter is very upset. It was her pony, and you know how it is with young girls and their horses. Pontus was everything to the poor girl. She just keeps crying and crying. I can't understand how anyone could do something like that. It's completely incomprehensible."

The words came pouring out, nonstop and all in one breath, and none of the officers had time to respond before the farmer started heading across the yard toward the pasture.

"Both my wife and the kids are really upset. It's a real mess. I think they're all in shock."

"Of course," said Knutas. "I understand."

"And Pontus . . . well, he was something special, you know," Larsson went on. "The kids could ride him whenever they liked, and they could do whatever they wanted with him. You couldn't find a more gentle horse. He was almost stupidly nice, you see. They would climb up on him when they were little and pull his mane and tug on his tail and things like that, and he let them do it. Well, he wasn't exactly a youngster anymore, fifteen years old, so sooner or later he would have ended up at the butcher's, but I like to think he still had a few more years left. Anyway, his life shouldn't have ended the way it did. I never could have imagined this."

"No," Knutas interjected sympathetically. "Do you know—"

"I bought that horse after we had our first son, thought it would be fun for him to have a horse to ride, you know. We don't have much else other than livestock out here in the country. Though we do have a dog, and she's had several puppies, you know. And we almost always have kittens—that cat must have had four or five litters by now, so we're going to have to get her fixed; well, you know what I mean. We also have rabbits, and baby rabbits, too. Well, the kids don't have much else to occupy their time, and besides, they're interested and they want to help out with the cows and calves, and that's something a man has to be grateful for. The fact that they're so interested."

"But—" Knutas ventured.

The farmer took no notice and just kept on talking.

"My oldest boy is sixteen and does the work of a full-grown hired hand when he comes home from school. Yes, he does. Every single day, too. He's as reliable as the amen in church. We have forty milk cows and twenty-five calves. My brother and his wife also work on the farm; we own it together. They live in the other direction, where you turned off the road. They have three kids, so it's a full house, and we take care of everything together. They're away right now, on vacation in Majorca, but they'll be back tomorrow, and I haven't called to tell them about the horrible thing that's happened. It would just upset them for no reason. It can just as well wait. But this whole thing is very unsettling, you know. I've never experienced anything like it before."

Knutas stared at Jörgen Larsson, who barely managed to take a breath before more words came pouring out of him. They had reached the gate, and the farmer pointed a thick finger toward the narrow grove of trees.

"The horse is lying over there, without a head. That's really the worst thing I've ever seen. The bastard must have had a hell of a time cutting it off. I don't know whether he sawed it off or hacked it off or what exactly he did."

"Where are the other horses?" barked Knutas to put an end to the farmer's unrelenting torrent.

"Oh, we took them inside. He might try to hurt them, too. You never know. Although we haven't seen any cuts on them. We let the sheep stay out," said Larsson apologetically. "They don't seem to be bothered by much."

Knutas had given up trying to ask the farmer any questions, so he said nothing. That could wait until later.

Larsson unhooked the latch and firmly shooed away the sheep that had crowded around his legs.

The detectives tried to keep up with his long strides through the pasture.

Over where the horse lay, a flock of crows was cawing above the cadaver.

In the midst of that bucolic summer scene of the horse pasture, the green-clad hillside, and the glittering bay lay a muscular pony with a plump belly and flowing tail, but his neck ended in a huge bloody wound.

"Who the hell would do something like this?" exploded Knutas.

For once the farmer was at a loss for words.

For TV reporter Johan Berg, the news situation looked anything but favorable on this Wednesday morning. There was absolutely nothing happening. He was sitting at his dust-covered desk in the small editorial office of Swedish TV in downtown Visby. He had paged through the morning newspapers and listened to the local radio station. He couldn't help feeling impressed with how the editors had managed to fill the papers and the broadcasts, in spite of the fact that they didn't contain even a shred of news. He had talked to Pia Lilja, the Gotland cameraperson with whom he was working during the summer, and told her that she could come in later. It was pointless for both of them to sit there twiddling their thumbs.

Listlessly he sifted through several days' worth of municipal documents and reports of proceedings, feebly hoping to find something. His boss, Max Grenfors, at the central editorial office back in Stockholm, had given him an assignment this morning that seemed fairly impossible. He was supposed to find a news story and do a report for the evening broadcast. "Preferably one we can lead off with. We haven't got much for the program, and we need something from you." Hadn't he heard this all before?

Johan had worked as a crime reporter for Swedish TV for twelve years in the Regional News division, which covered Stockholm, Uppsala, and the island county of Gotland. In addition, he was in charge of covering Gotland news, which could mean anything from runaway cows to a school that had burned down or the overcrowding of the hospital's emergency room. Previously the area's coverage had been handled from Stockholm, but Swedish TV had decided to reinstate the local editorial office on Gotland for a trial period this summer, and Johan had been assigned as reporter. For the past two months he'd been living on the island, and there was nowhere else he would rather be. Love had brought him here, and in spite of the numerous obstacles that still had to be overcome, he was determined that he and Emma Winarve, a teacher in Roma, would be together. They had met and fallen in love in connection with a murder case that he was covering a year ago. Emma was married and had two children when their relationship began. Now she was newly divorced and expecting their child at any moment. His baby and hers.

Johan still couldn't comprehend that he was going to be a father. It was too enormous a concept, too intangible. To his great disappointment, Emma wanted to wait to move in together, "to see how things go," as she said. Her other children, Sara and Filip, were still so young. They needed to have a chance to get used to the new situation, living half the time with their father and half with their mother. Now they were going to have a new brother or sister. Emma wanted to take things one day at a time, and Johan was forced to be patient. Just like so many times before. Occasionally it felt as if so far their whole relationship had consisted of him waiting for her.

In his heart he was sure that they were moving in the right direction, that one day they would finally be together. This was what he had believed all along, and he hadn't become any less convinced. Emma had chosen to carry his child to term; that was enough for him. At least for the time being.

As far as his work situation on Gotland was concerned, there was much that he liked, including the independence and his collaboration with Pia, which functioned well. It was great not to have an editor breathing down his neck, too, even though the pressure sometimes felt just as intense, even from a distance. Of course, he missed the big-time crime stories in Stockholm, as well as his apartment and his friends, but his life had taken new turns, which meant that Gotland was where he most wanted to be.

There were also numerous advantages to working as part of a small team in a local office. He had a lot of freedom, and he found great satisfaction in setting his own work schedules. He and Pia tried to do one story each day, and that was sufficient. They were on their own. As long as they delivered broadcastable and more or less relevant reports, the home office was satisfied.

Right now they were planning a series about the high cost of housing. Johan was fascinated by the fact that people would pay several million kronor for a small house in Visby inside the medieval wall, and the amount they had to cough up for an apartment could be as much as the price tags in the most fashionable sections of Stockholm. No matter how charming the old city of Visby was, there was a big difference in the choice of services, jobs, and entertainment, and Visby could only be reached by boat or plane. He wondered who the two thousand people were who lived inside the ring wall and could afford those incredible prices, at least by Gotland standards. The residents with normal salaries could only dream of living downtown, unless they had inherited a place.

Johan had been stationed on Gotland since May 1, and up until now he hadn't lacked for story ideas. Unemployment was a big problem on the island. During the past few years several large companies had cut back on the number of employees or had shut down completely. Some had moved their production to the mainland. The latest death blow came when the government decided to close P18, the old military base, as part of the big wave of cuts in the defense budget that had swept across Sweden.

Now, though, the team hadn't managed to squeeze out a single story for several days, and Johan was clearly feeling the pressure from Grenfors in Stockholm.

When the phone rang, he answered without much enthusiasm.

It was Pia, and there was an eager tone to her voice. He could hear that she was driving as she talked.

"Hey, a horse has been found in a pasture with its head cut off."

Pia had a habit of skipping any introductory greetings, which she viewed as unnecessary, especially when she was in a hurry and had something important to say.

"When?"

"This morning. Two little girls found it in a pasture out by Petesviken. Do you know where that is?"

"No clue."

"It's in southern Gotland, on the west coast—it's probably about thirty-five miles from the city."

"How did you hear about this?"

"I have a friend who lives there. She called me."

"Who owns the horse?"

"A completely ordinary farm family."

"We should drive out there right away. How soon can you get here?"

"I'm out in front now."

Johan hung up the phone and immediately called

Detective Superintendent Knutas on his direct line. He got no answer, and the switchboard told him that the entire investigative team would be tied up all morning.

A decapitated horse sounded weird, but that was exactly what he needed. He grabbed a notebook and pen and locked the door to the office. He decided to wait to call Grenfors in Stockholm; he had nothing against keeping the editor on tenterhooks for a while.

He sat in the kitchen, thinking about how palpably a room could change, depending on who was in it and what was taking place. The gloom that had previously emanated from the walls, and the guilt and shame that had fallen from the ceiling onto his head, were now gone. In the past the walls had pressed in and threatened him whenever he sat at his place at the table, which was always the same. Whatever food was served gave him no pleasure; it merely swelled up inside his mouth until he had a hard time swallowing. A plateful of anxiety lay hidden under the gravy.

Things were different now that he could do whatever he pleased. He had made himself a hearty breakfast. The exertions of the morning demanded a solid meal.

On the plate in front of him were three thick slices of toasted white bread with pieces of Falun sausage and eggs dripping with fat. He topped them off with a generous squirt of ketchup, along with salt and pepper. The cat was meowing greedily and rubbing against his leg. He tossed her a piece of sausage.

The clock on the wall showed that it was nine

forty-five. Through the dusty windowpane he could see the sun lighting up the yard outside. He ate the food with a good appetite and gulped down some of the cold milk. When he was done, he pushed away the plate and belched loudly. He leaned back in his chair and took a pinch of snuff.

His body was tired; his arms ached. It had been more difficult than he'd anticipated. For a moment he had even thought that he might not be able to do it. Finally, he had managed it. The finishing work had taken a good long time, but now it was done.

He stood up and picked up his plate. Carefully he rinsed off the scraps of food under the faucet and then washed the plate.

All of a sudden he felt very tired. He had to lie down and sleep. He let out the cat, who soundlessly slunk off. Then he went up the creaking stairs to the second floor and went into the far room, at the end of the house. The room had never been repaired after the fire. Patches of soot covered the walls, and even the burned bed was still there, like some sort of charred log in the corner. He thought he could even sense a faint whiff of smoke, but it was probably just his imagination. On the floor was an old mattress, and that was where he lay down. This room made him feel good. It gave him a sense of calm that he otherwise never felt, and he slept well.

Knutas never ceased to be amazed at how fast news traveled. Reporters from the local radio station, TV, and newspapers had all contacted him, wanting to know what had happened. On Gotland there was enormous news value in the fact that a horse had been decapitated. Experience had taught him that nothing stirred up the public as much as the abuse of animals.

The thought had barely appeared in his mind before the organization Friends of the Animals was on the line, and several other animal rights groups would undoubtedly be calling him soon. The police spokesman, Lars Norrby, was away on vacation, so Knutas had to handle the reporters on his own. He wrote up a brief press release and said that for a change he was going to be unreachable for the next few hours.

Back at the criminal investigation division after the morning excursion to Petesviken, Knutas bought a sandwich from the vending machine in the coffee room. There was no time for lunch. He had called in his closest colleagues for a meeting at one o'clock. Sohlman should be able to make it back from the investigation out at the crime scene to join them, thanks to the fact that there were now two crime techs in the police department.

They gathered in the bright, open conference room, which had a big table in the middle. Police headquarters had recently been remodeled, and new furniture, in a simple Scandinavian design, had been purchased. Knutas had felt more comfortable with their old worn furniture made of pine. At least the view was still the same; the panoramic windows looked out on the Forum supermarket parking lot, the ring wall, and the sea.

"The crime that has been committed is a particularly nasty one," Knutas began, and he told them about what they had seen out at Petesviken. "The pasture and the surrounding area have been blocked off," he went on. "There's a highway that runs past the pasture, and that's where we're looking for traces of any vehicles. If the person or persons who did this took the horse's head with them, they most likely had a car. The neighbors and other people who live in the area are being interviewed, so we'll have to see what turns up during the course of the day."

"How was the horse killed?" asked Jacobsson.

"Erik can tell us more about that." Knutas turned to the crime tech.

"Let's take a look at some pictures of the horse," said

Sohlman. "I have to warn you, Karin, that some of them are very unpleasant." He directed this comment to Jacobsson, not only because she was the most sensitive of his colleagues when it came to blood, but also because she had a great affection for animals.

He clicked through the photos of the horribly abused body.

"As you can see here, the head was severed from the neck, or rather, hacked and chopped off. A veterinarian, Åke Tornsjö, has already taken a look at the horse. He's going to do a more thorough examination later, but he was able to tell us how he thinks it was done. According to him, the perpetrator—if it actually was the work of one individual—presumably first knocked the horse unconscious by giving him a strong blow to the forehead, most likely with a hammer, a sledgehammer, or an axe. When the horse lost consciousness, he used a large knife, like a butcher knife, to slice through the neck, and that's what killed the animal—meaning, the loss of blood. To sever the head from the vertebrae, he had to smash them apart. We've found crushed pieces of bone, and I would guess that it was done by using an axe. Marks on the ground indicate that the horse was still alive after the first blow. He lay there, kicking in his death throes. The grass had been thrashed about, and the ground was churned up. The area around the neck is ragged and rough, which indicates that the perpetrator had to go at it for a while—he seems to have known perfectly well what to do, even if he lacked a more detailed knowledge of a horse's anatomy."

"How nice. Then we can exclude all veterinarians," muttered Wittberg.

"There's one thing that I can't make sense of," Sohlman went on, unperturbed. "When the carotid artery was severed, the horse should have lost an incredible amount of blood. We can see that blood did run out of the neck and body, but there's only a small amount accumulated on the ground. Almost negligible. Even if the blood had seeped into the ground, there should still be more of it."

The others gave the tech a puzzled look.

"How would you explain that?" said Jacobsson.

"The only thing I can come up with is that the perpetrator must have collected the blood."

"Why would anybody want to do something like that?" objected Wittberg.

"I have no idea." Sohlman stroked his chin meditatively. "The owner last saw the horse at around eleven last night. The vet estimates that the animal had been dead for at least five or six hours by the time the girls found him. That means that the crime was most likely committed sometime before four in the morning. As far as the pasture is concerned, it's being searched by dogs, along with the immediate vicinity, in an attempt to find the head. So far no luck. We'll continue to widen the area of our search."

Jacobsson grimaced. "How disgusting. So the perpetrator took both the head and the blood along," she said. "What do we know about the horse?"

Knutas looked down at his notes.

"A pony, fifteen years old, castrated—so it was a gelding. A gentle, friendly animal, with no previous police record."

Wittberg snickered. Jacobsson was not amused.

"What about the owner?" she asked.

"His name is Jörgen Larsson. Married, the father of three. He took over the farm along with his brother ten years ago. It's their childhood home, and their parents still live in one of the separate wings of the house. The farm is quite large. They have about forty cows and a lot of calves. There don't seem to be any conflicts within the family. They've run their farm in peace and quiet all these years. Neither Jörgen Larsson nor any other family member has a police record.

"The vet thinks that the crime was committed by someone who grew up on a farm or who has had previous contact with the slaughtering or butchering of animals," Sohlman went on. "He says that this isn't the sort of thing that can be done on the spur of the moment. It requires careful planning, nerve, and determination—as well as brute strength. You'd have to hit hard to make the horse lose consciousness, and you'd also have to know where to strike. The brain is located very high up on the forehead. According to Åke Tornsjö, the perpetrator must have done this sort of thing before."

Everyone seated around the table was listening with interest.

"Has the farmer or anyone in his family ever received any sort of threat?" asked Wittberg.

"No, not as far as we know."

"The question is whether this was directed at the farmer personally, or whether it's a madman who's attacking animals," said Jacobsson.

"Could this be some kind of boyish prank?" Wittberg tossed out the question.

"With a butcher knife and an axe and a means of transporting the head?" said Jacobsson. "Not on your life. On the other hand, I do wonder if there are any mental patients with a history of animal abuse who have been released."

"Actually, we've already managed to check up on that," said Knutas. "Do any of you recall Gustav Persson? The guy who used to roam around the pastures putting nails into horses' hooves? He would pound the nail in partway, and when the horse set his foot down to walk, the nail would go in farther and farther. Persson didn't just make do with one hoof, either. He would put nails in several so that in the end the horse couldn't stand upright. He eluded the police for several weeks until he was finally caught. By then he had injured a dozen animals. There's also Bingeby-Anna. She would kill any cat that she saw and hang them on the fence."

"But she's super tiny and thin," Jacobsson objected. "She'd never be able to carry out this sort of crime, at least not alone. I'm the size of an elephant compared to her. She can't weigh more than ninety pounds."

Knutas raised his eyebrows at the exaggeration. Jacobsson herself was small-boned and stood no more than about five foot three.

"I don't think this has anything to do with an impulsive act by some mental patient," Wittberg protested. "It was too well planned. To commit such a crime, during the lightest nights of the summer and with people and houses nearby, must have required meticulous planning, just as Erik said. I'm amazed that the perpetrator even dared, when there was such a big risk of being seen. The road to the pasture runs along all the farm buildings. It's practically like driving right through their yards. Anyone who woke up could have seen or heard the car."

"You're right," said Sohlman, "but we've discovered that it's possible to reach the pasture from another direction." He clicked through the pictures until he came to the ones showing maps of the area. "The road ends and splits in two when you reach Petesviken. Instead of turning right and driving past the farms, you go left. A short distance away there's a tractor path along the fields that circles the whole area and goes past the pasture on the other side. If the perpetrator chose that route, and I'm convinced that he did, then he would have avoided being seen from the farms. He could have driven out to the pasture and back in peace and quiet, with no risk of being discovered. From the farms in Petesviken you can't see if a car is driving along that path. We've checked. Right now we're examining the tire tracks out there, but it's difficult because the ground is so dry."

"Good," said Knutas. "We'll continue to interview the neighbors and anyone else in the area. Let's hope we find out something. The perp must have had a car. He had to transport an axe and a knife and possibly other tools as well, along with the horse's head."

"And he was probably covered with blood," Sohlman added.

"Maybe he took a dip and washed it off. The sea is so close, after all," Jacobsson suggested.

"Wouldn't that be kind of reckless?" Wittberg gave her a dubious look. "Would he really go for a swim, with a very strong risk of being discovered? Even though the crime was committed after eleven, on these light summer nights people go out for a dip at all hours. Especially since it's been so hot."

"On the other hand, the area is relatively isolated," Knutas interjected. "There can't be more than three or four families living on those farms and moving about, plus maybe a few people from the houses farther up the road. It's not an area that anyone would just happen to stroll through. Well, we're going to have to look more closely into the family background of the farmer. Either there's a particular reason why it was Larsson's horse that was killed, or else it was just by chance. We still have to investigate all possibilities."

"Do you think the guilty person is part of the family?" asked Jacobsson. "The wife taking revenge on the husband, or vice versa?"

"That seems rather far-fetched," said Knutas. "A person would have to be awfully sick to commit this type of crime. But we can't rule it out. We've been surprised before. We need to talk to the farmer again. He's unusually talkative, but we were there only a short time. I think someone needs to drive back out there. The girls who found the horse have to be interviewed as soon as possible."

"I can leave right now." Wittberg was already getting to his feet.

"I'll go with you," said Jacobsson. "If there isn't anything else you need me to do?"

"Go, both of you," said Knutas. "I'll stay here and deal with the press."

Martina Flochten rushed around the cramped room, grabbing up toiletries and a towel. She was going to take a quick shower and change her clothes. The students had the afternoon off from their excavating work, because an American archaeology professor was in Visby to give a lecture at the college. Martina was in a hurry for entirely different reasons, though, although her fellow students had no idea why.

They were going to take advantage of the situation. Her longing for him was burning and urgent.

She had suppressed all thought of the boyfriend she had back in the Netherlands. He kept calling her cell phone more and more often. The more she ignored her phone, the more persistent he became. One evening when she had left her phone behind in the room, he had called twenty-eight times. It was sick, and she found it embarrassing because her roommate, Eva, had been home that evening, lying in bed and trying to read. Martina planned to end the relationship when she got back home. She couldn't bring herself to do it over the phone. That would be too wretched.

Her father had also called. He was coming to Gotland the following week. He had business in Visby and was planning to kill two birds with one stone, so to speak. Maybe he was worried about her. Martina was close to her father, although she thought he could be rather overprotective. Then again, she certainly had given him reason to worry on numerous occasions. Martina was ambitious and a good student. She did well in school, but in her free time she never hesitated to go out partying, and there was no shortage of parties among the various student crowds at the university in Rotterdam. She had even tried drugs, but only the less serious kind.

Martina's interest in archaeology was sparked when she saw a TV program about an excavation in Peru. She was impressed by the archaeologists' patient, systematic work, and by what the earth could tell them.

When she began studying the subject, she quickly become intrigued by the Viking Age. She read everything she could get her hands on about the Vikings and how they had lived. Their religion, with its belief in numerous gods, appealed to her. And she was fascinated not only by the Viking ships and their plundering expeditions out in the world but also by the extensive trade the Vikings had carried on, especially on Gotland.

This course had definitely whetted Martina's appetite, and she had already decided to do further studies in the subject at the college in Visby after finishing her archaeology degree.

By the time she was done with her shower, the others had gone out to the bus that was going to take them to the lecture. She went out and explained that she wasn't feeling well and wanted to stay home. Eva seemed disappointed. They had all planned to have a beer somewhere afterward, to take advantage of being in town.

After the bus drove off, Martina rushed back inside to get her purse, casting one last glance at herself in the mirror. She looked good. The Gotland sun had given her skin a lovely sheen, and her long hair was blonder than usual.

He wanted to meet at the harbor. Walking briskly and full of anticipation, she strode across the wooden bridge behind the youth hostel, heading down to the harbor area.

Petesviken was a good distance from Visby, on the southwest coast of Gotland. Johan and Pia quickly left the city behind. Pia, who was driving, nodded toward the sign for Högklint as they passed the exit.

"That's a place we could do a story on, apropos the overheated real estate market. Sometimes I think all the hysteria of the eighties has come back. Have you heard about the luxury hotel they're going to build out there?"

"Of course. We've done lots of reports about it. I guess they're just waiting for the municipal council's decision in the fall before they get started."

"That's about right. They'll probably start building before the year's over. It's going to be a giant complex with hotel suites, condos, a gourmet restaurant, and a nightclub. Five star."

"I wonder if there's really a demand for something like that here."

"Of course there is. The mainland is swarming with people who have a romantic view of Gotland. People who vacationed here when they were younger and now want to come back with their families and experience the island in a more comfortable fashion. And there are plenty of people with money in Sweden."

"It'll create jobs, if nothing else. Although I can imagine there must be some opposition, too. Isn't Högklint a nature preserve?"

"They're not going to build at the edge of the cliffs—they wouldn't be allowed to do that—but it's still unbelievable that the building plans are probably going to be approved. Naturally the biggest protests are from the people who live in the area. They have fierce discussions even when someone just wants to paint their door a different color. Otherwise it's mostly nature lovers who are opposed—people who work to protect the flora and fauna. Lots of different kinds of birds breed on the hillside at Högklint in the spring-time, and it also has one of the most beautiful views on the whole island. Plus I think a lot of people feel that this side of Visby has been exploited enough with Pippi Longstocking's Kneippbyn amusement park and everything."

"Isn't the owner a foreigner?" asked Johan.

"I think it's a joint venture, between the municipality and several foreign investors."

"Let's look into it some more when we have time. It's definitely worth a longer story."

Forty-five minutes later they reached Petesviken.

The pasture had been cordoned off and was being

guarded by several uniformed police officers standing at the gate. None of them would answer any of Johan's questions about a decapitated horse. Instead, they referred him to Knutas.

Pia was already at work with her camera, which didn't surprise Johan. She never wasted any time. He had liked her from their very first meeting at the editorial office. She looked tough, with her straggly black hair cut short, the ring in her nose, and the heavy eyeliner highlighting her dark brown eyes. She had greeted him without any fuss and immediately offered some of her own ideas. That boded well for the rest of the summer. She had been born and bred in Visby, and she knew Gotland like the back of her hand. Through her large extended family she had relatives and friends scattered over many parts of the island. She had no less than six siblings, and all of them had stayed on Gotland and established their own families, so her network of contacts was enormous. In terms of quality, the shots that she took might not have been quite as top-notch as Johan was used to, but she took plenty of them, often from interesting angles. Over time she would undoubtedly be brilliant, as long as she kept her sense of commitment and strong drive. She was young, ambitious, and determined to get a permanent position with one of the big TV stations in Stockholm. She had been working less than a year, yet she'd already managed to get a long-term temporary job with Swedish TV, which was nothing to sneeze at. Right now she had disappeared around a bend in the road.

Johan had a real urge to crawl under the police tape farther away, but he knew that if he got caught, he would have burned his bridges with the police. And he definitely couldn't afford to do that. He was aware that his bosses back in Stockholm were considering reinstating the local news service on Gotland on a full-time basis, and the results of his summer assignment would weigh heavily in the balance. Johan wanted nothing more than to stay on the island.

He looked for Pia, but she seemed to have been swallowed up by the earth. Surprising, since the TV camera was so big and cumbersome—hardly something that you could carry around just anywhere. He started walking along the fence.

It was a big pasture, and he couldn't see where it ended. The wooded area was in the way. He surveyed the strip of trees and suddenly caught sight of Pia. She was inside the cordoned-off area and was busy getting a panoramic shot of the pasture. At first he was angry—he was going to pay the consequences if it was shown on TV—but the next second he changed his mind. She was just doing her job, getting good shots in the best way she knew how. That was exactly how he wanted a cameraperson to work. The danger of worrying about offending the police was that you could start being too considerate. Then the focus shifted from looking out for the best interests of the viewers to staying on good terms with the authorities. That was not at all where he wanted to end up. He was aware that he had to look out for himself. The irritation that had flared up inside him gave way to gratitude. Pia was a damn good camerawoman.

When she was finished, they stopped by the nearby farms. No one was willing to be interviewed. Johan suspected that they'd all been given instructions by the police. Just as they had decided to give up and were about to drive off, a boy about ten or eleven came walking along the road. Johan rolled down the window.

"Hi! My name is Johan, and this is Pia. We work for the TV station, and we've been here filming the pasture where the horse was killed. Did you hear anything about what happened?"

"Of course I did," said the boy. "I live right over there."

He nodded at the road behind them.

"Do you know the girls who found the horse?"

"A little. But they don't live here. They're just visiting their grandmother and grandfather."

"Do you know where their house is?"

"Yes, it's right nearby. I can show you."

The boy declined their offer to let him ride along in their car. He led the way down the road, and they drove behind at a snail's pace.

They quickly reached the home of the girls' grandparents.

A well-trimmed hedge surrounded the house, and outside sat the two girls on a big rock, dangling their legs.

Johan introduced himself and Pia, who was right behind him.

"We're not allowed to talk to reporters," said Agnes. "That's what Grandpa said."

"Why are you sitting out here?" asked Johan, ignoring her comment.

"No reason. We were thinking of picking some flowers for Mamma and Pappa. They'll be here tonight."

"How lovely for you," said Pia sympathetically. "After such an awful thing happened. I can't understand how anyone could do something like that to a horse. To such an innocent animal. And he was so adorable, a real sweetheart from what I heard."

"The world's sweetest horse, that's what he was. The world's most adorable pony . . ."

Agnes's voice faded away.

"What was his name?"

"Pontus," said the girls in unison.

"We're going to do our best to help out so that the police will catch the person who did this. I promise you," Pia went on. "Was it horrible when you found him?"

"It was disgusting," said Agnes. "The whole head was gone."

"I wish we'd never gone into that pasture," added Sofie.

"Now wait a minute—just think about it. You were the ones who went in, and it was actually a very good thing that you did, because otherwise it might have taken much longer before Pontus . . . Was that his name?"

The girls nodded.

"Otherwise it might have taken much longer before Pontus was found, and for the police it's really important to investigate these sorts of matters as quickly as possible."

Agnes looked at Pia in surprise.

"I guess that's right. We didn't think about it like that," she said, looking relieved. Sofie also looked happier.

Johan pondered for a few seconds the appropriateness of interviewing such young girls without first obtaining permission from their parents. He was always particularly cautious about interviewing children. This was a borderline case. He decided not to interfere. He would let Pia carry on with the conversation.

"Our job, mine and Johan's," said Pia in a soft voice, "is to make TV reports when something like this happens. We'd like to be able to give the viewers a story, but of course we would never force anyone to be on TV. Although it's best when we have eyewitnesses who can describe what happened, because that might prompt other people to come forward with tips for the police. We think that if people watching TV saw the two of you talking about how you found Pontus, they'd be more interested than if Johan just talks. They would care more, to be quite honest."

The girls were listening attentively.

"So we were wondering whether we could ask you a few questions about what happened this morning. I'll run the camera and Johan will ask the questions, and if you can't answer or you think it's too hard, we'll stop. You get to decide. Later we'll edit the interview, so it doesn't matter if there are mistakes. Okay?"

Sofie used her elbow to poke Agnes in the side and then whispered in her ear. "We're not allowed."

"No, but I don't care," said Agnes firmly as she jumped down from the rock. "It'll be fine."

When Pia and Johan drove off, they had an interview on film with the girls describing what they had seen. They had also revealed that the horse's head wasn't merely cut off—it had disappeared without a trace.

"It won't surprise me if we catch shit for this," Johan said to Pia as she drove.

"What do you mean?"

"The police are going to be mad. Not that I care, but I just thought I should warn you."

"I don't know what you're talking about." Pia cast an

indignant glance at Johan. "We're doing our job. That's all. There's no need to exaggerate. This is about a dead horse, damn it. Not a person."

"True, but interviewing children is a sensitive issue."

"If we started questioning them right after their mother died, I would understand your reasoning." Pia's voice sounded even angrier.

"Don't misunderstand me," Johan objected. "I just think we need to be careful about interviewing minors. As journalists we have a huge responsibility."

"It's not our fault if people want to talk. We haven't forced anyone. Besides, we found out some new information, thanks to talking to those girls. The part about the horse's head being missing."

She rolled down the window to toss out her wad of snuff. Then she deliberately turned up the music. The discussion was clearly over. Pia was intelligent and bold, but maybe she needed to be a bit more humble, since she was new at the game. Johan sensed that—for good or bad—his colleague was going to be a cameraperson to reckon with in the future.

Emma Winarve was sitting in the hammock in the yard of her house in Roma, leaning against the pillows propped behind her back. She was trying to find as comfortable a position as possible. In her extremely pregnant condition, that wasn't so easy. She was hot and sweaty all the time, even though she stayed in the shade. The high pressure of the past week had taken its toll. Right now she felt huge and shapeless, even though she weighed much less than she had with her other children. So far she hadn't put on more than twenty-five pounds, which seemed to fit in with everything else. This time the pregnancy was different. Previously the children had been eagerly awaited, and there was never any doubt that she would carry them to term. The baby that was now growing in her womb could just as easily have ended up as a bloody lump, scraped out while there was still time. Now, of course, she was glad that hadn't happened. There were still two weeks left before the birth, if everything went as planned.

She and the baby had just enjoyed a fruit salad,

consisting of melon, kiwi, pineapple, and star fruit. Tropical fruit never tasted better than when she was pregnant.

She watched Sara and Filip, who were busy playing croquet on the lawn. They had just finished first and second grade and had already been forced to endure their parents' divorce.

Sometimes the feelings of guilt were oppressive. At the same time, Emma didn't think she could have done anything differently. She usually consoled herself with the fact that at least they weren't alone. Almost half the children in their classes had parents who were divorced.

When she'd met Johan Berg during the previous summer, Emma had fallen passionately in love. Emma—who had never thought she could be unfaithful. At first she blamed it on the shock and the despair she had felt when her best friend, Helena, was murdered. She was the first victim of a serial killer, and Johan was one of the reporters who had interviewed Emma, in her role as friend of the victim.

That was when she began to have serious doubts about her marriage. The feelings that she developed for Johan were something she had never experienced before. Several times she tried to break things off and went back to her husband, Olle, who forgave her in spite of everything.

During one of the occasional relapses to which she later succumbed, when she met Johan in secret, she got pregnant. Her first thought was to get rid of the fetus. When she told Olle, he was even prepared to forget about her repeated infidelities, but the condition he laid down for saving their marriage was that she have an abortion. She made an appointment for the procedure and told Johan once and for all that it was over.

She and her family celebrated a quiet Christmas together. The children were overjoyed that everything was back to normal, and Emma received a much-longed-for puppy from Olle as a Christmas present.

Then Johan suddenly showed up at their home in Roma and turned everything upside down. When Emma saw the two men in her life together, the whole situation appeared in a new light that was blindingly clear. All of a sudden she understood why it had been so difficult to end her relationship with Johan. He was obviously the one that she loved. Her marriage to Olle was over, and it was too late to do anything about it.

Two days later she phoned Johan and told him that she was keeping the baby.

Now here she sat, newly divorced with two children living with her every other week, and a third child on the way. The fact that she had decided to have the baby didn't mean that she and Johan would automatically become a family, as he had apparently imagined. There was nothing Johan wanted more than to move into the house immediately and become a stepfather for Sara and Filip, but Emma needed time. She felt far from ready to throw herself into a new family configuration. How she was going to manage to take care of the baby all alone was something that she would deal with later.

She ran her hand over the lemon yellow cotton of her dress. Her breasts felt big and heavy, already set for their coming task. Her legs were partially numb. Her circulation had gone from bad to worse; this was at least something that she remembered from her previous pregnancies. It felt as if her blood were motionless inside her body. She was pale, her fingers and toes were cold, and the fact that she had become so sluggish and ungainly didn't make things any better. Emma was used to working out at least three times a week. She was an inveterate smoker, but she had stopped as soon as she learned that she was pregnant, just as she had done the other two times. She didn't have the slightest craving, but she sensed that she would start smoking again as soon as she stopped breast-feeding.

Her smoking went hand in hand with the level of problems in her life. To put it simply: The more problems she had, the more she smoked. She had to have some sort of solace when life was so hard. How she was supposed to handle the divorce was impossible to predict; that was something she had been ruthlessly forced to acknowledge.

She'd been prepared for things to be difficult with Olle, but she'd never anticipated that everything would become so nasty, bitter, and miserable. All the exhausting fights and his victim's mind-set had almost put her over the edge during the past spring. It was a miracle that she had managed to get through it without smoking.

At least they'd managed to find a good solution to the question of where to live. Olle had gotten himself a big apartment in downtown Roma, within walking distance of their house. They'd agreed to take turns having the children every other week, at least in the beginning. Later they would see how things went. The children would decide. At least Olle was reasonable enough to see to it that the children weren't affected more than necessary.

Emma raised her eyes from the crossword puzzle that she was staring at, the letters melting together into an incomprehensible blur. Sara and Filip were completely absorbed in their croquet game. They hadn't had a single fight. That was an unexpected benefit of all that had happened: The children seemed calmer now, as if they had taken on more responsibility. There was no longer the same amount of space for them to mess around in when everything else was falling apart. Her guilty conscience again tapped her on the shoulder. The divorce was her fault. That's what the whole family thought, including her parents, although no one would come right out and say so.

She had explained things to the children as best she could, without trying to make excuses. But was that good enough? Would they ever understand?

She looked at their smooth young faces. Sara, with the darker hair and intense brown eyes, was lively but meticulous. She was talking loudly to her little brother while he tried to concentrate on hitting the ball through the hoop. Filip had blonder hair and a fairer complexion; he was a prankster and the family rascal.

She wondered if she would be able to love her unborn child as unconditionally as she loved them.

Knutas's office was on the second floor of police headquarters. It was spacious and bright, with sand-colored walls and light furniture made of birch. The one exception was his old, worn desk chair made of oak with a soft leather seat. He hadn't been able to part with it when the building was remodeled the previous year and all the other old things had been replaced. Too many puzzle pieces had fallen into place while he sat in that chair for all those years. He felt that he wouldn't be able to think as well in a new chair, even though it might be better for his back.

He rocked gently back and forth as he pondered the case of the decapitated pony. Crimes against animals were extremely rare on Gotland. Of course, there were incidents of neglect—people who forgot to feed animals or clean out their cages or boxes—but this was something different. Possibly a madman who enjoyed hurting animals. Knutas had dealt with cases like that before, although not of this caliber. Maybe the horse was killed in a fit of rage. If so, who was the actual target of the anger?

At the same time, the whole thing seemed the result

of cold-blooded calculation. The crime had been committed at an hour when everyone was in bed asleep but it was still light enough outdoors. According to the farmer, the perp must have fed the other animals, to ensure that he'd be able to commit the deed without commotion. It gave him the opportunity to kill and butcher the horse in peace and quiet. The question was: Why had the killer taken the head away? It was hardly for the purpose of fishing for eel, the way Knutas had seen someone use a horse's head in a movie long ago.

He took out his pipe, filling it with great care. Then he sucked on the stem without lighting it. That was what he usually did whenever he needed to think. He seldom lit his pipe, and besides, smoking wasn't permitted indoors. By turning his chair slightly he could see the overcrowded parking lot at the Forum supermarket. The tourist season had started in earnest after the Midsummer holiday. The island had fifty-eight thousand permanent residents, but during the summer months the population increased by another eight hundred thousand. In mid-August it all ended as suddenly as it had begun.

He had asked Wittberg and Jacobsson to take a closer look at the horse owner's background that afternoon. The techs, with Sohlman in charge, were out at the crime scene, and officers had started interviewing neighbors and anyone else who might have seen something.

Lina called. He could tell from her voice that she was stressed. She was going to be late. They were extremely busy at the maternity ward. Knutas told her that he was busy, too.

Knutas's Danish wife, Lina, was a midwife at Visby Hospital, and the Gotland women were giving birth like never before. A new baby boom seemed to have swept the island. Lina had worked late every single day for several weeks now, and it never seemed to let up. He and the twins had to manage as best they could. Not that it was a problem. For the most part the children did a great job all on their own. So far Petra and Nils had spent their summer vacation swimming and playing soccer. They had no objections to receiving money to buy pizza and hamburgers instead of eating their father's poorly cooked meals. The last straw came when he once again offered them what he proudly presented as "Pappa's special macaroni and cheese." It was a tasteless, mushy dish and, on top of everything else, it was burned around the edges.

For Knutas's part, the spring had been relatively uneventful. He hadn't felt well for a while after a high-profile murder case in the winter, when a girl had disappeared and was later found dead. The case had gotten under his skin, and he had become involved in a highly personal manner. In hindsight it was impossible to say how that might have affected his judgment, but he was afraid that it had failed him. If so, he had contributed to the girl's death. The guilt he felt was hard to bear.

For a while he thought he was sinking into a depression of the very worst kind. Insomnia was the clearest sign—and the fact that he often felt dejected and listless wasn't like him. Suddenly he had also acquired a temper that made Lina's loud outbursts seem like mouse squeaks in comparison. He lost his temper at the slightest things, and when his family members reacted to his unprovoked anger, he felt offended and wronged. Like a damn martyr. It ended with Lina dragging him to see a psychologist. For the first time in his life Knutas had accepted professional help for his personal problems. His expectations were low, but he'd been surprised. The therapist was there to help him, and she gave him her undivided attention, listening without offering advice or criticism. She took in what he said, then asked a few questions here and there, which led him onto new avenues of thought. Through the therapy he had gained new insights about himself and his relationship to those around him, and the feelings of guilt gradually decreased. It was actually only recently that he'd started feeling better.

His thoughts were interrupted when the phone rang again. The switchboard wanted to know if he was willing to meet with the team from Swedish TV. With a sigh Knutas agreed. He had an ambivalent relationship with Johan Berg. The reporter's persistence could infuriate

Knutas, although he had to admit that Berg was good at his job. Berg often managed to dig up information on his own, plus he had a confounded talent for getting people, including the superintendent, to reveal more than they'd originally intended to say.

Johan seemed stressed when he appeared in the hallway. He probably was in a rush to do his broadcast. His black hair was plastered to his forehead, and his cotton shirt was rumpled and stained. It occurred to Knutas that the reporter had probably already been out to Petesviken and had just come back from there. If only he hadn't found anyone who had agreed to an interview. Knutas didn't want to say anything; he had no right to interfere with the work of journalists. Their job was to find out as much as possible, while his was to make sure that information didn't leak out. He prepared himself for some difficult questions, noticing how his jaw tightened before the interview even began.

Johan had brought with him that new camerawoman, who looked like a punk with her black hair sticking out in all directions. She also had a ring in her nose.

Pia refused to make do with standing in the hallway. She directed them out to a balcony that had been built when police headquarters was remodeled. She wanted Knutas to talk about that horrible crime against the idyllic backdrop of the summer greenery, the ring wall, and the sea. Typical TV people—the only thing they thought about was their camera shots.

Johan started off with the usual questions about what had happened. Then came something unexpected—or maybe not totally unexpected.

"Have you found the head?"

Knutas clenched his teeth and didn't answer. The fact that the head was missing was something the police had decided to keep secret. Those who knew about it had been given strict instructions not to divulge anything about the matter.

"I wonder if you've found the head," Johan repeated stubbornly.

"I have nothing to say on that topic," said Knutas, annoyed.

"I've been told by a reliable source that it's missing," said Johan. "So you might as well confirm it, don't you think?"

Knutas's face turned bright red with anger. He realized that the police no longer had anything to gain by denying the fact.

"No, we haven't found the head," he admitted, giving a sigh of resignation.

"Do you have any theory about what happened to it?"

"No."

"Does that mean that the perpetrator took it with him?"

"Probably."

"Why would he do that?"

"Impossible to say at the moment."

"What do you think the person or persons who did this will use the head for?"

"It's all speculation, and speculation is something that we police don't waste much time on. Right now it's a matter of trying to catch the guilty party."

"What's your personal reaction to the crime?"

"I think it's terrible that someone would do such a thing to an animal. It goes without saying that the police are taking the matter very seriously, and we're going to devote all possible resources to finding out who's to blame. We're appealing to the public to call the police with information if they saw or heard anything that might be connected with the crime."

Knutas ended the interview.

He was hot and annoyed. Even though he knew it was fruitless, he tried to get Johan to leave out the information about the missing head. Not surprisingly, the journalist refused to budge. He thought the information was of such general interest that it had to be made public.

By the time Pia and Johan got back to the office, they had to hurry to put together the story in time to make the evening news. They sat down to work in the only editing room. Johan called Grenfors, who thought it was okay that they had interviewed the girls. They were old enough, and he was of the same opinion as Pia—it was just a horse, after all. On the other hand, Grenfors wasn't known for being the most cautious of news editors.

"I just hope that no one else finds out the part about the missing head," murmured Pia as she focused on pushing buttons. They had half an hour left before it was time for the first spot from Regional News, and they had promised the editor to deliver at least a minute and a half. At five fifty they were ready, and they sent the digital story by computer to the home office in Stockholm.

After the broadcast, Grenfors called. "Well done," he said appreciatively. "Great that you got the girls. They were damn good, and I don't think they've been interviewed by anyone else."

"No, as far as I know, we were the only ones they talked to."

"How did you get them to talk, by the way?"

"The credit goes to Pia," said Johan. "She was the one who persuaded them."

"Is that right?" Grenfors sounded surprised. "Give her my best and tell her that she did a damn fine job. What are you doing tomorrow to follow up?"

In his mind Johan pictured the editor as he sat there, tilting his chair back at his desk in the Regional News offices in the TV building in Stockholm's Gärdet district. He was a tall, trim man of fifty, with dyed hair and a blatant sense of vanity.

Johan thought that things had been getting worse lately. Grenfors had grown more and more nervous. His anxiety about not getting usable stories delivered on time manifested itself in different ways: constant phone calls to ask how the work was proceeding and long discussions about how the report should be done. The editor often made his own calls to individuals who had been booked for an interview, just to double-check that it was actually going to take place.

Of course, Grenfors had always had a tendency to meddle too much, but not to this extent. Johan wondered whether it had to do with the increased stress and shrinking profits at the editorial office. Cutbacks were frequent at the news divisions. Resources were constantly being reduced, while fewer and fewer people were being asked to do more stories, at the price of stressed-out colleagues and reduced quality.

That was one of the big advantages of working on Gotland—not having to take the brunt of the editor's constant anxiety. Right now Johan could at least keep it at a distance.

THURSDAY, JULY 1

Exactly as Knutas had expected, there was strong reaction to the news about the decapitated horse.

Ever since he had arrived at work at seven thirty that morning, the phone had been ringing off the hook. In the wake of the reports in the media came reactions from municipal politicians, horse lovers, animal rights activists, vegans, and the general public. Everyone wanted the police to hurry up and catch the scumbag who had committed such a crime.

As Knutas entered the room there was a rustling of morning newspapers from everyone who had gathered for the next meeting of the investigative team.

Lars Norrby was back from his two-week vacation to the Canary Islands. He had arrived home late last night, and he was deeply engrossed in the morning paper. The police spokesman was tall and dark, and now he also had an attractive suntan. He had worked at Visby police headquarters just as long as Knutas had, and he served as the superintendent's deputy. Norrby was phlegmatic but scrupulous and reliable. He was not a man of surprises; Knutas always knew where he stood with him.

The meeting started off with a discussion of what the local media had publicized.

"I can't understand how the girls wound up on TV," said Jacobsson. "We expressly told them not to give anyone an interview."

"That Johan Berg from Regional News is an asshole to manipulate children that way," raged Wittberg. "A damned idiot."

"We can't stop anyone, whether they're children or adults, from talking to the press if they want to," said Knutas. "At the same time, it may not be such a bad thing. The fact that the girls spoke out will hopefully lead to some sort of tip, and that's what we need. So far they've been few and far between. Even worse is the fact that everyone now knows that the horse's head is missing. That's going to stir up a lot of speculation."

Sohlman looked tired. He had probably worked late into the night.

"We've examined the tire tracks more closely and were able to distinguish sets from two different vehicles. One of them was easy to identify; it's from the farmer's car. We've compared the tread on the tires to the tracks, and they're a perfect match. As for the other set of tracks, it's more difficult. The tires have big tread and are worn almost bald. They're probably from a small truck, maybe a pickup, but they might also belong to a van."

"Any other evidence?" asked Jacobsson.

"We've picked up a lot of things: plastic bags, Popsicle sticks, cigarette butts, a few bottles. Nothing especially interesting."

"We should go visit other horse owners in the area and find out if they've seen anything fishy," she suggested. "Sometimes you have to ask people directly."

"Although I don't know how much energy we should invest in this matter," said Knutas. "It *is* just a horse, after all."

"What do you mean 'just'? It's a disgusting case of animal abuse," said Jacobsson indignantly. "Should we forget about the whole thing simply because no human being was harmed?"

"Anyone who could do that to an animal might definitely be a danger to people as well," added Wittberg.

"If nothing else, the TV news really managed to stir people up after the story last night. The public is demanding that we do everything in our power to find the person who killed the horse. The phone has been ringing nonstop. I think we may need to spend as much time calming down all the outraged people as we do on the actual investigation. But no matter what, we do need to discuss the part about the decapitation. What sort of person do you think would do something like that?" Knutas let his gaze move from one colleague to the next.

"I think it seems as if someone is out for personal revenge against the farmer. Or maybe against the wife. Or why not the eldest son?" Norrby rubbed his hand meditatively over his clean-shaven chin. "It's definitely a warning, no doubt about it. Some bizarre sort of vendetta."

"Or maybe the whole thing has to do with what we can't find in the pasture, meaning the horse's head," Knutas countered. "What's the perp going to use it for? Maybe we should start over from that angle instead. He can't very well be thinking of making it into a trophy and hanging it up over the fireplace like a moose head. Someone who doesn't have a thing to do with the Larsson family might have reason to be afraid."

"The whole thing is starting to sound like *The Godfather*," said Jacobsson. "Don't you remember the man who woke up to find the horse's head in his bed?"

Everyone around the table grimaced.

"Maybe a Gotland Mafia has secretly taken root down there in the south of the island," snickered Norrby. "Just like in Sicily."

"Oh, sure, there are lots of similarities between Gotland and Sicily," added Knutas with a wry smile. "We have plenty of sheep. And sheep heads."

FRIDAY, JULY 2

The prop plane landed at the Bromma domestic airport outside Stockholm just after 3:00 P.M. The man with the dark blue sports bag stood up the minute the plane stopped moving. He wore tinted glasses and a cap pulled down over his forehead. He'd been lucky enough to have two seats to himself, so there was no risk that someone might try to converse with him. The flight attendant must have sensed his antipathy because she came by only once to make him a discreet offer of coffee; after that she left him in peace. As his cab headed toward Stockholm, he let out a quiet sigh of anticipation. He was looking forward to the meeting.

He asked the driver to stop several blocks from his destination. There could be nothing that would trace him to the address. It was the height of the summer, and Stockholm was trembling with heat. Outdoor cafés filled the sidewalks, where customers were enjoying a caffe latte or a glass of wine. The water glittered down by Strandvägen. At the wharf old sailboats were moored side by side with luxury yachts and passenger ferries, which during the peak hours would transport

Stockholmers and tourists out to the archipelago.

He had never felt comfortable in the capital, but on a day like today, even he could almost understand why some people loved Stockholm. Everybody in the part of the city where he now found himself was well dressed, and almost everyone he saw was wearing sunglasses. He smiled in amusement—how typical for city dwellers. As if the slightest encounter with nature made them want to protect or equip themselves in some way.

In the city he was a stranger, an outsider. It was hard to comprehend that these well-dressed people who walked with such purpose along the street all around him were actually his fellow countrymen. Here everyone knew where they were going.

The quick pace made him nervous. Everything had to move so fast, so very fast. When he stopped to buy a can of snuff at the Pressbyrån kiosk and searched for change, he could feel the impatience of the clerk behind the cash register as the line behind him grew longer.

The building was one of the city's most exclusive addresses, and the trees that lined the street lent it an imposing frame. He had memorized the code, and the massive oak door slid open with an ease that surprised him. The stairwell inside was empty and silent. A crystal chandelier hung from the ceiling, and on the floor lay a thick red carpet that continued up the entire staircase. The ceiling height was impressive. The austere grandeur and permeating silence made him uncertain. He stood there for a moment, staring at the names on the elegant sign on the wall: von Rosen, Gyllenstierna, Bauerbusch.

Suddenly he felt like a timid little boy. He had the same sense of submissiveness and lack of self-esteem that he'd had when he was growing up. He didn't belong here; he was a house cat among ermines; he wasn't good enough or distinguished enough to be in this luxurious marble foyer among the refined people who lived behind these dark-varnished doors. For a moment he stood there, struggling with himself. He couldn't just turn around and leave, not after he'd come so far. He had to pull himself together, muster his courage. He'd done that before. He sat down on the bottom step, put his head in his hands, and shut his eyes tight. He needed to concentrate, although at the same time he was worried that someone might come in the front door. Finally he felt able to stand up.

He chose to walk up the four flights of stairs, even though there was an elevator. He'd never been able to tolerate elevators. Outside the apartment door he stopped to catch his breath. He fixed his eyes on the shiny brass plate with the name engraved in elegant script. Again he felt uncertain. Of course, they had met before, but not here. They barely knew each other. What if the man waiting for him was not alone? He fumbled to pull a handkerchief out of his inside breast pocket. Not a sound came from the neighboring apartments. Not a sign of life.

Uneasiness struck him once more and quickly grew stronger; he felt dizzy. *Not again,* he thought.

The muted walls began to shrink around him, coming closer. Thoughts raced back and forth in his head. He couldn't do it; he had to turn around. The doors were enemies, barriers that were keeping him out; they didn't want him here. The porcelain pot in the window with the magnificent white azalea seemed to be staring at him with hostility: *You have no business being here. Go back to the alley where you came from.*

He stood there paralyzed, concentrating on his breathing, trying to regulate his heartbeat. He had suffered from panic attacks for as long as he could remember. He had to leave—that's what he had now decided. First he just needed to marshal his forces and concentrate so that he wouldn't faint. What a fine mess that would be—to be found here, lying stretched out on the marble floor. What an impression that would make.

Far below he heard the front door open and close. He waited tensely. The building had five floors, and he was up on the fourth. If he was unlucky, the person who had just come in would be heading for the top floor.

Suddenly he heard footsteps coming up the stairs. The footsteps got louder. Someone was about to appear on the stairs at any second, and he wanted at all costs to avoid being seen here. Swiftly he wiped the worst of the sweat from his forehead and took a deep breath. He had to go inside now; he had to force himself to act normal. Resolutely he rang the doorbell.

One hospital delivery room was like any other. Emma wondered if this was the same room in which she had given birth to Sara and Filip. That was almost ten years ago. It seemed to her an eternity as she was maneuvered inside and expert arms moved her over to the birthing bed. Her cervix was now dilated to almost three inches, and everything was happening fast. The nurse was young and dressed in white. She had kind eyes, and her blond hair was wound into a knot on top of her head. She gave Emma's arm a reassuring pat as she recorded the contractions on a chart.

"We've brought you in here because it won't be long now. Soon you'll be all the way open."

The contractions came rushing over her like an earthquake, gradually increasing in strength; everything went black when they exploded into fireworks of pain, only to slowly fade away into a brief respite before the next one rolled through her. They came and went, like swells on the sea outside the window.

Even though Johan was only five minutes away from the hospital, Emma hadn't called him as she had promised to do when the labor pains started. Everything was so complicated, and she had convinced herself that it would be best if she handled the birth on her own. Now she regretted her decision. Johan was the father of her child; that was an irrevocable fact. What did it matter if she allowed him to give her some support? Her pride bordered on pig-headed stupidity. Here she lay, at the mercy of her pain, and she had only herself to blame. She had chosen not to summon him here, to share the moment with her. He could have held her hand, consoled her, and massaged her aching back.

She breathed according to the instructions she had been given in the prenatal course she had attended when she was pregnant with Sara. How different things were back then. They had been so happy—she and Olle. His face flickered past. They had practiced breathing together, they had spent weeks preparing for how they would handle the labor pains, and she had taught him how she wanted to be massaged.

"It's only a matter of minutes now," said the nurse gently as she wiped the sweat from Emma's brow.

"I want Johan to come," whimpered Emma. "The father."

"All right. How do we get hold of him?"

"Call his cell phone. Please."

The young woman didn't waste any time. She rushed out and came right back with a cordless phone. Emma rattled off Johan's number.

* * *

She didn't know how much time had passed before the door opened and she saw Johan's face, looking worried and tense. He took her hand.

"How are you?"

"I'm sorry," she said before the pain overwhelmed her again with even greater force, making any further conversation impossible. She clutched his hand as hard as she could. *Now I'm going to die,* she thought. *I'm going to die.*

"You're open all the way now," said the midwife. "Breathe now, breathe. Don't start pushing yet."

Emma panted like a thirsty dog. The bearing-down contractions tore at her, trying to pull her along with them. She had to use all her strength not to give in.

"Don't push," she heard the midwife urging her.

In a haze she noticed the obstetrician come in and sit beside the midwife, down there somewhere between her white legs, spread wide apart. A sheet covered her, so at least she didn't have to look at all the misery. She had intended to stand up to give birth, or at least to squat down. How shameful this was. She had absolutely no strength left in her legs.

Every now and then, in her groggy state, she was aware of Johan next to her, his hand holding hers.

She lost all sense of time and space as she listened to

her own hysterical breathing—it was the only thing that could stop her from pushing.

Suddenly Emma heard a voice that she had heard before. Another midwife had come into the room. She recognized the woman's Danish accent from one of her previous births.

"All right, here's what we're going to do."

Emma no longer cared about what was happening around her; she had slipped into a vacuum in which she felt no pain. It didn't matter whether she died right here and now. There was something liberating about that thought.

A woman is never so close to death as when she gives life, thought Emma.

Night arrived with unusually high temperatures. The air was oppressive, and the ventilation in the building, which was more than a hundred years old, was all but nonexistent. Warfsholm's youth hostel resembled a merchant's villa from the nineteenth century, but it had originally been built as a public bathhouse. It stood off by itself, right near the water, as an annex to the main building, which housed the hotel and dining room and was several hundred yards farther out on the promontory.

In front of the youth hostel was a neatly mown lawn with some garden furniture, a small parking lot, and an area with juniper shrubs nearly six feet high that grew in a labyrinth before giving way to tall reeds and the water. Behind the hostel was a wooden footbridge that extended three hundred yards out over the water and led to the harbor and the road to the town of Klintehamn.

At this time of day it was tranquil and quiet.

The guests had sat outside for a long time, enjoying the warm night, but now they had all gone off to bed.

Outdoor lamps lit up the building. Not that it was needed—the nights at this time of year were very bright. It never really got completely dark.

The hallway on the ground floor was deserted. The doors to the rooms had been decorated with hand-painted signs: GRÖTLINGBO, HABLINGBO, HAVDHEM. Each of them had been named for a parish on Gotland. The doors were closed, and not a sound penetrated through the solid walls.

Martina Flochten was sweating on her bed. She wore only a pair of panties. She had pulled the duvet out of its cover and tossed it aside. The window was wide open, but it made little difference. Eva seemed to be sleeping soundly on the other side of the room.

Something had made Martina wake up. Maybe it was the heat. She lay motionless, listening to her friend's steady breathing. If only she could sleep like that. Martina was thirsty and had to pee. Finally she gave up trying to go back to sleep. With a sigh she got out of bed, pulled a T-shirt over her head, and looked out the window. A dark haze covered the foliage on the trees, the lawn, and the reeds farther away at the edge of the water. The sun had sunk below the horizon, but the light was still holding on.

Silence reigned. Not even a seagull could be heard at this late hour. A glance at the digital clock on the table told her that it was ten minutes past two.

Martina went to use the bathroom that was halfway

down the hall and then padded up the narrow spiral staircase to the kitchen and got herself a glass of water. She opened the freezer and took out a few ice cubes, dropping them into her glass with a discreet plop. She opened all the windows and left them ajar, to let in the warm night air. She had a hard time imagining that she was so far north.

In one hand she held the glass of water and in the other a cigarette that she stole from a pack on the kitchen counter. She went outside and sat down on the creaky wooden steps.

The lush, overgrown summer greenery was beautiful in the glow of the night. She had really come to love Gotland.

Martina's mother had left the island at the age of eighteen to work as a nanny for a family in Rotterdam. She had planned to stay in the Netherlands for a year, but then she met Martina's father, who was studying to be an architect. They got married, and it didn't take long before Martina and her brother were born.

The family had come to Gotland every year on vacation. They would stay with Martina's maternal grandparents in Hemse or at a hotel in the city. Her grandparents had passed away long ago, and her mother had died in a car crash when Martina was eighteen, but the rest of the family still came to Gotland every year.

Now she was more in love than she had ever been

before. A month ago she didn't even know he existed, but now she felt that he was the very breath of life for her.

A rustling in the grove of trees next to the youth hostel interrupted her thoughts. She lowered the hand holding the cigarette and looked in that direction. Not a sound. Probably a hedgehog. They always came out at night. Then she heard a twig snap. Was someone there? Her eyes swept over the expanse of lawn in front of the house, the tables and benches, the playground, the clothesline with a solitary blue-and-white-striped bath towel hanging from it, and the juniper bushes that stood like lonely soldiers on parade. Suddenly the silence seemed menacing.

She put out her cigarette and remained seated for a moment, listening hard, but once again quiet had settled in. She stood up. Maybe she was imagining things. She wasn't used to these bright, bewitching nights. Wasn't used to being alone. *You nitwit,* she thought. *You're in safe and secure Sweden. There's nothing to be scared of here.*

She pressed down on the handle and the heavy door opened with a creak.

More rustling, but she didn't even turn around to see where the sound was coming from.

SATURDAY, JULY 3

Morning light seeped through the thin curtains. It was very quiet. Johan was sitting in an armchair next to the window with his newborn daughter in his arms, a little bundle in the soft cotton blanket that had been wrapped around her. Her face was tiny and flushed; her eyes were closed, her mouth slightly open.

He thought she was breathing very fast—her heart was beating in her breast like a baby bird's. He held her without moving, feeling the warmth and weight of her body. He couldn't get his fill of looking at her.

Johan didn't know how long he'd been sitting in this position, staring at the baby. His legs had fallen asleep long ago. It was incomprehensible that this little person in his arms was his daughter, that she was going to call him Pappa.

Emma lay in bed, sleeping on her side. Her face was smooth and peaceful. She had been through so much pain only a few hours ago. He had tried to help her as best he could. He had never imagined that a birth could be so dramatic. In the middle of everything, as he held Emma's hand and the midwife issued orders and guided her through the delivery, he was suddenly seized with the enormity of the event. Emma was producing life with her body; another human being was going to come out of it and continue the cycle. That was nature's proper order. He had never felt so close to life before—and yet it was actually a fight between life and death.

For several terrifying moments he was afraid that Emma might die. She seemed to lose consciousness, and the midwife's worried expression didn't bode well. The problem was that vaginal swelling had formed an obstruction so that the baby couldn't come out. That was why Emma wasn't supposed to push, even though she was wide open, because then the vagina swelled up even more. It was turning out to be a difficult delivery until Knutas's wife, Lina, showed up and managed to move the obstruction aside.

After that everything went fine, and it was all over in less than a minute. The second the baby started to cry, Emma relaxed. The first thing Johan did was kiss her. At that moment he admired her more than he had ever admired anyone else.

Johan looked down at his daughter again. Her chin quivered, and she spread out the tiny fingers of her hand like a fan, then curled them up again. He already knew that he would love her all his life, no matter what happened.

On Saturday morning, as Knutas took the turnoff to Lickershamn, he heaved a sigh of relief. A weekend at the summer house was just what he needed after spending the whole week sweating in overcrowded Visby.

Their summer place was no more than fifteen miles from the city, yet out there he felt as if his daily life back home were far away. On the way into Lickershamn proper was an area of erosional rock remnants called rauks where he usually stopped. There were a dozen large rauks and a number of smaller ones. Some were eighteen to twenty feet high, and a number were covered with ivy, the official plant of Gotland. An informational sign posted by the county commission explained that these rauks had been formed by the Littorine Sea seven thousand years ago. Knutas was fascinated by the rauks, which looked like some sort of clumsily shaped stone sculptures. The story of their origin was quite interesting, too.

The Gotland bedrock was largely made up of coral reefs that were created in a tropical sea four hundred million years ago. Between the reefs were layers of limestone, and when the ice that covered Gotland during the last ice age retreated ten thousand years ago, uplift began to occur. Where land and sea met, the waves eroded the bedrock. The reefs withstood the wear and tear of the waves better than the various kinds of rock surrounding them, so that was what remained as isolated stone pillars.

The most impressive rauk was called the Virgin, and it towered up from a plateau eighty-five feet above the sea, right next to the inlet forming the harbor. With its height of forty feet, the Virgin was Gotland's tallest rauk, and for that reason it had become the symbol of Lickershamn. It was a peaceful area with a cluster of houses around the little bay and two docks jutting out into the sea where fishing boats and pleasure craft were moored.

The family's summer place, half a mile away, was a two-story house made of gray-plastered limestone with the window frames, doorframes, and other trim painted burgundy. The surrounding landscape was barren, with stunted and windblown pine trees and juniper bushes. The property was enclosed by a stone fence. There were plenty of stones on this side of Gotland. The stretch of land from Lummelunda all the way up to Fårösund in the north was called the Stone Coast.

Petra and Nils had reluctantly agreed to come along. Knutas had enticed them by promising they would go out in the boat to fish that evening. Lina got out of the car and let out a delighted shout.

"Oh, how lovely," she said, taking in a deep breath. "Feel the air. Look at the sea."

They all helped to bring in the bags of food. Lina and the children were eager to go down to the beach and swim, but Knutas chose to stay behind and mow the grass, even though the summer had been so dry that it was hardly necessary.

At home in the city, Lina was usually the one who took care of the yard. The difference was that out here in the country he was left in peace. It was calm and quiet, with no neighbors to disturb him. He opened the door to the tool shed, and musty air came billowing out. He dragged out the cumbersome lawn mower and filled it with gasoline. It started up nicely after two tries.

He enjoyed making one lap after another, listening to the clattering of the mower and not thinking about anything in particular. Everyone heard the racket and refrained from bothering him while he was at it. That was why he didn't hurry. He mowed the whole lawn with great care.

The house stood off by itself; there were no neighbors within sight. Outside the fence at the back there was a protected beach cove that was used only by his family, a few neighbors, and occasionally a tourist who had gone astray. The large beach near Lickershamn was far enough away so that they weren't disturbed by any other swimmers, yet it was close enough that the children could walk there on their own if they liked. Knutas thought it was a perfect location.

By the time he was done, his shirt was soaked with sweat, even though the task really didn't require any great physical strength; the lawn mower practically ran itself.

He quickly changed into bathing trunks, grabbed a towel, and went down to the beach, where his family's towels and bathrobes were piled up in a heap. He smiled to himself, studying his family as he waded into the water.

Lina had her long, curly red hair pinned up with a barrette on top of her head. Her swimsuit was brightly colored, with big and little polka dots in various shades of pink against a light blue background. Her fair skin was covered with freckles. She often complained about her weight, and once he had taken her complaints seriously—a mistake that he would never make again. For her birthday he had bought her workout equipment, a gym membership, and an introductory package at Weight Watchers. It was an understatement to say that his wife did not appreciate the gift.

After more than fifteen years together, Knutas could still find himself surprised that they were married when he looked at her. He loved her and her boldness. She cleaned house and cooked with equal frenzy—everything was on a grand scale with Lina. Big carrots, sweeping gestures, lots of noise and commotion. She liked to be seen and heard. She took up a lot of room. Like now, as she splashed around in the water.

After their swim, they had coffee on the porch.

When Knutas saw Lina kick off her wooden clogs and gracefully stretch out her feet, he noticed that even her white ankles had freckles. She closed her eyes and tilted her face toward the sun. He decided not to talk about his job during the weekend.

Smoke from browning meat and the smell of strong spices wafted out of the kitchen and found its way into every nook and cranny. The archaeology students were cooking dinner together. Chili con carne was simmering in a giant pot on the stove, and everyone was pitching in.

They had kept the menu simple so that they'd have time to make Eldkvarn's concert at the hotel's outdoor stage at nine o'clock.

Martina was standing at the counter with Steven and Eva. They were peeling onions, and tears were running down their faces—not just from the onions. After having downed a number of shots of tequila, they were in high spirits and kept laughing at each other's bad jokes.

Twenty students were staying at the youth hostel, and right now they were all in the kitchen. Other guests who popped their heads up the spiral staircase saw at a glance that it would be better to come back later. The three tables were being set, and the coffee table in one corner was littered with bottles and glasses. Someone had brought in a boom box; the volume on the old tape player was obviously turned up too loud and was starting to distort the sound. The heat had prompted someone to open all the windows, and the festivities in the kitchen could be heard far and wide.

Martina was wearing low-cut jeans and a black camisole. Her blond hair hung loose. She rarely used much makeup, well aware that it wasn't necessary. A little mascara and lip gloss, nothing more. She was looking forward to seeing him, and she didn't think that anyone else in the group knew what was going on between them. Occasionally she flirted with someone else, just for the pleasure and amusement of seeing his frustration. They trudged around the excavation site, casting stolen glances at each other. Sometimes he happened to stroke her arm or leg with his hand.

"Come on and help me taste this," said Eva, giving her a poke in the side and holding out a spoon. "Is it spicy enough?"

"It needs a little more," said Martina, adding more chili powder. "It shouldn't be bland."

The concert evening couldn't have been more magnificent. The fiery red ball of the sun balanced on the horizon, turning the sea into a gleaming carpet. The aroma of newly grilled lamb still hovered over the concert area from the dinner that had been served at the hotel, and a diverse audience had gathered in front of the stage. Children ran around playing between the blankets; others were swimming in the mirror-smooth water. A group of older motorcyclists had settled down with beer cans in their hands, waiting to enjoy the music. The soft pop-rock tones of Eldkvarn grabbed hold of the listeners and eventually induced nearly everyone to get up and dance.

Martina was enjoying the intoxicated and relaxed feeling in her body after a whole day of hard work in the field. She was more than a little pleased with herself. Right before they were going to pack things up for the day, she had found an Arabic silver coin, dated 1012. Everyone had congratulated her, and she had been tempted to slip the coin into her pocket so that she could show it to her father. Instead she had made do with holding the Viking Age coin in her hand for a moment to admire it.

The singer's soft, raspy voice was uttering words that she didn't understand. No matter how hard she tried, she caught only a few disconnected words. She quickly gave up and concentrated on listening to the beat instead as she danced with the others.

Every once in a while during the evening she had looked for him. Several times she thought she caught a glimpse of his face, but the next second she realized that she was mistaken. She wondered why he hadn't shown up. Jonas distracted her by offering her a cold beer, which she gratefully accepted.

* * *

Several hours later she was sitting squeezed in between Mark and Jonas, and she realized that she was very drunk. Some of their group had gathered on the hotel porch to continue partying with the bikers. It was still hot, even though it was almost one in the morning. Martina had given up hoping that he would appear. At least he could have called her. She dug around in her bag for her cell phone, only to discover that it was missing. Oh well. It was probably somewhere in the grass. She would look for it later. She downed the rest of her drink and got up to go to the bathroom, which was near the main entrance, around the corner.

She had a craving for a cigarette, but she had run out and the pub didn't sell them. She had a whole carton up in her room, and she decided to go get a pack.

After using the toilet, she headed over to the youth hostel. She could hear everyone merrily laughing and talking on the porch. Someone was strumming on a guitar.

When she came out onto the path that ran along the sea, she realized how deserted the area was. She hadn't noticed before that there were no buildings nearby. The desolation was palpable. Bushes and trees lined the path, and from the darkness that was finally descending, she could hear the crickets' invisible orchestra.

On the other side of the water, machines were screeching from the nightly work going on at the harbor. A truck fully loaded with timber drove along the wharf, past the white wind-power station, whose blades were hesitantly turning in the feeble wind. A monstrous crane with a huge iron claw rose up into the air like some strange beast. The activity down at the harbor never seemed to cease.

Farther along, the vegetation was thicker. The willow trees on either side had been allowed to grow unchecked. Their curving branches stretched over the path and reached for each other like lovers hungry for an embrace. They formed a natural tunnel, which, in the solitude of the night, seemed frightening. Martina had sobered up as she walked, and now she regretted that she had come out here alone.

She turned around and realized that the distance back to the others was farther than it was to her room. She might as well keep going. Besides, she had such a craving for a cigarette. She walked faster, doing her best to shake off the feeling of uneasiness.

After she had gone partway into the tunnel of trees, she discovered a silhouette outlined against the light at the exit, about thirty yards ahead. Fear gripped her, and her mind was suddenly stone-cold sober. The figure was coming straight toward her, getting bigger with every step.

She suppressed her first impulse to turn around,

squinting her eyes to see better. At first she wasn't sure if it was a man or a woman. All she could see was a dark figure wearing a cap, a black jacket, and black pants.

No footsteps were audible. The ground was damper here.

The second she realized that it was a man coming toward her, terror lurched in her stomach.

He was walking with his head bowed, and the bill of his cap hid his face.

Mechanically she continued moving forward—as if there were no going back, no alternative. Her thoughts rushed around in her head like frightened sparrows. What was he doing here, in the middle of the night? The concert had ended long ago. Panic shot up inside her, without enabling her to act. Like a robot, she walked forward, rigidly programmed for her own doom.

She didn't dare glance up to see his face now that he was so close. The second they passed each other, she stopped breathing. He was several inches away from touching her arm. She sensed a rank, slightly stale smell that she couldn't place.

To her surprise he walked past and nothing happened.

The distance between them grew. The stranger continued on at the same pace, getting farther and farther away. She cautiously dared to take a breath.

All of a sudden she felt ashamed. It was stupid to scare

herself like that. Good Lord, a poor innocent man who probably worked at the hotel and was on his way home. Sometimes she actually felt sorry for men; they were suspected of all sorts of things, just because they were men.

The path widened, and she could see the light from the front door of the youth hostel. Relief made her dizzy. He wasn't dangerous. She had been imagining things. *But I'm not going out again,* she thought. Now all she longed for was the safety of her bed.

The fact that the man behind her had turned around was something that she noticed only when it was too late.

SUNDAY, JULY 4

Eva woke up because it was unbearably hot in the room. With great effort she turned onto her stomach and placed the pillow over her head to escape the relentless light. The pain was somewhere behind her eyes, and it wouldn't let up. How long had she been asleep? It was Sunday, which meant no excavating, thank God. She had a churning feeling in her stomach, reminding her that she had drunk much more than she could tolerate. Judging by the sunlight, it must be at least noon. She squinted her eyes at Martina's bed. It was empty, just as it was when Eva came home in the wee hours of the morning.

She yawned, climbed out of bed, and went down the hallway to take a shower. When she came back, she discovered that it was only ten o'clock.

Mark and Jonas had both had a hard time hiding their disappointment when they realized that Martina wasn't coming back after going off to use the toilet last night. It was obvious that they were both hoping they could get it on with her. Eva had assumed, as they had, that Martina had gone to bed. She had been far from sober. Apparently that was not what happened. She must have met someone.

Eva looked out the window, as if expecting Martina to come walking along the path. She went up to the kitchen, got out some things for breakfast, and made a pot of strong coffee. Jonas turned up after a while and sat down next to her with a cup of tea and a few pieces of toast. They chatted about the previous evening, and it wasn't long before he asked her where Martina was.

"I actually have no idea where she is. She didn't sleep here last night, anyway."

That would serve him right. She didn't like Jonas. He was a conceited and stubborn kind of guy. It would do him good to suffer a little.

"She didn't?" He paused with the glass halfway to his lips.

"No. Her bed wasn't slept in," Eva told him with ill-concealed glee.

"But that means something might have happened to her."

"Oh, cut it out. She slept with some guy she met, of course. There were several who seemed interested in her at the concert. Didn't you notice that tall blond guy from Stockholm that she was dancing with? He's probably the one she's with. She thought he was cute."

Jonas's face grew pale. "Who knows what kind of guy he is, a complete stranger like that. Is he staying here?"

"My dear boy, she wasn't born yesterday, you know.

Martina can take care of herself. She's a grown woman, for God's sake. Besides, I have no idea where he's staying."

Unperturbed, Eva went back to her yogurt.

On Sunday afternoon the students gathered to play volleyball on the beach. Martina still hadn't made an appearance. Eva had tried calling her cell phone several times but got no answer. *She could at least give us a call,* she thought with annoyance. She didn't really know Martina very well; they had only met a few weeks ago. Of course, they'd had fun together, both at the excavation site and during their off-hours, but Eva didn't really know much about her. None of the others seemed to think there was anything strange about the fact that Martina still hadn't shown up.

Eva tried to shake off a growing sense of concern. Maybe she was being silly, yet she couldn't help feeling seriously worried that something might have happened to her friend. It didn't help matters that Jonas and Mark kept hovering around, asking her where Martina could be.

MONDAY, JULY 5

When Martina still hadn't come home by the following morning, Eva decided to call the excavation leader, Staffan Mellgren, even though it was only 6:00 A.M. She didn't care whether she woke him up. She had lain awake most of the night, gripped by a growing sense of dread. Staffan answered the phone after a dozen rings, sounding bleary with sleep. He came wide awake when he heard that one of his students was missing.

"She's been gone since Saturday night?" he said angrily.

"Yes." Eva regretted not calling Staffan earlier. "We went to the concert, and then a bunch of us sat out on the hotel porch afterward. Martina left to go to the bathroom, but she never came back. We thought she had gone to bed."

"What time was that?"

"Maybe one or two in the morning. I didn't notice the time."

"What did the rest of you do?"

"We stayed where we were, talking."

"Didn't anyone go looking for her when you noticed that she hadn't come back?"

"No."

"How long did you stay there after she left?"

"An hour, maybe two."

"Has anyone seen her since then?"

"No, at least nobody who was sitting on the porch that night."

"And Martina hasn't been heard from since?"

"No."

"Are you sure that she hasn't slept in her bed these past two nights?"

"Of course I'm sure," Eva said in a voice that started to quaver. She couldn't hold back her tears any longer. She was frightened by the fact that he sounded so serious. His reaction confirmed her own feelings, that her concern was justified.

"We need to call the police. It's the only thing to do."

"You think so?"

"Absolutely. Something must have happened, otherwise she would have called. Have you talked to anyone at the front desk in the hotel?"

"No."

"Do that. In the meantime, I'll call the police."

Her legs trembling, Eva ran over to the front desk, which was in the main building. The clerk knew who Martina was but hadn't seen her. She offered to ask the rest of the staff during the course of the morning. Eva sank onto a chair. She punched in the number of her friend's cell phone but no longer got her voice mail. Now a monotone voice informed her: "The party you are trying to reach is temporarily unavailable."

Knutas and Jacobsson decided to drive out to Warfsholm, since Martina Flochten had been missing for more than twenty-four hours and no one seemed to know where she had gone. She hadn't contacted either her family or her boyfriend back home in the Netherlands.

Besides, they didn't have anything better to do. The summertime drought had set in, and the investigation of the decapitated horse had come to a standstill. It was a mystery who the perpetrator could be and where the head might be found.

They first checked at the front desk to see whether Martina's valuables were still in the safe where they'd been kept. Everything was there: her passport, her Visa card, and her insurance documents. So she hadn't left the country—at least not voluntarily.

They met Martina's roommate, Eva Svensson, on the stairs of the main building. She had shoulder-length ash blond hair, and she was wearing a white cotton camisole, a skirt, and sandals. As she led the way over to the youth hostel, they asked her about Martina.

"Does she have a boyfriend?" asked Jacobsson.

"She's seeing this guy back in Holland, or at least she was when she left home. But I actually think she met someone else here on Gotland."

"Why do you think that?"

"She's been gone a lot, and sometimes she slips away without giving any explanation."

"So this isn't unusual? For her to be missing?"

"The difference is that she hasn't called anyone. She always calls."

"How well do you know Martina?" Knutas carefully studied the young woman.

"Not too well. We liked each other at once, and we had a lot of fun right from the start. The course began with two weeks of theory at the college in Visby, so we were in town all the time. Then Martina started going off on her own in the evenings. During the second week I hardly saw her at all."

"Did you share a room in Visby, too?"

"No, we all had our own dorm rooms, so we didn't keep tabs on each other the same way we do here. Since we've been here at Warfsholm, she's often gone off on her own. Her excuse is that she has errands to run or that she wants to meditate, but I don't believe it. She's not the type."

"Has she ever been gone for a whole night before?"

"One night last week she slept somewhere else. She claimed that she was going to meet some friends of her family in Visby. They usually come here on vacation."

"Do you know who they are? These friends?"

"No. I never asked her, and she never told me. I'm not from here, so I wouldn't know them anyway."

"Couldn't that be what's happened now? That she's simply visiting friends?"

"I don't think so. She would have called."

"If she has a boyfriend here, who could it be?" asked Jacobsson.

"I actually have no idea. I've been trying to figure it out, to see if there's something going on between her and someone in the group, but it's hard to tell because she jokes around with everybody."

"Why didn't you ask her?"

"I've tried, but she always changes the subject as soon as I bring it up."

"Who would she have an opportunity to meet other than the students in the course? You don't have contact with many other people, do you?"

"No, although there are other guests staying at the hotel and the campground nearby. And she might have met someone in Visby earlier."

When they stepped into the entryway of the youth hostel, they could tell at once that the building was a venerable old place, even though it had been re-modeled. In the hall hung a bulletin board with instructions for everything from parties to fishing trips to the laundry room. From upstairs came the smell of toast, and subdued voices could be heard conversing. The room that Eva and Martina shared was on the ground floor, almost at the end of the corridor. It was long and narrow and cramped, with a window on one wall. A modest, iron-framed bunk bed stood on each side of the room, with barely enough space to walk between them. A sink with a mirror above it was fastened to one wall. Every nook and cranny was filled with clutter. A tape player stood on the wide windowsill along with bottles of hairspray, cosmetic bags, perfume, nail polish, bags of chips, and CDs. Clothing was either strewn about or hanging from the posts of the top bunks. Several books about the Viking Age signaled that archaeology students were staying in the room. Knutas gave up as soon as he stood in the doorway and saw all the mess. He let Jacobsson search the place on her own. There wasn't enough space for both of them anyway.

He sat down outside, actually lit his pipe for a change, and made a number of phone calls to see to it that the site was secured. He spoke to Erik Sohlman, who wanted to wait to do a technical examination of Martina's room. For the time being, they had no reason to suspect that a crime had been committed.

Meanwhile, Jacobsson did her search of the room. Eva had told her which side was Martina's, and Jacobsson began systematically going through the girl's belongings.

Her toiletry case was there, containing her toothbrush and a pack of birth control pills, which revealed that Martina hadn't taken any pills since Friday, July 2—which was several days ago. *If she had left voluntarily, she would have taken her toiletry case with her,* thought Jacobsson as she opened the suitcase that had been shoved under the bed. In addition to clothing it held a number of books, an unopened carton of cigarettes, and some makeup. In a slot she found a photograph of a young man with dark hair and brown eyes. Jacobsson turned it over, but there was nothing written on the back.

She slipped the picture into her pocket so she could ask Eva about it later and then looked around the cramped room. There wasn't much else to search. Except for the bed, of course. Carefully she removed the floral-patterned cover. There was a rustling sound, and under the pillow she found a page torn out of a newspaper. She sat down on the edge of the bed and unfolded the page. It was an article from *Gotlands Allehanda,* which had done a story on the first excavation course of the summer. The article was about what the students would be doing and where they came from. A picture showed the excavation leader, Staffan Mellgren, and several of the students in action out in the field. Jacobsson studied the article with surprise. Why would Martina keep it under her pillow?

That was where someone would usually keep something that was especially precious, maybe even hiding it there.

Staffan Mellgren was smiling broadly at the camera; the others could be seen in the background. He had to be twice as old as Martina. Jacobsson knew that Mellgren was married and had children. He was well known on Gotland because of his work at the college and at the archaeological excavations. Had they been seeing each other? Was he mixed up in her disappearance?

She hurried off to find Knutas.

Johan was awakened by a bang outside the window. With great effort he got out of bed and pulled aside the curtain.

The pastry shop across the street was getting its daily delivery. The bakery truck was parked in the narrow alley, and the driver was taking out boxes, which he loaded onto a hand truck. The owner of the pastry shop then took the hand truck and with a clatter disappeared through the back door. That meant that it couldn't be more than six in the morning. With a groan Johan went back to bed and pulled the covers over his head. The deliveries were made at six on weekdays, at eight on the weekend. He had learned that by now. If he had known in advance that this upheaval was going to take place every single morning, he would have made Swedish TV arrange for a different apartment.

Wrapped up in the warm covers, he lay there thinking about Emma and their newborn child. He had spent nearly the entire weekend over at the hospital. He wasn't allowed to sleep there, since it was already overcrowded, and Emma had to share a room with two other women who had just given birth.

The delivery of their baby was the biggest event of his life so far. The experience of becoming a father was more overwhelming than he could have imagined.

His mother and youngest brother had flown over from Stockholm on Saturday. She could hardly contain her joy at becoming a grandmother. Her first grandchild. Ever since the death of Johan's father a couple of years ago, her life had been very lonely. Johan had always been close to his mother, and he knew that she missed him now that he was working on Gotland. In his role as the eldest son, he had largely functioned as a replacement for his father after his death.

With the birth of the child, Johan realized that everything was going to be different. From now on he had to make his own family his first priority. He had suddenly become a family man with all new responsibilities. He found the thought both appealing and frightening.

The head office in Stockholm had sent flowers, but Grenfors expected Johan to be back at work right after the weekend. He had been assigned to cover the island, and they had agreed that he would wait to take any paternity leave until fall. He now regretted that decision. All he wanted to do was spend time with his new family.

The insistent buzzing of his cell phone interrupted his ruminations. *I really need to change the ringtone,* he thought as he flew out of bed to grab the phone from under his clothes, which were piled in a heap on the chair. He now paid attention to his phone in a whole different way. Emma might be calling him.

Instead the call was from Niklas Appelqvist, one of the few personal friends Johan had on Gotland. Even though Niklas was ten years younger, they enjoyed each other's company, mostly because they shared an interest in sixties rock 'n' roll. Johan had gotten to know the young archaeology student a year earlier, in connection with a murder case. Niklas lived in the same building as a newspaper photographer on a disability pension who had been found murdered in the basement. Niklas had helped Johan by giving him a number of tips during the investigation. When Johan moved to the island, they started spending time together.

"Hi, how're things going?"

"Fucking great," Johan managed to say. He cleared his throat and wearily sat down. "I became a father on Friday."

"Really? That's great! Congratulations! Boy or girl?"

"A girl," said Johan, feeling himself smile.

"Did everything go all right?"

"Well, it was a little dramatic for a while, but she got here just fine. So beautiful. Eight pounds two ounces, and twenty inches long."

"Wow. How's Emma?"

"Good, although she's really tired, of course."

"We need to celebrate this." Niklas sounded

enthusiastic. "Let me take you out for a beer tonight."

"Thanks, but I can't. I'm going to bring Emma and the baby home from the maternity ward. Maybe another time."

"Okay. By the way, I heard about something that might interest you."

"What's that?"

"A girl who's studying archaeology has disappeared. She's taking an excavation course at the college. Students from all over the world come here to work on a dig during the summer."

"How long has she been missing?"

"Since Saturday night. They're really upset about it over at the Warfsholm youth hostel where she's staying. Apparently she disappeared after the Eldkvarn concert on Saturday, and no one has seen her since. I know a girl who's helping out with the course, and she just told me about it."

"Do you have someone visiting you this early?"

"You mean this late."

"What's her name?"

"The girl who disappeared or my visitor?"

"The one who's missing, of course."

"Martina something or other." Johan could hear Niklas murmuring to someone in the background. "Martina Flochten. She's from the Netherlands."

"Flochten," repeated Johan. "How old is she?"

"Young. Twenty-something."

"Okay. Thanks."

Shit, what bad timing. There was nothing he would rather do than go over to see Emma and the baby, but he was the only TV reporter on the island. The story of a missing girl had to be checked out, even though the whole thing sounded a bit vague. He called the hospital, and according to the nurse who answered, Emma and the baby were fine. Both were asleep at the moment. They had stayed at the maternity ward longer than planned because the breast-feeding hadn't started the way it should.

His concern must have been audible in his voice, because the nurse assured Johan that it was completely normal and nothing to worry about: The breast-feeding would undoubtedly proceed as it was supposed to within a few days. He wondered if this was how his life was going to be, now that he'd become a father. Constant worry about all sorts of things.

It was eight forty-five. He phoned Knutas but was told that the superintendent would be busy all morning, and no one could or would say anything about the missing young woman. He took a shower, shaved, and gulped down a cup of coffee and ate a piece of toast. Then he called Pia. She could pick him up in fifteen minutes. They decided to drive straight out to the Warfsholm hotel and youth hostel.

* * *

The hotel consisted of a late-nineteenth-century wooden building painted yellow, with a lovely tower. It stood on a headland overlooking the sea. On one side of the building was an idyllic sandy beach. Beyond it could be seen the bird sanctuary at Vivesholm, where the spit of land stuck straight out into the water. On the other side of the building was the harbor, which, with its silos and wind-power station, formed a sharp contrast to the beach.

When Johan and Pia got out of the car in the parking lot, they discovered a police car. Two uniformed officers were walking along the beach and talking to families with children. The news team went down to the water and admired the view of the nature preserve on the islands of Big Karlsö and Little Karlsö.

"What's that?" asked Johan, pointing at something that was sticking out of the water just beyond the harbor entrance.

"That's the wreck from a freighter, the *Benguela,* that went aground out there. It must have been at least twenty years ago now."

"What happened?"

"The freighter was coming from Södertälje, on its way to Klintehamn. The accident happened in the winter. I think it was early morning. It was foggy, with a strong wind, and the vessel went aground so hard that they couldn't get her to budge."

"What about the crew?"

"I think they all made it, actually."

"Why hasn't she ever been salvaged?"

"There was something about a loophole in the law that meant the shipping company couldn't be held responsible, and the owner didn't feel he could afford to have the boat towed away. That's why it's still there."

"Incredible." Johan shook his head.

"Yes, isn't it? You used to be able to see a lot more of the boat. She seems to be rusting apart. It won't be long before she completely disappears below the surface."

For the time being they decided not to bother the police officers and walked up to the hotel entrance. They had made an appointment to meet with the manager, Kerstin Bodin. She was a slender, dark-haired woman who gave them a smile but looked tired.

They sat down in the outdoor section of the restaurant, with a view of the harbor. Pia didn't have the patience to sit still, so she went off with her camera.

"This is so unpleasant," said Kerstin. "Of course, it's not certain that anything awful has happened to her, but what if it has? I'm terrified that they're going to find her drowned out there. It's impossible to say what happened. She was apparently very drunk when she left."

"Do you know Martina?"

"We've talked a good deal. I've had more contact with her than with many of our guests. She's extremely nice. A very happy and open sort of girl. Her mother's from Gotland, you know. Martina has been to the island quite often."

"Where is her mother from?"

"Hemse. Both her mother and her grandparents are dead now, and Martina told me that she doesn't have any other relatives on Gotland. But she usually spends a week here every summer, on vacation."

"Do you know where she usually stays when she's here?"

"From what I understood, her family usually stays at the Wisby hotel. Apparently there's a special suite that they always reserve. She told me that her father knows the owner."

"I see. What's his name? Or her name?" Johan quickly added, realizing that he was in fact sitting across from a female hotel manager.

Kerstin smiled. "His name is Jacob Dahlén. We were in the same class in middle school."

"Maybe that's where Martina is."

"I don't think so," said Kerstin, shaking her head. "If so, why hasn't she called anyone? Surely she would know that everyone is worried."

"Yes, you're right," Johan agreed.

The link to the hotel owner in Visby was interesting. He would follow up on it later.

Kerstin took her cell phone out of the pocket of her linen shirt and punched in a number. When someone answered, she got up and went over to the railing that surrounded the restaurant area. She hopped up to perch on the railing as she talked. Sitting there and dangling her legs like that, she looked like a young girl. Johan instantly started thinking about his newborn daughter. In a few years she would be able to sit like that.

Kerstin came back to the table. "Jacob Dahlén doesn't know anything," she said. "He was shocked. He said he didn't even know that Martina was on Gotland."

Because of the photo torn out of a newspaper that Jacobsson had found under Martina's pillow, they decided to drive farther south to Fröjel, which was about six miles from Warfsholm. They wanted to have a talk with the excavation leader, Staffan Mellgren.

At the church Knutas turned off from the main road and parked outside the former school building, which now contained a café and a small exhibition space with a display about the excavations.

A ladder led down to the dig area, and as they approached, they saw Mellgren walking among the students, who were hard at work. The ground had been divided into rectangles that were about a foot and a half deep. In several of the pits, portions of skeletons could be seen, along with other objects that Knutas had a hard time identifying. On a long table in the middle of the area lay folders, maps, and plastic bags marked with various labels. Mellgren had stopped and was writing some notes in a folder. He looked up when Knutas and Jacobsson greeted him. A tall, athletic man with thick, dark brown hair with a touch of gray, he had to be in his forties, Jacobsson guessed. His eyes were an intense brown, and she concluded that he was good-looking—more attractive than in the photos she had seen.

"We'd like to talk to you about the disappearance of Martina Flochten," Knutas began.

"Of course. Just a minute," said Mellgren. He turned to a younger woman in the next pit, asked her a question that they couldn't hear, and jotted down some illegible squiggles.

There were objects inside the plastic bags on the table—bone fragments or tools. Jacobsson exclaimed with surprise when she saw a bag containing a silver necklace and another with silver coins.

"What are you going to do with all this?" She turned to Mellgren, who now seemed to have finished writing his notes.

"Every item we find is documented." He gestured to the ground behind them. "These spaces are called pits. We divide up the ground to facilitate both the excavation and the documentation. The items we find are placed in a bag on which we record the exact location and time of the find, in which pit and at what depth. When the workday is over, we lock up everything in those carts you walked past on your way here. Later the material is taken to our office at the college, where it's sorted and examined. Finally it ends up in the Antiquities Room for storage."

"Could we sit down somewhere and talk?" asked Knutas.

"Of course."

Mellgren led them to a corner of the excavation area where there was a plastic table and a few simple chairs.

"How long have you been digging here?" asked Knutas after they sat down.

"You mean during this course? We're just starting our third week of excavation."

"So by now you've all gotten to know each other well, is that right?"

"Of course. We've spent an intense amount of time together."

"Also in the evenings?"

"Not always, but there are a number of evening lectures and other activities, and sometimes we eat supper together. My responsibilities as the leader don't end when the workday is over." Mellgren smiled.

"What do you think of Martina?" asked Knutas.

The excavation leader turned serious again. "She's very knowledgeable for someone so young. She knows a surprising amount about the Viking Age in particular. Other than that, she's a lively person with a lot of enthusiasm, which rubs off on the others. So she's definitely an asset to the group."

"What do you think about her disappearing like this?" asked Jacobsson.

"It's incomprehensible. I'm sure that she would have called if everything was okay. Now I'm worried that she's in some kind of trouble. I don't know how much longer we can keep digging if she doesn't turn up soon. The fact that she's missing has created an enormous sense of uneasiness among all of us."

"When was the last time you saw her?" Knutas looked at the excavation leader attentively.

"On Saturday, after we finished digging for the day. She rode home in the bus with the rest of the students, the same as usual."

"What time was that?"

"It was around four, I think. Everybody was going to the concert that evening, and they were in high spirits when they left here."

"You didn't go?"

"No. I stayed home with my family."

"I see." Knutas wrote something in his notebook. "Could you describe your relationship with Martina?"

"We get along well. As I said, she's doing a great job."

"And you don't have a more intimate relationship?"

"No, we don't."

Jacobsson took the newspaper clipping out of her bag. "We found this under Martina's pillow on her bed."

Mellgren glanced at the article. His face was expressionless. "What am I supposed to say?"

"Why do you think she had a picture of you under her pillow?" asked Knutas.

"I have no idea. And by the way, the article is about what we do in the course. It's not just about me."

"Do you think that it's out of devotion to her archaeological work that she keeps a photo of the excavation under her pillow?" Knutas's voice was heavy with sarcasm.

Mellgren shrugged his shoulders. "How would I know? I don't know my students very well."

"So you don't have a closer relationship with Martina? That would be easy to assume, from looking at this."

"Absolutely not. Don't you understand that? I'm married and have four children. Besides, naturally I could never get mixed up with my students in that way."

Jacobsson tried a different tactic. "Could it be that Martina is in love with you?"

"I really don't think so."

"Has she given you any signs to that effect?"

"No."

"Maybe you've encouraged her in her work, and she misinterpreted what you said?"

"Of course that's possible, but not as far as I know, at any rate."

"Has anything happened between the two of you?"

"What do you mean by 'happened'?"

"Well, is there anything going on between you?"

"No. And now that's enough."

Mellgren was about to stand up, but Knutas took his arm to stop him.

"You haven't had a fight? Some sort of confrontation?"

"Let's drop this topic. I have exactly the same relationship with Martina as with all the others. No more, no less."

"Then what about someone else?" asked Jacobsson to ease the tension. "Do you know whether she's with someone else in the group?"

"I don't really keep tabs on their relationships with each other."

"You haven't noticed that she's had a fight with anyone?"

"No. Martina was as happy as always when I last saw her. I just hope that she turns up soon."

Jacobsson could see that they weren't going to get any further and changed the subject. She had become quite curious about what was going on around them.

"Could you tell us a little about this site and the excavation work?"

Mellgren sighed and leaned back in his chair, as if to collect himself after the assault on his integrity. Apparently he saw that Jacobsson's interest was genuine, because as he began talking a new gleam appeared in his eye.

"The fields that you see all around here, which to the

naked eye look like ordinary fields and meadows, conceal a Viking Age settlement extending over what we estimate to be a hundred and twenty thousand square yards. In other words, the area is huge. Excavations have been carried out here since the late eighties, and so far we've explored only a small section."

"How did you know that this would be an interesting area to excavate in the beginning?" asked Jacobsson.

"Several reasons. A farmer who was planting his crops discovered something glittering in the soil. It was a bracelet from the tenth century. In addition, the location of the church interested archaeologists." He pointed toward the lovely whitewashed Fröjel Church, which stood on a hill. "It wasn't built in the middle of the parish where people live, like other churches. Instead it's on the edge of Fröjel parish, near the sea. Archaeologists pondered that and came up with the idea that it was probably because there was a harbor down here that was very busy, with people coming and going, and so the church was built nearby. You can also tell from the color of the soil that people and animals have lived here. It's rich in phosphate, which manifests as a darker color in the soil. After the discovery of the bracelet in the field, we initiated some test digs, and that led to the discovery of traces of a trading site with a permanent settlement—rather like Birka on Lake Mälaren on the mainland. We've found the remains of houses, several gravesites, a picture stone, coins, tools, and jewelry. Since we started excavating, we've found a total of thirty-five thousand artifacts."

Jacobsson whistled.

"From what time period?" asked Knutas.

"Mostly the Viking Age, meaning around A.D. 850 to 1050, but we've also found artifacts from the seventh century and the twelfth century, so altogether we're talking about a period of five hundred years."

"How do you know where to dig?"

"When we start an excavation, we decide on a specific area that we think is interesting. Then we divide it into various pits that are each twenty-four square yards, as you can see here."

The quadrants were marked off with string.

"Each participant is given several areas, and then we dig until we reach a depth of ten to twelve inches. That's necessary if we're going to find the artifacts at their proper location; everything above that has usually been disturbed by working the earth, by plowing, for instance. After we've dug down a ways, we slice off the earth, almost like using a cheese slicer, very carefully, half an inch at a time, so as to minimize the risk of disturbing anything. It takes a few weeks to reach the level where it starts getting interesting."

"I had no idea that you had found so much," said Jacobsson, fascinated. "Of course, we've all read and heard about the excavations, but I at least hadn't realized the extent of them until now."

"Good Lord," said Mellgren with a sigh, looking at Jacobsson with amusement. "Nowhere else in the world have there been as many Viking Age coins discovered, for instance, as here on Gotland. The island was in the middle of the trade route between Russia and the Continent, after all, and the islanders were masters at trading goods from various regions."

"What did they trade?" asked Jacobsson.

Knutas was beginning to get a tense look on his face. They weren't here to listen to a lecture on archaeology. They were here to find out facts that might help them locate Martina Flochten. He made a deliberate show of leaving the others to get a firsthand look at the area. Jacobsson seemed completely captivated by Mellgren, hanging on every word he was saying. Knutas hadn't realized that Jacobsson was so interested in history. Yet another side of her that he knew nothing about.

He sat down on a bench that stood next to the area. Below him gaped a pit with a skeleton that lay completely exposed to the air.

It was incredible to think that he was sitting here looking down at the skeleton of a human being that hadn't seen the light of day for a thousand years. How many people had walked across this field since then? Even he felt a certain fascination with the whole thing.

So this was where Martina had sat, scraping away at the earth with the others a few days ago. Where in the name of heaven had she gone? Had she committed suicide? That seemed highly unlikely. She was so full of life, or at least that was the image she presented. Had she been the victim of an accident? She was apparently drunk. Maybe she had simply fallen into the water. So far they had only searched on land. Maybe it was that simple.

Knutas decided to bring in divers on the following day if Martina hadn't turned up.

In the car on their way back, Jacobsson was full of enthusiasm.

"Just think how fantastic that is, all the things they've found. It's unbelievable. I was allowed to hold an amber charm from the tenth century. Can you imagine that? In my next life I'm going to be an archaeologist, no doubt about it."

"At one point I thought we were going to spend all day there," muttered Knutas. "My stomach is completely empty. Don't you ever need to eat?"

"Don't be so grumpy. I thought it was incredibly interesting. We'll pick up some food along the way. What do you think about Mellgren and his relationship with Martina?"

"He seems sincere. I don't think he'd get himself mixed up with one of the participants in the course. It's not just his marriage that would be at stake, if you can use the word 'just.' He'd be risking his whole professional career."

"Maybe he's tired of his job," said Jacobsson matter-of-factly. "Maybe it's a form of self-destructive behavior, although it could also be unconscious. Maybe deep inside he wishes that the whole thing would go to hell."

"Another possibility is that he's fallen head over heels in love," suggested Knutas, who had a more romantic outlook than his colleague.

"Sure," she said, smiling, "but the one doesn't have to exclude the other."

Back at police headquarters they were stopped by Lars Norrby.

"I've talked to a witness who had something interesting to say."

"Let's take it in my office," said Knutas.

They sat down on the little sofa group that stood over by the wall.

"It was a man who called. One day he was biking along the road toward the Warfsholm hotel. He was actually going over there to have dinner. Apparently that's what he does every Monday, and this happened to be a Monday. Suddenly he caught sight of Martina walking along the road. He described her in great detail. He seemed positive that he had seen her."

"And?" Knutas sounded impatient.

"She was walking away from the hotel, along the edge of the road. The man said that he thought it was the left side of the road, but he wasn't positive. She was wearing a blue skirt; he remembered that quite clearly, but he couldn't remember what kind of top she wore at all."

"Get to the point," barked Knutas.

His colleague's long-windedness and tendency to report unnecessary details could drive Knutas crazy. Norrby glared at him, looking insulted.

"Well. In any case, she got into a car that was parked right at the entrance to the mini-golf course."

"How can he be so sure that it was Martina he saw?"

"Apparently her archaeology colleagues have been going around showing people pictures of her. Or maybe it was just one picture."

"I see. So they're doing their own investigative work?"

"Exactly, and it has actually produced results."

"Did he see who was sitting in the car?" asked Jacobsson.

"He thinks it was a man about thirty-five or forty. Maybe older. He was wearing dark glasses, so it wasn't easy to tell. He wasn't sure about the man's hair, but he didn't think it was blond. Closer to brown."

"When did this happen?"

"A week ago. Last Monday, around five or five thirty."

"Martina has been missing for three days. No longer than that," interjected Jacobsson.

"Yes, but this could still be of interest," Norrby protested. "Obviously someone was waiting by the side of the road for her."

"And we might ask ourselves why he didn't drive up

to the hotel parking lot. Clearly he didn't want to be seen," said Knutas.

"It seems that she has some sort of secret relationship," said Jacobsson, "and it wouldn't take much to conclude that he had something to do with her disappearance. Whether she went with him voluntarily or not."

"It couldn't very well be voluntary," Norrby objected. "Otherwise why hasn't she called?"

"Everyone is speculating that she's been kidnapped," Knutas said. "We can only hope that nothing worse has happened to her. What kind of car was it?"

"The witness knows nothing about cars. He doesn't even have a driver's license. This much he could say: it was an ordinary blue sedan, and it didn't look new."

Jacobsson turned to Knutas.

"What color car does Mellgren drive?"

"No idea, but we'll find out, of course."

"Has the man ever seen her at any other time?"

"No, just that once."

"Which way did they drive off?"

"The car headed toward the main road."

"I don't suppose he got the license plate number?"

"No." Norrby gave them a little smile. "We're not that lucky."

"I want to talk to this witness as soon as possible."

"He lives and works in Klintehamn, so that should be easy to arrange."

"Good."

The phone rang, and Knutas answered. There was a roaring in the receiver, and it took several seconds before Knutas understood that it was Martina Flochten's father on the line. In stumbling English, Knutas did the best he could to answer the anxious father's questions. They agreed to meet the following day, when Patrick Flochten would arrive in Visby to take part in the search for his daughter.

The door was locked when he tried the handle. He got out the key and unlocked it. Everything looked the same as when his parents were alive: The bureau in the hall was just as brightly polished now as it was back then; the kitchen clock was ticking off the seconds with the same regular clacking sound; the Chinese plates hung in the same place on the wall where they had hung all those years; even the paper towel holder on the table was the same. He went into the living room and silently looked around. It was different from other Swedish living rooms, above all because there was no sofa. Everyone else had a sofa, but in their house there had never been one. A sofa was meant for socializing, something to sit on while you relaxed in front of the TV. There was no sofa here because that would have been an impossibility. A sofa presented the risk that they might sit so close together that their bodies touched, and that was a sin. Most things that were fun were sins. They had no TV because it was a sin. They never listened to music on the radio because it was a sin. Comic strips and party games were sins, along with laughing on Sunday. Although there wasn't much risk that anyone in that house would laugh on a Sunday. There was little chance that anyone would ever laugh at all. He couldn't recall ever seeing his father or mother smile even once. Their home was marked by silence and seriousness, prayer, discipline, and punishment.

It had taken him time to muster the courage to drive out here, but each time he did, he lost a little more of the guilt and shame that he had felt since childhood. The influence of his parents was slowly being erased.

He had come up with the idea a few months earlier. It would be the ultimate betrayal of his parents, the fact that they were going to hold their meetings here. This was the first time, and he was full of anticipation. He'd made all the preparations, down to the last detail. He went into the next room and opened a big cupboard. He took out the figures one by one, holding them carefully before lining them up on the table in the living room. This was where it would happen, right here and nowhere else. When he was done, he stuck his feet into his wooden clogs and went out. Inside the barn was a door that led to a storage room. That's where the bowl was. He went to get it, carrying it cautiously because the contents were precious. It was now going to be put to use; next time it would be even better.

He went to stand at the window and looked out. The evening sun colored the sky red, and it was so warm that they'd be able to conduct a number of the exercises outdoors. No one would see them or notice what they were doing.

The sound of an engine interrupted his thoughts, and the next instant a car appeared around the curve, a car that he recognized. How nice that he had arrived first. Maybe they'd have time to talk and settle a number of things. They had been more and more at loggerheads lately, and their differences of opinion had grown deeper, which concerned him. Now that they had come so far, he didn't want any monkey wrench in the machinery.

The power battle between them had been going on for a long time. It had to end. The moment was fast approaching when the whole situation would become untenable. He had always believed that they shared the same commitment, but lately he'd been forced to see that this wasn't the case. He hoped that the other man's reluctance was based on things that wouldn't play a major role in the long run. He hoped that he would be able to convince him that there was only one way and that the wheel had already started to turn. They were under way, and now there was no going back.

TUESDAY, JULY 6

The following day was the first cloudy day in two weeks. Knutas arrived at work early. It was no more than seven fifteen when he entered police headquarters and said hello to the duty officer. They chatted for a moment, as they always did before Knutas continued up two floors to the criminal investigation division. He got himself a cup of coffee and leafed through the local morning papers.

It wasn't long before Jacobsson, who was also an early-morning person, stuck her head in the door.

"Good morning," she greeted him. "Would you like some coffee?"

"No, thanks. I've already got some."

She looked tired.

"How are things?" Knutas gave her a searching look.

"Okay, but I hardly slept last night."

"Is that because you were worrying about Martina Flochten?"

"That was one reason," she said curtly and then took a sip of her coffee.

She had a very particular way of letting him

know that he shouldn't ask any more questions.

"Have you come up with any ideas?" he asked instead.

"Not exactly, but I've been thinking about that car."

"And?"

"She apparently got in the car of her own free will. She had arranged to meet the unknown man, so he's clearly someone she got to know here on Gotland. But why be so secretive? Of course, she does have a boyfriend, but he's back home in Rotterdam. If she wanted to have a little fun over here, he at least wasn't going to notice."

"What are you getting at?"

"There must be something strange about the man she met. If they're having, or had, a love affair, why keep it under wraps? Well, there are two reasons why they might want to hide it. Either he's married or else there's something about him—maybe he's a teacher or has some connection with the course—that makes it a sensitive issue for them to be together."

"Or both," suggested Knutas.

"Exactly. Staffan Mellgren seems the most likely candidate, of course, but it could also be someone else. I've checked on the color of his car, and it's not blue. It's a silvery gray. Either he used someone else's car, or he's not the one that Martina met. The students spent two weeks studying theory in Visby before they started on the actual excavation work here. During that time they had several different teachers. Plus they evidently went out and partied almost every night. Martina has had all sorts of opportunities to meet someone.

"Another thing I think is strange is that she didn't contact the family of Jacob Dahlén at the Wisby hotel. The manager of the Warfsholm, Kerstin Bodin, said that Dahlén is a family friend. Martina's family comes here once a year, and they always stay at his hotel. Of course, he's probably mostly a friend of her father, but it's still odd that she didn't at least stop by to say hello, don't you think? She's been on Gotland for more than four weeks, two of them in Visby. Why didn't she contact him? The hotel is right downtown, for God's sake, just a stone's throw from the college."

"Have you talked to Jacob Dahlén?"

"Only on the phone. He's out of town."

"Maybe she did intend to contact him but hadn't gotten around to it yet. You know how it is when you're someplace where you know someone only superficially. And the course continues until the middle of August. Maybe she thinks she has plenty of time to look him up."

"Sure," Jacobsson conceded. "You might be right."

"By the way, where did she stay during those two weeks when she was studying theory in Visby?"

"The same place as all the others. Student dorms on Mejerigatan."

"Let's drive over and have a talk with the lodgers, also

the landlord. Someone might have noticed something. I'll make the arrangements," said Knutas and reached for the phone.

Patrick Flochten was a stately man with dark brown hair that stuck out in all directions. Judging by the color of his complexion, the weather had been nice in the Netherlands. He wore glasses with black frames that looked expensive, and he had on a light linen suit. His handshake was damp and his expression tense as he sat down on the visitor's chair in Knutas's office.

"Martina's brother and I are, of course, beside ourselves with worry. I'd like you to tell me everything that led up to my daughter's disappearance," he said in perfect English. *"Everything!"*

Knutas, whose command of English was far from sufficient for conducting an interview, had already anticipated this problem. That was why he had asked Jacobsson to join them. She began by describing what the police knew so far about Martina's disappearance. Jacobsson kept wondering why there was something familiar about the man sitting across from her. Maybe it was just that he and his daughter looked alike, judging by the photos that she'd seen of Martina.

"I'm familiar with Warfsholm. I've gone out to the

hotel with the children for dinner several times when we've been here on Gotland. How could Martina disappear from there without a single person seeing her? There are cottages and people everywhere. Besides, the nights are so bright here; it never gets really dark."

"It was late at night when Martina left the others. The hotel guests were in bed asleep. She went to the bathroom around one o'clock, and by then almost everyone who had been to the concert had gone home. The few who were still awake were sitting in the bar."

"Didn't anyone see anything?"

"Apparently not, unfortunately. A full-blown search is under way, of course. We're using dogs and helicopters. A search party is also being organized today. The search area is gradually being expanded."

Jacobsson deliberately neglected to mention the divers. It sounded too horrible, as if they'd already given up hope of finding Martina alive.

"Could she have gone to the mainland?"

"There's no indication that she has left the island. We've checked the passenger lists with the company that operates the ferry service, as well as the airlines. In any event, she didn't travel under her own name. The front desk at the hotel holds on to the students' valuables for safekeeping, and nothing was missing—not her passport or her Visa card or the cash that she had stowed away."

Patrick Flochten gave both officers a look of despair.

"It sounds as if you're assuming that she's been involved in some sort of crime."

Knutas and Jacobsson exchanged glances.

"Let's not rush ahead and assume the worst," Jacobsson urged him. "We have no idea what may have happened. Sometimes people disappear under the most peculiar circumstances, only to show up later without any sort of drama. That may well be the case here. We shouldn't forget that Martina has only been missing for a few days. Who knows? Maybe she fell head over heels in love, or something like that. Right now we need to take one thing at a time. First and foremost, we need to concentrate on finding her as quickly as possible. Has Martina ever disappeared before without letting anyone know?"

Patrick Flochten thought about that for a moment.

"Well, yes . . . She was sometimes pretty wild as a teenager. And yes, a few times she didn't come home at night, but not for several days in a row like this. And she's calmed down over the years."

"Does she use drugs?"

"Not that I've noticed. She may have tried them—that goes without saying—but she has never used drugs in the sense that I think you're implying."

"No other addiction problems or illnesses?"

"No."

"What's her relationship like with her boyfriend?"

"Good, as far as I know. They've been together for

over a year, and it seems to be very stable. He's quite a bit older."

"Has she told you about some new man that she's met?"

"No, why would she do that?"

"Several circumstances indicate that she has a new relationship. A witness has also suggested that she may be in love with someone."

"Really? That's odd. She's usually so open about things like that. We have no secrets from each other." Patrick Flochten's expression grew wary.

"We know that you regularly come here on vacation and that you usually stay at the Wisby hotel—is that right?"

"Yes. I've known the owner for a long time. Jacob Dahlén. We're business acquaintances, and we've also been friends for many years."

Tears welled up in Patrick Flochten's eyes, as if he suddenly remembered that his daughter was missing.

No one said anything for a moment.

"What kind of work do you do?" Knutas asked.

"I'm an architect. I run an architectural firm in Rotterdam along with a partner. We also own several development companies, including one here on Gotland."

"Is that right? Which one?"

"Our firm helped design the new condos at

Södervärn, and we're involved in the big hotel project that's being planned."

"The one at Högklint?"

"Exactly. I designed the hotel, and we're also investors."

Jacobsson suddenly remembered where she had seen Patrick Flochten before. One of the local newspapers had done a story about the project and included the name of the architect along with his picture. She now recalled that his children were also mentioned. It was reported that his late wife had been from Gotland.

"So you're going to be working over here a good deal?"

"I would think so."

"But you've been here a lot before?"

"Yes. During the past year I've spent a great deal of time in Visby." His voice faded away. Patrick Flochten hid his face in his hands.

"Maybe that's enough for now," Knutas interjected. "Is there anything else you would like to know?"

"Yes," replied the man tonelessly. "Where can I start searching?"

When Emma woke up in the morning, it took a moment before she realized that she was back home again after giving birth. The tenderness in her abdomen reminded her of what she'd been through. The sunlight coming through the curtains rested on the face of her newborn baby as she lay there, so very small, surrounded by pillows and covers. Emma turned onto her side and placed her hand gently on the tiny, downy shoulder poking out from under the knitted shirt.

The baby's face was a blotchy red. Emma looked for signs of herself and Johan in their new daughter's features. He was going to drop by for a while before work. She wanted to see him, and yet she didn't.

The silence in the house was palpable; it gave her a feeling of unreality. Under normal circumstances there would have been a lot of commotion from the children and the dog, but now the links to the past had been broken; the traditions no longer existed. It was frightening not to know how the rest of her life was going to proceed. She still hadn't gotten used to the fact that Sara and Filip also lived somewhere else. Right now she longed for them and didn't want to wait until the next day to see them, as planned. After that they were going abroad on vacation with Olle for two weeks.

The divorce had been worse than she could have imagined. The fact that in the end she decided to have the baby, even though she and Olle had agreed to try saving their marriage, had at first made him furious. Over time he had realized that he had no other choice but to accept her decision, even though it made a divorce inevitable. Like two automatons they had filled out the papers and taken care of practical matters. He had moved into an apartment, and suddenly she was living alone in a big house with the children there only every other week.

As her belly got bigger and bigger, Olle had become more and more difficult. The slightest little thing could erupt into a problem, anything from how they were going to split up the Easter holidays to who should buy shoes for Sara or drive Filip to soccer practice. Everything had to be thrashed out ad nauseam. It felt as if Olle wanted to punish her. In his eyes she saw accusations and wounded pride.

At first Olle wanted to be so strong. The practical matters had to be handled in the most adroit manner, almost as if he were trying to make the divorce as gentle as possible for himself when he was faced with the fait accompli. But when almost everything had been worked out and decided, and the train started rolling in a new direction, his emotions finally caught up with him. To deal with his own pain, he shifted all the blame and responsibility onto her. He refused to have anything to do with the puppy that he had bought for her in an attempt to patch up their marriage. Fortunately one of Emma's women friends had taken care of the dog while she was in the maternity ward.

She had no plans for the summer. The children would be staying with her for a few weeks later on, but first they were going abroad with their father. He had rented a house in Italy for two weeks, along with a friend who was also a single parent. They were going to fly to Nice, rent a car, and stay in an Italian mountain village. *If only he'd thought up fun things like that when we were married,* she thought enviously. *Now he decides to be creative and full of ideas.*

Johan had mentioned that he wanted them to go somewhere together. Right now it felt impossible.

Through the bedroom window she caught sight of him as he came walking up the garden path. In his hands he was holding a paper bag and a bouquet of flowers. He noticed her in the window and smiled and waved.

Maybe it wasn't so strange that she didn't want to throw herself into a new living arrangement with Johan. That comforting thought suddenly took root, and she felt the guilt she carried on her shoulders lighten. *One step at a time,* she thought. *One step at a time.*

Johan had warned Pia that he would be arriving late for work. Nothing special was going on, and he longed to take a walk with Emma and their newborn baby. They went out through the gate and continued along the residential street. It was a quiet neighborhood with little traffic. That didn't stop Johan from looking several times in both directions each time they had to cross the street before he ventured across with the baby buggy. Emma, who'd been through all this before, was significantly calmer.

"Does it feel strange to be out with me and a baby buggy?" he asked. "I mean, you and Olle have walked around here with the kids all these years, taking them to the playground, dropping them off at day care or picking them up, and spending time with the other parents in these houses."

"No, actually it doesn't feel strange." Emma looked surprised, as if it hadn't even occurred to her that this area belonged to her and Olle.

They walked in silence for a while. Johan was overwhelmed by the unfamiliar situation and felt no need to talk.

Last night he had driven Emma and their daughter home from the hospital, and it had been unbelievably hard to leave them. Emma didn't want him to stay overnight. It was still too early, she told him when he objected. He couldn't help feeling hurt. He hadn't yet spent a night in the house in Roma. That was one of the boundaries he longed to cross, one of the obstacles that Emma had set up and that stood in the way of their having a chance to strengthen their relationship.

They continued through the neighborhood. It was good for the baby to be out and get some fresh air. She looked so little as she lay under the cotton blanket. Her head was covered with a turquoise cotton cap even though it was seventy-seven degrees outside. Her dark hair stuck out from under the cap. When Johan poked his head inside the buggy and placed his cheek against her body, he noticed how rapid and light as a feather her breathing was.

He could see that Emma was tired. Her face was very beautiful—those high cheekbones, dark eyes, and distinct eyebrows that had enchanted him so much. Now her complexion was paler and her cheeks slightly rounder than usual. He liked that; it gave her a softer appearance.

He had loved her before they had the baby, and now, after the birth, his love had grown to a painful level.

They'd been through periods when he felt that there was a balance between them, that they loved each other equally, that Emma, too, wanted them to be together. Now he found himself at a disadvantage. Emma didn't want him in the house. Not yet, she said. The children had to get used to things; it was all too much for them at the moment, with the new sister and everything else. They would see each other when they could, which meant when Sara and Filip were staying with their father. Nothing had turned out as he'd hoped.

Johan had been looking forward to the baby's arrival, to taking care of Emma and the child and simply enjoying things. How wrong he had been. The fact that Emma had decided to have the baby didn't mean that she was ready to regard them as an established couple. She had explained to him that she just couldn't throw herself into a new relationship. So much had happened during the past year. Her whole life had been turned upside down. It would take time to digest and rearrange everything, to cut off all ties with her old life.

Now she was walking along beside him and looking very content, in spite of everything. He stopped pushing the buggy to stroke her cheek.

"I love you," he said, feeling how true that was.

Emma looked away without saying a word. In the past she would have told him the same thing, or at least something similar.

They continued on toward the sports field as they chatted about all sorts of things, mostly about the baby and what name they were going to give her. Johan wanted her to be called Natalie, while Emma preferred Elin.

"But she looks like a Natalie," said Johan. "With her dark hair and brown eyes. Slightly exotic. She's going to be a real beauty—with us as her parents," he added and grinned. "Just picture a cute girl with long dark hair named Natalie."

Emma couldn't help smiling. "Maybe right now, yes. At the moment she has dark hair and eyes, but she could just as well end up blond and blue-eyed. Maybe then the name wouldn't suit her as well."

"Oh, what does that matter? It's a beautiful name."

"Sure, but I'm allergic to the idea of giving Swedish children names that try to be as international as possible. Names like Nicole, Angelique, or Yvette. We live in Sweden, not France."

"Don't you think you're being a little narrow-minded? Did you know that one in five Swedes has foreign heritage? Sweden is no fair-skinned paradise anymore, with rye bread dancing the Hambo. It's multicultural. Even though I admit that the development seems to be happening slower over here on Gotland," he teased, giving her a little poke in the side.

"I still think that Elin is nicer," insisted Emma.

Johan stopped again and took her face between the palms of his hands.

"If you feel so strongly about it, then Elin it is—as long as you're happy."

"But I want you to like it, too."

"I do, I assure you I do. I'm so happy to have a daughter named Elin with you, believe me."

WEDNESDAY, JULY 7

Kalle Östlund's parents had bought the summer house near Björkhaga, just north of Klintehamn, in the fifties. Their family was one of the first to move into the small summer-house area. Most of the residents were islanders—some who had moved to the mainland but wanted to keep their summer house, and others who lived in Visby and felt it was the right location for a country place, about twenty miles away. It was a peaceful area for most of the year. During the summer it got livelier when tourists headed out there to walk along the Vivesholm promontory and admire the countless birds that frequented the shoreline. It was also a popular place for watching sunsets, when the whole sky would be colored crimson, with a view of the open sea in both directions. Kalle thought it was splendid, too, even though he had seen the drama thousands of times from here. For him there was no lovelier place on earth. He enjoyed fishing, and on this morning he was going out to pull up his net, which he hoped would be filled with flounder.

He had set the alarm clock for 5:00 A.M., and his wife,

Birgitta, was sound asleep when he got up, but the dog was happy and wide-awake. Their Italian retriever, Lisa, was like a whirlwind. She loved to go everywhere with him, which she did. She scampered around his legs as he trudged off.

He opened the big gate facing the promontory, where the dairy cows were grazing in the summer pasture. The sky was a bright blue, and the clouds were woolly and harmless, hovering above the boathouses over by Kovik on the other side of the shore. The dirt road that ran along the promontory was light in color, bearing witness to the fact that the soil was rich in lime. Out here the landscape was heathlike. The vegetation was low-lying and consisted mostly of juniper and short-stemmed flowers.

At the moment the meadow along the shore shimmered with flowers of sea thrift, which looked like little pink balls.

He had brought Lisa's leash, just in case, but he let her run free on the path down to the boat. The birds' breeding season was over, so she wouldn't find any bird eggs. The promontory was the breeding ground for a large number of herons, cormorants, and various kinds of gulls.

When they had reached the middle of the shoreline meadow facing the sea, Lisa caught sight of a rabbit and took off in the opposite direction. He glimpsed the little bunny bounding away for dear life with the dog barking wildly right on its heels. Kalle called several times, but the dog was much too engrossed in the chase to pay any attention. He shook his head and kept on going. She'd come back soon enough. He got the boat ready, now and then casting an eye over the promontory and calling the dog, but Lisa was nowhere in sight.

Kalle decided to wait. He sat down on a rock and took out a can of Ettan snuff. He put a thick wad under his lip. Every now and then he heard a rustling in the grass and bushes from birds or from rabbits scampering in and out of their holes. A couple of shelducks with their characteristic red bills swam along the shoreline. Cows occasionally walked past the wooded area in the middle of the promontory, although right now they were out at the very end of the point. That was lucky. Lisa was so frisky today that she might even start chasing cows, and then she could end up getting kicked to death.

After Kalle had been sitting there for well over fifteen minutes without any sign of the dog, he decided to go and look for her. He was annoyed. If he didn't find her soon, it would be too late to go out fishing. He walked back across the meadow, over the cattle grid in the fence surrounding the woods, and in among the trees. Then he heard Lisa barking. She must have gone a good distance into the woods since he hadn't heard her until now. The fenced-in area contained remnants of a moat, a reminder of the days when Vivesholm was a

Viking harbor and a defensive fort had stood on the site.

The woods got denser. He passed the old, rickety bird observation tower that stood on the edge of the woods. Farther along, the ground turned to marsh and then the sea began. He could glimpse the Warfsholm hotel from here, and the bird path wasn't far away. The barking got louder. The dog must be very close now. Then he caught sight of something champagne-colored between the trees, and there stood Lisa, barking wildly at a pine tree. What in the world could be so interesting?

He walked forward another ten feet and then stopped short. For several trembling seconds he tried hard to comprehend what he was looking at. He couldn't make himself take in the image of the young woman who was swaying freely in the air, naked, with a noose around her neck. Her head was bent forward, and her long blond hair hid her face. Kalle's first thought was that it must be a tragic suicide. He suddenly felt violently ill and was forced to sit down on the ground. Then he noticed that the woman was covered in blood. Someone had sliced open the lower part of her belly with a knife.

Just over an hour later Knutas turned onto the dirt road that ran past the summer houses to the sea and Vivesholm. With him were Karin Jacobsson and Erik Sohlman. Before they left, Knutas had gotten hold of the medical examiner, who was going to fly over from the mainland later in the day.

Standing next to the gate was a man of about sixty-five. He was wearing shorts and a knit shirt, and with him on a leash was a dog with curly, light-colored fur. The detectives parked outside the gate and walked on the grass next to the dirt road leading out to the promontory so as not to disturb any tire tracks.

Kalle Östlund raised his hand and pointed. "He must have driven past the turnoff," he said. "Otherwise he would have been seen from the houses that are closest to the water."

They followed the older man toward a small wooded area and continued along a well-worn path that ran parallel to the old moat. Here and there grew sloe and rosehips.

There was almost no wind, and the only sound was

the screeching of the birds above the sea. They didn't see the body until it was right in front of them.

Dangling in the air, surrounded by the lush summer greenery, was a young woman. Her hair fell over her face, and the slender body that hung lifelessly from a noose was a blotchy red. Across the smooth abdomen someone had made a cut over a foot long. Blood had run out of it and down over her crotch and legs.

There was a brutal contrast between her youthful beauty and the violence that she had suffered.

The detectives studied the body in silence.

"Well, this was how I found her," said Kalle Östlund at last.

"And you haven't left the area since?" asked Knutas.

"No, I called my wife, but I didn't dare leave."

"Did you see or hear anyone on your way here?"

"No. I was here alone. Along with Lisa," said Kalle, patting the dog.

Knutas called to the police officers who had now joined them and were beginning to put up crime-scene tape.

"We need to cordon off the fenced-in area. I want some of you to start knocking on doors at the nearby houses right away. What about the canine unit?"

"It's on the way," said Jacobsson.

"Good. There's no time to waste. You can go home in the meantime," he told the man with the dog, "but stay there. We'll be talking to you and your wife shortly."

"It can't be anyone but Martina Flochten, can it?" said Jacobsson. "The body matches the age and the description."

"Yes, it's her. Without a doubt," Knutas agreed.

"What the hell kind of lunatic did she run into?" said Sohlman tersely. "Why would anyone hang a person after he'd already killed her?"

"Or why slash a person you've already hanged?" countered Jacobsson.

Knutas moved cautiously around the body, studying it from every angle. Martina looked like a terrifying doll. Her face was bright red, as if she had been straining hard. Her eyes were open but dull and lackluster. Her lips were brownish black and dry, her skin blotchy red, her calves and feet a mottled purple.

Flies were visible in the incision in the lower portion of her abdomen. Knutas's stomach turned over when he saw little maggots squirming in the wound.

"I wonder if she's been hanging here since Saturday," murmured Jacobsson behind the handkerchief that she had pressed to her mouth.

"What day is it today? Wednesday. If she was murdered on Saturday night, that would mean that it's been over seventy-two hours," said Sohlman. "It's possible."

"She'll have to stay like this until the ME gets here," said Knutas. "I want him to see how she looks at the scene."

Curious spectators had already gathered at the gate. Knutas declined to answer any of their questions as he and his colleagues hurried past.

They drove straight back to police headquarters.

He stood in the middle of the woods, leaning against the rough bark of the tree. His eyes were closed and he was listening. The wind rushing through the trees, a pine cone that fell to the ground with a soft thud, a crow cawing. There was a strong fragrance here in the shadows. Resin, pine needles, dirt, and blueberries. Slowly he bent his knees and slid his back down the tree trunk until he ended up in a sitting position. The uneven surface of the tree didn't bother him. He began muttering to himself, quietly and monotonously. Gradually he sank into the state that he was trying for, into a trance. He merged with the tree. His soul could stay there while he projected his consciousness into something else.

The transference was important for him; it was actually essential if he was going to complete his task.

He became one with the tree. There were no boundaries, none at all. He had slipped into another reality. The rest of the world no longer concerned him. Whatever had been worrying him before no longer had any importance. He had freed himself from all commonplace and trivial problems—everything that had to do with other people. He no longer needed to care about them, because he had entered into a different alliance that had nothing to do with human relationships. It was as if walls had fallen, obstacles had been swept aside, and the path lay straight and clearly marked before him. He realized that he possessed unusual powers.

Suddenly a twig snapped and a fox emerged from a thicket. It sat down like a cat right in front of him and began to wash, taking its time. Now and then the fox glanced up and studied him for a moment. When it headed back into the woods, it passed quite close without paying any attention to him. He took a deep breath.

That was the final proof that he had succeeded.

Knutas's phone rang nonstop after he got back to his office. He had his hands full dealing with questions from the press about the murder of Martina Flochten. Finally, after calling Patrick Flochten and notifying him of the discovery of his daughter's corpse, he was forced to tell the switchboard not to put through any more calls. He needed time to concentrate on his work.

It was decided that a press conference would be held later that afternoon. Lars Norrby offered to make the arrangements instead of taking part in the investigative meeting.

Knutas had notified the prosecutor, who took a seat next to him in the conference room. Birger Smittenberg was an experienced chief prosecutor, and he had worked for the Gotland district court for many years. Over time a solid trust had been established between him and Knutas. They had a long series of investigations behind them. Smittenberg was originally from Stockholm, but in the late seventies he had married a Gotland woman who was a ballad singer. He was deeply committed to his work, and he participated in the investigative meetings as often as he could.

"As you all know, twenty-one-year-old Martina Flochten from Rotterdam in the Netherlands was found murdered out at Vivesholm," Knutas began. "She was found around five thirty this morning by the owner of one of the summer houses in the area. A man named Kalle Östlund. There is no doubt that she was murdered. Erik will describe the injuries in a moment. The ME is on his way from Stockholm and will be examining the body at the scene later today. The fenced-in area has been cordoned off and is now being searched by the canine patrol. We're also searching for clues around Warfsholm, as best we can. We can't very well demand that they close up the whole place. I think that's where I'll stop for the time being."

He nodded to Sohlman, who got up and went over to the computer. He clicked on a key and an aerial view of the area appeared on the white screen at the front of the room.

"This is Vivesholm. The land is privately owned by a farmer who lets his cows graze out here, but the area is open to the public. Lots of people come here to watch the birds or to see the view."

"It's also popular with windsurfers," interjected Thomas Wittberg. "I've been out there to surf several times. A hell of a great place."

"Out on the promontory there's a small wooded area

surrounded by a fence. There's also an old birdwatching tower."

Sohlman changed pictures.

"This was where the body of Martina Flochten was found, hanging from a tree. Generally only the farmer or someone who might want to get a better view from the bird tower would enter this area at all. That's why it's not so strange that it took several days for the body to be found. Let's take a look at the injuries. This isn't exactly your usual sort of murder."

Several of the detectives began to fidget as soon as the pictures of Martina appeared.

"What's significant is that she seems to have been killed in more than one way," Sohlman went on pensively. "The victim was both strangled and knifed. One qualified guess is that she was first hanged from the noose, and afterward the perpetrator slashed her with a knife. The appearance of the incision indicates that it was probably done after death. Since she has no other injuries, it looks as if the perpetrator was able to cut her open in peace and quiet, so to speak. She didn't offer any resistance. But there's another issue."

Sohlman paused for effect and looked at his colleagues pointedly.

"We're not positive that she died from hanging. There are several indications that she was already dead when she was hung up in that tree."

"What sort of indications?" asked Knutas, looking startled.

"As I said, this is just a hunch—I'll gladly leave the confirming analysis to the ME—but I've seen quite a few hanging deaths when people committed suicide by kicking away the chair or whatever they were standing on and then were strangled by the noose. The deceased typically has specific types of injuries. These include bruises along the groove on the neck where the rope dug in, as well as hemorrhaging at the base of the neck muscles along the collarbone. These signs of vitality, as they're called, are easy to detect. You notice them at once if you've been at that type of death scene before. Martina doesn't have any of them. Something doesn't add up."

Jacobsson looked in surprise at the crime tech.

"So that means the murderer might have used several methods to kill Martina instead of settling for just one—and the hanging and stab wound in the abdomen were two of the methods. But what actually killed her?"

A tense silence followed. Wittberg was the first to speak.

"It's one thing when a killer stages an assault by using a knife, for example, to stab the victim and then continues to hack away even though the person is already dead. Or he keeps firing unnecessary shots at the victim. That's something that occurs in a fit of rage or because the killer is under the influence of drugs or has simply gone berserk. But this seems to be a different story."

"The murder feels ritualistic," murmured Knutas as he looked at the pictures.

"Yes," agreed Smittenberg. "The perpetrator would have had time to stop and think between the various steps; he should have calmed down."

"What about the motive?" said Jacobsson meditatively. "He had a definite reason for killing her in several ways. It symbolizes something. The modus operandi seems like some sort of ceremony, just as Anders said. The question is: Why is she naked? What does it mean?"

"There are no outward signs of sexual assault, but if she was assaulted it will show up in the autopsy. Yet the fact that she's not wearing any clothes clearly has sexual connotations."

"What sort of evidence have you found?" asked Wittberg.

"Not much so far," said Sohlman. "We're in the process of searching the entire promontory, and there's a lot of area to cover."

"We're continuing to go door to door in the summer-house area," interjected Knutas. "Let's hope it produces some results."

"How many summer houses are there?" asked Smittenberg.

"About twenty."

"Was the murder committed at the site where the body was found?"

"It's hard to say at the moment," said Sohlman. "I didn't see any signs of a struggle at the site. On the other hand, we haven't yet had a chance to examine everything thoroughly. The ME has to make his examination before we can move the body. Since the decomposition process has already set in, I would guess that she's been dead for two or three days. I can't give you a more specific time of death at the moment—but it seems likely that she was killed late Saturday night or early Sunday morning. It's virtually impossible to drive into the wooded area, so the perp probably carried her there if he killed her somewhere else. It's at least a couple of hundred yards away on foot, which means that we're dealing with someone who's quite strong. Martina was not a petite girl. She was both tall and muscular."

"I'm thinking about the decapitated horse in Petesviken," said Jacobsson. "I wonder if there's some connection. That seemed ritualistic, too."

"Of course we'll look for points of connection between the two cases," said Knutas. "We need to find out more about Martina Flochten's past. Who was she? What was she doing before the murder? Did anything unusual happen? Did her behavior change in any way? What sort of person was she? Can you take responsibility for finding out these things, Karin?"

"Sure."

"It's also important that we talk with every single summer-house owner around Vivesholm as soon as possible, and even more important, the guests who were staying at the hotel over the weekend. I'll leave that to you, Thomas. All the archaeologists have to be interviewed, too—the students taking the course, the teachers, and the others at the college. Since I don't want the press to get wind of this ritualistic angle, no one should say anything about it, and I mean not to anybody at all."

Knutas gazed sternly at his colleagues sitting around the table.

"If this gets out, we're done for. Then we'll have reporters chasing us all day long."

He stood up.

"At four o'clock this afternoon we're holding a press conference. Lars and I will handle it."

Staffan Mellgren looked haggard when Knutas met him in the reception area of police headquarters. His face was pale and his eyes red-rimmed and shiny. There was something jumpy about him, and his clothes were so wrinkled that it looked as if he had slept in them. They went up to Knutas's office where they could talk undisturbed. Mellgren declined the offer of coffee.

"How are you doing?" asked Knutas after they sat down across from each other.

"This is so terrible, what happened to Martina. I can't understand it."

"I want to start by talking some more about the student group. We understand that Martina was quite popular. Was there anyone who didn't get along with her?"

Mellgren shook his head.

"No, not as far as I know."

"Do you know of anyone who was particularly fond of Martina? Or maybe even in love with her?"

"Not exactly," he replied hesitantly, "but there are two guys who paid a lot of attention to her."

"Who are they?"

"Jonas is a Swede, from Skåne, probably no more than twenty years old. Mark is American, a little older, about twenty-five, I would guess. Those two really get along—Mark and Jonas, I mean. They're as thick as thieves."

"In what way did they show an interest in Martina?"

"Well, they were always hovering around her. Both of them liked to talk and joke with her."

"Did one of them seem more fond of her than the other?"

"No, I don't think you could say that. I think they both liked her equally."

"Was the interest mutual?"

"I think Martina thought they were fun and nice as friends, but nothing more than that."

"How do you know that?"

"It's just a feeling."

"Are the two of them also staying at Warfsholm?"

"Yes."

"Have you noticed any strangers hanging around the excavation site?"

"Just the usual. People we know or one of the neighbors who drops by to talk for a while. Small groups of tourists show up several times a week, but they usually keep a safe distance away."

"As the leader of the course, do you have any idea who might have murdered Martina?"

"No."

"I've asked you this question before, but I'm going to have to ask it again: What was your relationship with her?"

"She was a student that I liked and respected, as a *student,*" said Mellgren in a sharp voice. "Of course there was nothing going on between us. I've already told you that."

"Where were you on Saturday night?"

"I was actually out having a beer."

"Alone?"

"Yes."

"Where?"

"First at Donner's Well and later at the Monk's Cellar."

"Did you meet anyone you know?"

"I always run into a few acquaintances."

"When did you get home?"

"I don't know. I didn't look at my watch."

"But you must be able to say whether it was 9:00 P.M. or 3:00 A.M.," said Knutas impatiently.

He was starting to be genuinely annoyed, and he wondered what a married father of four was doing out on the town alone on a Saturday night. Why wasn't he home with his family if he hadn't planned to meet someone?

"I guess it was almost three."

"What's your marriage like?" asked Knutas.

Mellgren was slow to answer. His jaw visibly tightened.

"You'll have to excuse the question, but I need to ask it," Knutas went on as he stared back at the man.

"Things are fine between Susanna and me. Did she tell you otherwise?"

Knutas raised his hand in protest. "Absolutely not. I was just wondering."

The room in which the press conference was going to be held was buzzing with life. The reporters were taking seats in the rows of chairs, and microphones were being set up on the podium at the front of the room. Up until now the police had declined to issue any statement, so everyone was very curious about what they were going to hear about the murder of the young archaeology student.

The murmuring automatically stopped when Anders Knutas and Lars Norrby took their places up front.

"Welcome to the press conference," Knutas began. "The young woman who has been missing since Saturday, Martina Flochten, who was born in 1983, has been found dead outside of Vivesholm. That's just outside of Klintehamn, approximately nineteen miles south of Visby on the west coast. There is no doubt whatsoever that she was murdered."

He glanced down at his notes.

"The body was found at 5:45 A.M. by an individual who was out walking in the area. Many of you already know that Martina was born and raised in the Netherlands, but her mother was from Hemse here on Gotland. The mother died three years ago. Martina has lived in the Netherlands all her life. She came here in early June to take part in a course on archaeological excavation that is offered by the college. She had been on Gotland for a month before she disappeared on the night that a concert was held at Warfsholm. July third. We'll now take questions."

"Can you tell us anything about how she was murdered?"

"No."

"Why not?"

"Because the investigation is ongoing."

"Was some sort of weapon used?"

"Yes, but I don't intend to say anything more on the subject."

"Was she sexually assaulted?"

"We won't know until an autopsy is performed on the body."

"When will that happen?"

"The body was examined by the ME at the site this afternoon. Tonight it will be transported to the forensic medicine lab in Solna. The autopsy will be done in the next few days."

"Do you know how long she's been dead?"

"Not yet. The autopsy report will tell us that."

"Surely you must be able to say something about how long she'd been dead when she was found. Was it a matter of an hour? Or had she been dead since she disappeared?"

"This much I can tell you: It was most likely that she'd been dead at least twenty-four hours."

"Is it a question of one killer, or were there more?"

"We don't know at the present moment."

"So there could have been more than one?"

"That's possible."

"Do you have any suspects?"

"Not at the moment, no."

"Are there any witnesses?"

"We've been knocking on doors all day, and we're compiling statements from everyone in the area who might have seen something."

"Martina Flochten was half Swedish, and her mother was from Gotland. Is that significant?"

"Of course we're working on a broad front and will follow up on all possible leads."

"Does she have any relatives here on Gotland?"

"No. Her only relatives here were her maternal grandparents, and they've been dead for years."

"Has the area out there been cordoned off?"

"The wooded area where the body was found has been cordoned off."

"For how long?"

"Until the technical work is completed."

"How much contact did she have with Gotland?"

"She used to come here once a year on vacation."

"What could be a possible motive for the murder?"

"It's much too early to speculate about a motive," snapped Knutas.

"Was Martina Flochten known to the Dutch or Swedish police?"

"No, not as far as we know."

"She'd been missing for several days—why wasn't Vivesholm searched by the police earlier? It's so close to Warfsholm, after all."

"We didn't see any reason to do so. The police have to work on one area at a time, so we start with the location where the individual was last seen, and then we gradually expand our efforts from there."

"Was there any evidence left by the murderer?"

"A perpetrator always leaves evidence. I can't discuss what it might be, since the investigation is ongoing."

"What are the police going to do now?"

"As I said, we're working hard to interview people and take their statements. The police would like to appeal to the public for any tips, both from those who were at the Warfsholm hotel on the evening when the Eldkvarn concert took place, and from others who may have seen Martina with someone who could be of interest to the investigation. It's especially important at this early stage."

Knutas stood up to indicate that the press conference was over. He ignored the flood of questions directed at him. Various journalists began taking him aside for separate interviews.

An hour later the whole spectacle was finally over, and he could escape to his office. In all his years as a police officer he had always found it trying to deal with the press whenever major events occurred. It was a balancing act, trying to tell reporters enough without giving away too many details that might harm the investigation.

When Knutas was back in his office, the ME called. He had finished examining the body at the site.

"I must say that I've never seen anything like this before. We're dealing with a truly deviant killer."

"We've already realized that."

"I've done a preliminary examination, and I don't want to draw any definite conclusions, but there are a number of things that I can tell you."

"Let's hear it."

"I would say that she's been dead for at least three or four days."

"So it's possible that she was killed on the same night that she disappeared?"

"That might very well be. She was subjected to several types of violence, and I won't be completely sure of the cause of death until after the autopsy. Judging by the look of the injuries, I would guess that she was not killed by the knife wound in her abdomen."

"Sohlman suspected as much."

"On the other hand, there are signs that she may have died from drowning."

"Is that right?"

"I've found residue of a certain type of foam. When the victim drowns, foam gets whipped up in the windpipe and lungs. It gathers around the mouth and looks a bit like egg whites that have been whipped and then hardened. In addition, she has traces of seaweed and sand in her hair, as well as under her fingernails, which indicates that the killer may have pushed her head underwater somewhere along the shore. When she struggled, she buried her fingernails in the sea floor—that's where the seaweed and sand came from. She also has hand and fingernail marks on the back of her neck and on her upper arms. I've found sand and sludge from the sea floor in her mouth. And there are tiny specks of blood in her eyes, which she could have gotten from fighting back or from lack of oxygen. As I said, I don't want to be more specific about the cause of death right now, but judging by appearances, she was dead before she was hanged from that noose. The most probable scenario is that he first drowned her by holding her head underwater. In all likelihood she was drowned somewhere else. Her body was then transported out to Vivesholm."

"Why do you think she was killed somewhere else?"

"Simply because that type of sand isn't found out at Vivesholm."

"So she was killed near a sandy beach?"

"Not necessarily, but the sea floor was sandy. Out at the bird promontory where she was found, it's mostly rock. She would have had more injuries to her hands if she'd been drowned there."

"I see."

Knutas was taking copious notes. He was impressed by how much information the ME could read from a body.

"There's one thing that surprises me. How did the perpetrator manage to hang the body up there? He must have hoisted her up in some way, or else he didn't do it alone," the ME went on. "She looks as if she weighs between 130 and 145 pounds, at any rate. That much dead weight is difficult, if not almost impossible, to hoist up single-handedly."

"So you think there were more people involved?"

"Either that, or else we're dealing with a physically strong man with some sort of ingenious hoisting method." The ME cleared his throat. "There's something else that has me confused. It's that incision she has in her abdomen and the blood from it."

"What about it?"

"The incision looks to be deep enough to have damaged the aorta, which would result in a great deal of blood loss. The accumulation of blood on the ground under the body should have been bigger. It's almost as if the killer collected some of the blood."

"Is that right? Sohlman said the exact same thing about another recent case. Do you know about the horse that was decapitated a little more than a week ago?"

"Sure."

"The perp did the same thing."

"I didn't hear about that." The ME sounded surprised.

"Well, it's true. According to the veterinarian who examined the horse, the blood had been collected and removed. When can we get a preliminary autopsy report?"

"The body is being taken to the lab now. I'll try to finish the whole autopsy by tomorrow, so I can fax over a preliminary report to you tomorrow evening."

"That's great," said Knutas gratefully. "One more thing—could you tell if there was any sign of a sexual assault?"

"She has no external injuries to indicate that. Whether she'd had intercourse is something that we will hopefully know by tomorrow."

Knutas thanked him and put down the phone. He leaned back in his chair. A perpetrator who killed horses and women and drained the blood from their bodies. A ritual murderer.

It pained him to think about Martina Flochten. She'd had her whole life ahead of her. She was a student interested in archaeology. She had come to Gotland to help out on an excavation of the island's cultural treasures—and here she had met with such a cruel fate.

Patrick Flochten had fallen to pieces when the police told him the news of his daughter's death. Knutas was going to visit him later in the day, and he shuddered at the thought of seeing him. Dealing with family members of a victim was one of the most difficult parts of his job; he'd never gotten used to it. It was worst of all when young people were involved.

Possible connections between the decapitated horse and the murder of Martina were now being investigated. The question was: What kind of person would drain the blood out of his victim?

The police had to start by looking at the circle of people surrounding Martina, which included the students taking the course and their teachers. Knutas had gone over the list of students. Most of them were young, and there was almost an equal number of Swedes and foreigners.

He looked at the names and addresses and birth dates. Nearly all were between the ages of twenty and twenty-five, with a few exceptions. One woman from Göteborg was only nineteen, the British woman was forty-one, and one of the Americans was fifty-three. Knutas slowly spun his chair around.

Who was present during Martina's stay here? The students in the course, the teachers, the staff at the Warfsholm hotel and youth hostel. Surely she couldn't have met very many other people. That was where they had to start. Take them one by one as fast as possible, and at the same time find out who she'd met during the weeks she'd spent in Visby studying theory. Knutas sighed. He realized that his upcoming vacation was going to have to be postponed. Lina had probably already realized as much. He knew that it would be difficult for her to change her vacation, so she and the children would probably take the planned trip to Denmark. He could join them if the case was solved quickly. Even though at the moment it seemed very complicated, he could always hope for a miracle.

He might as well contact the National Criminal Police at once; they were going to need help. He thought about Martin Kihlgård. Although the inspector from the NCP had his bad points, they knew each other so well by now that he would probably be the easiest person to deal with. Knutas picked up the phone and punched in the number. It surprised him how relieved he felt when he heard his colleague's voice on the line.

Anyone who passed by the building wouldn't suspect a thing. It looked like any other dreary warehouse made of gray sheet metal with several parking slots near the unremarkable entrance. No one would believe that inside those walls were unimaginable treasures that had lain buried and forgotten for thousands of years, treasures that had been used by people in a different era, a different life. Utterly unlike anything that was familiar to people nowadays.

He used to come over here late at night when he was sure that all the employees had gone home. Then he had the whole place to himself. The same feeling of reverence struck him every time he opened the door and entered the first room.

He could roam up and down the aisles for hours. Pull out an archive storage rack here and there, take out something at random: an animal bone, a bead, a spearhead, or a nail. It didn't matter. For him no relic was more valuable than any other. Sometimes he would sit on the floor, holding an artifact in his hand. Everything around him would melt away, and the treasure in his hand became the focus. It spoke to him, whispered to him. He thought he could hear voices, echoes from the past. It was the same magical experience each time. Occasionally he had tried to transport himself into the same state as he did at home, but it never worked. This place had something different about it, maybe because it contained so much history from so long ago.

He was convinced that spirits lived in these objects. In here he also sensed a contact with the gods—they listened to him, and he heard their voices. They told him what he was supposed to do, gave him solace, and stood by him when he needed them. Nor did they hesitate to give him praise when he'd done something that was to their liking. He received guidance from them; he didn't know how he could have managed without their help. They told him what they wanted for themselves and what things they thought he could keep. He gladly did their bidding and was offered rewards when the time was ripe. His relationship with them went both ways, based on give and take, just like any human relationship.

Some of the artifacts he kept at home; others he sold off. That was a necessity. He had a responsibility, and he didn't hesitate to accept it. All the hidden things that were dug out of the earth belonged to him and his kinsmen; that was a feeling that had become stronger and stronger over the years. It was better for him to take care of the relics than for them to end up in a display case in some museum in Stockholm. If they were going to disappear from the island, he might as well be the one who decided where they would go. With his fingertips he caressed the shelves in the aisles. They were neatly marked with stickers and numbers, yet it was seldom that anyone checked to see that the drawers actually contained what was listed on the labels. That was why he was able to keep going, undetected. He had started out slowly many years ago and then just kept on. This was his world, and no one could take it away from him. He would never let go of his hold on it.

For the first time in his life he felt that he truly had something important to do. It was a task that he undertook with the greatest seriousness.

The investigative team had decided that all the students in the course, along with their teachers, should be interviewed before the night was over, so they had divided up the individuals for questioning. Jacobsson and Knutas took one of the students with whom Martina had had the most contact: Mark Feathers, an American. They also had one of the teachers in the group assigned to them: Aron Bjarke.

The long workday was drawing to a close, and Knutas was genuinely tired. He was in charge of questioning Bjarke; Jacobsson was present as a witness. When they sat down in the interview room, Knutas couldn't hold back a yawn. He immediately apologized.

Bjarke had taught landscape reconstruction and phosphate analysis during the introductory two weeks of theory. He was a tall, middle-aged man with dark blond hair and a nondescript face. His hairline was receding a bit; otherwise he looked younger than his forty-three years. His chin was adorned with a well-trimmed beard, and his eyes were green with thick, curling lashes.

"What do you know about Martina Flochten?" Knutas began.

"Not much, I have to admit. She was a sweet, lively girl who showed a great deal of interest in the Viking Age in particular. I had the impression that she was more knowledgeable than most of the others. In general, she seemed extremely engaged in the subject."

If the teacher hadn't spoken with such a marked Gotland accent, Knutas would have sworn that he was from the mainland. There was something about his clothes and his style of wearing them, something slightly elegant and big city–like about his neatly pressed slacks and jacket. His voice and manner of speaking, strangely enough, didn't match his appearance. At the same time, there was something disarming about him. He gave Knutas a friendly look as he waited for the next question.

"Did you socialize with her outside of class?"

"No, at least not alone. But the whole group got together several times. We had dinner at the home of one of the other teachers, we went out for a beer, and we played a game of *kubb* in Almedalen. But we were all together, as a group."

"Were you at Warfsholm on Saturday night?"

"No, I've hardly seen the students since they moved out to Fröjel and started excavating."

"Where were you on Saturday night?"

The soft-spoken teacher looked surprised at the question. "Am I a suspect?"

"Not at all. This is purely a routine question that we're asking everyone," Knutas explained. "What were you doing on Saturday night?"

"Nothing special. I was home watching TV."

"Alone?"

"Yes."

"Do you live alone?"

"Yes."

"Do you have any children?"

"No, not yet, anyway."

"Were you home all night?"

"Yes. I think I stayed up quite late. Then I went to bed around midnight. That's what I usually do."

"Did you notice whether Martina was ever together with anyone in the group or with one of the teachers?"

Aron Bjarke suddenly looked embarrassed. "Well, things like that are so hard to judge. Because you never know. It's possible that you imagine one thing and then maybe it's not true at all. I'd prefer not to say anything about it," he explained, putting on a pompous expression.

"What do you mean?" asked Jacobsson from the corner.

"I think that Martina liked to flirt and show off for the men in the group. It was quite obvious. They all fell for it."

"Was there anyone who seemed especially interested in her?"

"Hm . . . I don't know," he said hesitantly. "Maybe there was one person that I thought showed her a little too much attention, but I could be mistaken, of course."

"Who was it?"

Bjarke squirmed. "This is embarrassing because it's one of the teachers. I'm thinking actually of the excavation leader, Staffan Mellgren."

"Is that right?"

"At the same time, you need to know that he often has romantic escapades with cute young female students. It sounds awful to say this, but he has a hard time keeping his hands off them. This isn't the first time that he's shown an interest, so to speak, in a female student."

The man sitting across from Knutas leaned forward and lowered his voice.

"Staffan Mellgren is a lecher, a sex addict. Everyone knows that. He hasn't been faithful to his wife for even a week since the day they got married. And since he prefers"—here Bjarke held up both hands in the air and made the sign for quote marks—*"lamb flesh,* he usually goes for young female students who look up to the teacher and are easy conquests for him."

Bjarke certainly didn't mince words. The teacher's candor surprised both detectives. Knutas perked up.

"Do you mean to say in all seriousness that Mellgren has previously had relationships with students?"

"Of course. It happens all the time. It would be strange if Staffan gave a course and didn't get mixed up with at least one of the female participants."

"How long as this been going on?"

"For ten years at least."

"Does Mellgren's wife know about his affairs?"

"It would be hard for me to imagine that she'd accept something like that."

"You seem to know Mellgren well."

"We've worked together for over fifteen years."

"How has he managed to keep his love affairs a secret from his wife all these years?"

"He and Susanna lead separate lives. She stays home with the kids and takes care of the house and the farm. His job takes up a lot of his time. I don't think they actually see much of each other."

"What was it about Mellgren's behavior toward Martina that attracted your attention?"

"I can't say with certainty that there was actually anything going on between them. The whole group didn't get together very often. I taught my classes, and he wasn't part of that. But when the course started, when everyone was in Visby, we did have a number of group activities. Since I've seen Staffan in action, so to speak, numerous times before, I can tell at once when he goes into pursuit mode."

"In what way?"

"Well, it's really the same old story. He laughs and

jokes a lot with the person he's interested in at the moment. He gives her long looks without saying anything. His old tricks are so obvious that it's ridiculous."

"You seem quite certain about this."

"Let me put it this way: A young woman has been murdered, which is an enormously serious matter, of course. Obviously I don't want to single anybody out or make any claims that might make the person suspect in your eyes. To do that, I realize that I'd have to be absolutely positive about my claims. This much I can tell you, though: He at least tried to get together with Martina Flochten. Whether his advances were returned, I can't say. I don't know anything about that. After the two weeks devoted to theory, the group moved out to Fröjel, and I haven't seen Martina since then."

Jacobsson and Knutas took time out for a cup of coffee before the next interview. Both of them felt the need for a break after their meeting with Aron Bjarke.

In the corridor other students and teachers from the college were going in and out of the various interview rooms. There were many that had to be dealt with.

"Considering what that teacher told us, it's going to be damn interesting to hear what the other interviews have produced," said Jacobsson as they waited for their plastic cups to fill with coffee from the machine. "Do you think he's credible?"

"Hard to know. He was undeniably candid. That always makes me suspicious."

"Why's that? I thought you valued openness," said Jacobsson with a smile.

The interview with the American student Mark Feathers was conducted by Jacobsson. Once again Knutas's command of English wasn't sufficient.

At first glance Feathers looked like the archetypical American guy: close-cropped hair, baggy knee-length shorts, and a big, wrinkled T-shirt that was not tucked in. On his feet he wore tennis socks with a blue border and the obligatory sneakers. He was tall and muscular with an angry expression. He looked more like a baseball player than someone who patiently devoted himself to archaeological excavations.

He seemed upset.

"I just can't believe that she's gone. The whole thing is sick. What did that bastard do to her?" Feathers spoke in a loud, forceful voice, and he glared at Jacobsson aggressively.

"I'm afraid I can't tell you how Martina died."

"Was she raped? Was it a sex crime?"

"No, we don't think so, but it's too early to say for sure."

"If only I could get my hands on that monster." He clenched his fist in a threatening gesture.

"We understand that you're shocked, but you really need to calm down," Jacobsson admonished him. "The important thing right now is that we find out as much as we can about Martina and what she was doing during the days before she disappeared. Can you help us with this?"

"Sure. Of course," he said, sounding a bit more subdued.

"How would you describe Martina?"

"Smart, nice, cute, and damned good at anything having to do with the Viking Age. She knew more than anybody. She was very energetic. She worked harder than any of us. Above all she was loyal, as a friend, that is."

"Was there anything flirtatious or provocative about her behavior?"

Feathers hesitated for a moment before replying.

"I wouldn't really say that. She was lively and open—but flirtatious . . . no."

"Did you notice any change in her behavior lately?"

"No. She was the same as always."

"So there wasn't anything special that happened before she disappeared?"

He shook his head.

"Do you know whether she has a boyfriend here?"

"I'm not sure, but I think so."

"What makes you think that?"

Feathers gave both officers a solemn look. "Jonas and I share the room next to Martina and Eva's. Every day after excavating, we take a bus back to Warfsholm. After working in the heat and dirt for eight or nine hours, everyone is really eager to take a shower and change clothes. But Martina would often disappear as soon as we got home."

"Where did she go?"

"I have no clue."

"Did you see which direction she went?"

"Yes. The bus would pull up right in front of the youth hostel and stop. Then everyone rushed out to get to the shower first. In the beginning I didn't give a thought to the fact that Martina didn't go inside with the rest of us. It took a few days before I noticed. She headed over to the hotel instead."

"Did you ever ask her where she was going?"

"Once. She told me that she was going to buy some ice cream. There's a kiosk next to the restaurant."

"Did she usually go off alone?"

"I never saw anyone go with her."

"And you think that she was meeting someone?"

"Yes, because she always came home at the same time, a couple of hours later."

"Did you mention this to any of the others?"

"To my roommate, Jonas, of course. He had a better handle on what Martina did than anyone else."

"What do you mean by that?"

"He was in love with her, although that's not something that he wanted to talk about."

"Did anyone else know about this?"

"Sure. It was really obvious."

"Were his feelings reciprocated?"

Feathers shook his head. "No, not a chance."

Jacobsson decided to change tack. "Is this your first time in Sweden?"

"Why do you ask?"

"Why shouldn't I ask?"

"Er, I don't know . . . It just seems so unrelated to what's happened."

"How about answering the question?"

"Well, no, I've actually been here before."

"When was that?"

"I was here on Gotland last year, and also the year before."

"How did that happen?"

"The first time, I was with a friend whose girlfriend was from here. They met when she was an exchange student in the States. I hung out with him, and we had such a good time that I wanted to come back. So when it was time for him to come back, I came along."

"Isn't it awfully expensive for a student to come over here?"

"My parents pay for it," said Feathers, unperturbed.

"How long have you been studying archaeology?"

"About three years, off and on."

"What do you mean by 'off and on'?"

"I've dabbled in a little of everything—traveled, sailed. I compete in a lot of windsurfing contests."

That's the reason for the muscles and the athletic look, thought Jacobsson.

"Have you made any friends here during your visits?"

"I've met a lot of people, of course, but the ones you meet in the summer, at the beach or in a pub, are often from somewhere else. So I haven't met very many people who actually live on Gotland."

"Can you mention any at all?"

"Sure. A few who live in Visby."

Jacobsson took down their names and phone numbers.

"How long are you planning to stay here this time?"

"The course goes until the middle of August. After that I plan to stay a couple more weeks."

"Where are you going to stay?"

"With friends in Visby."

"The ones you gave me the phone numbers for?"

"Yes. I'm going to stay with Niklas Appelqvist."

"Did you meet Martina during your previous visit to Gotland?"

"No."

"What were you doing on the night she disappeared?"

"Why do you ask?"

"It's routine."

"I was drinking beer with some others in the group on the hotel porch after the concert. Martina was there, too."

"How long did you stay?"

"As long as the others did, until three or four or so. After that we all went to bed. Jonas and I share a room, so we were together all night."

"So he can confirm that you were with him all evening and all night?"

"Sure. I can vouch for him, too."

THURSDAY, JULY 8

The next day Martin Kihlgård arrived, accompanied by an NCP colleague. The forensic psychiatrist Agneta Larsvik had been called in to help with interpreting the special circumstances surrounding the murder, in particular the modus operandi.

When Kihlgård showed up in the corridor of the criminal investigation division, he was greeted with enthusiastic shouts and slaps on the back. The jovial inspector had become very popular in Visby during his previous visits to assist Knutas with homicide investigations. Jacobsson seemed especially delighted to see him.

"Hey there," she cried when he appeared in the doorway. She threw herself into his arms and was completely swallowed up by his massive body.

"Good gracious, what a reception," he said happily. "How are things out here in the country?"

"Well, one strange thing after another seems to be happening," said Jacobsson. "We're having a meeting in a minute, so you'll get to hear more about it."

"I've already heard a lot. Sounds damned nasty."

"It really is. Come and say hello to Anders. I think he's in his office."

She took her stout colleague by the arm and escorted him to her boss's office.

"Hi, Knutie." Kihlgård's face broke into a smile when he caught sight of Knutas sitting at his desk.

Knutas shook hands with him, keeping a straight face. Martin Kihlgård was the only person who would even consider calling him by that disgusting nickname.

Kihlgård's colleague Agneta Larsvik had a gentle and less brusque manner. A tall and slender brunette with her hair pulled back into a knot, she greeted Knutas pleasantly.

After a little small talk the investigative team gathered to inform the detectives from the NCP about the latest events.

"Do you need to have to something to eat?" Jacobsson knew what sort of appetite Kihlgård had.

"Yes, that would be great. Don't you think?"

He turned to Larsvik, who looked surprised. She made an attempt to say something but was stopped by Jacobsson.

"I'll order sandwiches."

"Thank you."

With a pleased look on his face, Kihlgård sat down between Lars Norrby and Birger Smittenberg. It didn't take long before all three were engrossed in a lively discussion about which of the Greek islands was the best vacation destination.

Someone came in with a platter loaded with open-face shrimp sandwiches, as well as a tray with light beer and Ramlösa mineral water. A moment later chocolate cookies and coffee also appeared on the table. The team wasn't used to such extravagance. Knutas cast a glance at Jacobsson. She certainly hadn't spared any expense to make Kihlgård feel welcome.

He looked at his colleagues. Everyone was talking and laughing with the jovial inspector from the NCP, eager to hear the latest gossip from Stockholm. It was always the same thing. As soon as Kihlgård showed up, the meetings were transformed into some sort of social gathering.

Knutas loudly cleared his throat to get their attention. He welcomed Martin Kihlgård and Agneta Larsvik.

Then the team devoted more than an hour to going over what the investigation had produced so far. The interviews from the previous day were reviewed. The most interesting item that had emerged was the news about Staffan Mellgren's infidelities, as reported by the teacher Aron Bjarke. They agreed that it was a lead that merited investigation.

When they were almost finished, there was a knock on the door and Erik Sohlman came in. Judging by his expression, he had something interesting to tell them.

"I have something to add," he said when Knutas paused.

"Let's hear it."

"The divers who have been dragging the bay near Warfsholm have found a ring that belonged to Martina."

"Where?"

"In the water near the youth hostel, on the sea floor near the reeds, meaning in quite shallow water. It's a big, rather ungainly silver ring with several stones of various colors. We've cordoned off the area and are presently looking for more evidence. I have to go back."

"Where's the ring?"

"In the lab."

Knutas leaned back in his chair. "It matches the ME's theory. That's where she was drowned. Then the perp stuffed her body in his car and drove out to Vivesholm to complete his work."

"Presumably he held her head underwater for the requisite amount of time," said Sohlman. "She had sand and sludge under her fingernails. Most likely it got there when he was holding her under. The bottom is swampy there, so her fingers would have sunk in a bit. That may have been how she lost the ring. It's the kind with an opening in the band and has to be squeezed tight to fit."

A gloomy mood had settled over the room. Maybe they were all thinking about the same thing: the image of Martina, futilely fighting for her life in the reeds while her friends were partying only a few hundred yards away, having no idea what was happening.

"It sounds premeditated," said Kihlgård, "and ice cold. He must have counted on getting her alone so that he could carry out the deed. I mean, who goes around with a knife and a rope and things like that in his car for no reason?"

"Maybe he'd been spying on her for a while," Jacobsson tossed out. "We don't know how long he may have been waiting for the right opportunity. Maybe it was just a lucky chance that it happened that night."

"Can we be sure that it was Martina he was out to get?" asked Kihlgård. "Who's to say he wasn't just after some random victim, anyone at all?"

"That might also be the case," Knutas admitted.

"Another thing that strikes me is that this crime required time," Kihlgård went on. "He must have needed at least a couple of hours to get everything done."

"Then there's the ritualistic element. What does that tell us?" said Knutas. He turned to look at the forensic psychiatrist.

"It's much too early for me to make any sort of evaluation," said Agneta Larsvik. "I want to see more pictures of the victim and study more of the facts. I also need to wait for the autopsy report. In addition, I'd like to see the crime scene before I say anything specific."

"But what's your first reaction?" Knutas ventured.

"What we see here," she said with a glance at the photo of Martina, which filled the entire screen, "is an expression of extreme and improbable violence. It's a very strange act, which makes me think of a solitary, gravely ill perpetrator with a strong hatred for women. Possibly inexperienced sexually. The knife wound in the abdomen may signify a curiosity about the female body in the same way that other perps insert objects into the vagina to examine it. The fact that the victim is naked might imply a sexual association, but as I said, at this stage it's impossible to draw any definite conclusions."

"Do you think this is the perp's first crime?" asked Jacobsson.

"Probably not. I would guess it's a young killer who has committed violent crimes before. This sort of macabre crime is not something a person would do his first time out."

"Why do you think he's young?"

"An individual who is sick enough to be capable of a crime of this nature wouldn't be able to get along in society for very long. To put it simply, he wouldn't get very old before he was caught. But keep in mind that these are only my initial thoughts."

Knutas was looking resolute. "Can you say anything about the modus operandi?"

All eyes were fixed on Larsvik.

"The fact that the perpetrator hung the body up in

the tree may mean that he wants to be seen. By exposing his victim, he's saying to us that he's dangerous, almost like 'Look what I can do!' It may indicate that the murderer wants to tell us that we'd better stop him in time, before he does the same thing again."

Late that afternoon the preliminary autopsy report arrived by fax from the forensic medicine lab in Solna. In his mind Knutas sent the ME words of thanks; then he closed the door to his office and started leafing through the pages.

It turned out that Martina had died from drowning after all. Her lungs were severely inflated; she had foam in her windpipe and seawater in her stomach. Traces of sperm were found in her vagina, but there were no injuries to indicate a sexual assault. The sperm sample had been sent to the Swedish Crime Laboratory in Linköping. The knife wound in her abdomen was deep; it had injured the aorta and intestines. Her blood alcohol level was .12, which meant that she was definitely intoxicated when the murder was committed.

The discovery of the ring and the autopsy results indicated that the murder had occurred at Warfsholm—to be more precise, at the shoreline in front of the youth hostel, not far from the front door and the parking area but hidden by the surrounding juniper bushes. The killer had presumably been so bold as to park right there. When Martina was dead it would have been a simple matter to carry her to his car. The bushes would have hidden him from view. After that he most likely drove straight out to Vivesholm. It would have been about 2:00 or 3:00 A.M. At that hour all the summer guests would have been sound asleep in their houses.

The perpetrator must have parked his car near the fence, far enough away that it wouldn't be seen from the gate or the summer houses. Then he lifted out the body and carried it into the grove of trees.

He had probably prepared the site earlier. Hoisting up a corpse was heavy work. It was unlikely that a woman could have done it, unless she'd had help. Of course, there could have been two or more perpetrators.

Why had the killer chosen to hoist up the body, thereby making it visible and easier to discover? For one thing, it decreased any lead he may have had. For another, executing the maneuver itself entailed a risk of discovery. Was it as the forensic psychiatrist had thought: that this was a way for the perpetrator to call attention to himself? Knutas had his doubts.

Then there was the matter of the abdominal wound. If it didn't have anything to do with Larsvik's assumption about sexual curiosity, what did it mean? Was the killer trying to desecrate his victim? Was it the assault itself that gave him some sort of satisfaction?

Otherwise, as Knutas saw it, there was only one other reason: to drain the body of a great deal of blood, just as had been done with the horse. The blood would then be used for some specific purpose.

The question was: What?

Gunnar Ambjörnsson, Social Democrat and local politician, lived alone. He had done so all his adult life, and that was how he preferred it. To be his own master, to avoid always having to negotiate with others about one thing or another, to compromise, to give and take. He'd done enough of that while he was growing up with four siblings in a cramped row house on Irisdalsgatan in Visby. He'd always had to share a bedroom. The sofa in front of the TV in the living room was always occupied. The chairs around the dining room table were always crowded together. He never had even a corner to himself. The only place he could find any peace was in the bathroom, but never for very long.

When he moved away from home, he first went to Göteborg to study at the university. There he lived in a student dorm with a shared shower and kitchen, so there wasn't much private space there, either. When he finished his degree, he immediately got a job with the county of Gotland, and he'd been on the island ever since. He found an apartment on Stenkumlaväg—centrally located but not in the middle of downtown. A two-room place with a kitchen and a view of the street. On the fourth floor of the building. He would never forget the feeling when he entered his apartment for the first time. Empty, newly remodeled, and fresh. He remembered how he ran his finger over the shiny tiles in the bathroom, sniffed at the new paint in the kitchen, and admired the pristine moldings in the living room. He was delighted by the solitude and by how orderly it all was.

Gradually he worked his way up to better apartments, and for the past twenty years he had lived in his own small house with a garden surrounded by a wall—in Klinten itself, the picturesque residential area across from the cathedral, which was the most attractive area in all of Visby. In the past it been the poorest neighborhood, with a gallows hill so that the condemned could be seen from all over the city and serve as a deterrent. The view was magnificent, with the entire medieval city spread out below with its narrow lanes, its ruins, and the ring wall. On the other side of town was the sea, forming a blue backdrop.

Gunnar Ambjörnsson had never married, nor did he have any children, and at the age of sixty-two he realized that he never would. He'd had women in his life, but the relationships had never resulted in living with any of them. A few had tried to get him to do so, but each time he had backed out at the last minute. Of course he had been interested, and even in love, but he didn't think it was worth giving up his solitude.

For the past few years he'd had a steady relationship with a woman from Stånga. Berit was a teacher, and she was very busy with her job and the small farm where she lived. She would never give up her life in the country to move in with him in the city, and that suited him perfectly. They each lived their separate lives and got together on the weekends. That was precisely the way he wanted it.

Right now he was on his way home after taking part in a golf tournament in Slite. Golf was one of his great passions in his free time, aside from politics. He'd been a Social Democrat since childhood, having grown up in a true working-class family; he was a member of the city council, belonged to several commissions, and served on various boards of directors. He didn't work during the summer, so he took the opportunity to travel a great deal. In a few days he would be heading for the Moroccan city of Marrakech. He had fallen in love with the place as a teenager and had gone back regularly over the years. He always traveled alone. That was the whole point, in his opinion. That made it possible for him to meet new people in an entirely different way than if he'd had a traveling companion. Berit didn't care; she was so busy with her farm, her animals, her children and grandchildren.

He barely managed to maneuver his car between the small, low buildings and turn onto Norra Murgatan, which was up the hill next to the northeastern section of the ring wall. He parked the car in the slot reserved for him. He was looking forward to taking a shower and then sitting in the garden reading *Aftonbladet* with a shot of whiskey. It was a warm evening with no wind. He glanced at his watch as he climbed out of the car. Nine fifteen and as bright as daylight. The Swedish summer was unbeatable when the weather was good. He opened the trunk and took out his heavy golf bag. Then he got out his key and unlocked the gate in the seven-foot-high fence that shielded his property from view. The garden consisted of several beds of roses, a rectangular plot of grass with patio furniture, and a barbecue area. There was also a shed where he kept his gardening tools.

This was his oasis, a little piece of green paradise in the midst of the city. He had even put in a pond with a fountain that murmured in blissful tranquility.

After he closed the gate behind him and walked along the well-weeded gravel path to the front door of his house, something made him stop short. Something had changed since he left the house early that morning.

Ambjörnsson was a very meticulous person with set routines; he always did everything in exactly the same way each day. Something was different, but he couldn't figure out what it could be.

He set down his golf bag and scanned the deep red climbing roses on the trellis that separated the sitting area from the lawn and the facade of the house. The neighbor's black cat was perched on the fence facing the street, watching him from her elevated position.

Then he realized what was out of the ordinary. The fountain wasn't on. He didn't hear it splashing. At first he thought that some problem must have arisen to shut off the water. Then he saw that the broom wasn't in its usual place, leaning against the wall where it normally was. Now he was certain: Someone had been here. He was positive. Had there been a break-in? He hurried over to the door and tried it. No, it was locked and undamaged, as far as he could tell. With fumbling fingers he unlocked the door and went in. The house had only one floor, so it didn't take long to search it. His original painting by Peter Dahl hung undisturbed on the wall above the sofa in the living room, along with the Zorn etching. He pulled out the drawer in the chiffonier; the silverware was still there, as was his coin collection.

Everything seemed untouched. He went back outside and caught sight of the broom, leaning against the shed. He never left it there. Cautiously he approached the shed, listening for any sound. There was a risk that someone might be hiding inside. The intruder had apparently not bothered with the house itself. Maybe he had been surprised to hear someone show up and had taken refuge in the shed. Since Ambjörnsson always locked the gate, he sometimes left the shed door open. He was on the alert and moved as quietly as he could. It was extremely uncommon to have a burglary in this neighborhood. He'd never known it to happen in all the years he had lived here. If only it wasn't some junkie who was high and might do anything at all. Occasionally one of them would sit and drink with the local winos on the lawn across from the Rackarbacken ring wall when the weather was good.

Cautiously he climbed the steps, just enough so that he could reach out and slowly press down the door handle. Something was there, he could clearly sense it; he hardly dared breathe. Now it was too late to change his mind.

At first he didn't comprehend what it was that came rushing out at him when the door opened. He fell over backward, and he could feel something big and bloody come toppling over him. He screamed when he looked into the dead eyes of a horse's head.

He washed his hands with great care, rubbing on the soap and scrubbing with the stiff brush so that his skin hurt. Then he continued up along his arms, brushing so vigorously that his skin stung and layers were gradually scraped off. He started to bleed. By that time he no longer felt any pain. The water didn't flow properly from the faucet, nor did it ever get truly hot. He didn't care; in some way that was all part of the whole process. He bled into the sink, and he liked seeing the blood splash up on the stainless steel sides. Then he scrubbed his chest, his stomach, his legs, and his arms in the same rough manner.

He came out here every time. This was his starting point, the center of his circle, the hub in his life. Here the present shook hands with the future, stood eye to eye with the past. Everything became knotted together into one entity. It was only in this house that he could feel peace.

The turning point had occurred here, and he knew exactly when it had happened. He now understood that he had been chosen, but also that this had not occurred by mere chance.

He had arranged it himself by finally taking command of his own life. He would never have to wonder what it was that had prompted his actions from the very beginning. Perhaps it was merely a feeling of satiety, that now it was enough. From being a victim, he had now gone on the attack. Once and for all.

There was something painful yet at the same time liberating about getting older. Life's insights caught up with you, and there was no avoiding them. They nudged the back of your knees, breathed down your neck until you let them emerge, and then it was like a dam bursting. All the torments that he had hidden under his skin came to the surface and broke through the wall of defenses that he had so carefully constructed since the very first violations in his childhood. To live was to suffer, but he had been punished enough. So one day when he was wandering through the woods alone, he confronted them eye to eye. They spoke through pine and spruce, juniper and blueberry branches. He could hear their whispering voices in the crowns of the trees, in the marshy ground, and in the overcast sky. When he trudged along the shore he heard their cries from far off in the foamy white wave tops and in the sandy dunes.

He screamed and drowned out the roar of the waves.

"I hear you, I hear you. I'm here, I'm yours! I'm your eternal servant, I offer my blood, my life!"

They answered him quickly and firmly. It was not his blood they were interested in.

The call came into police headquarters at 9:15 P.M. Speaking in a distressed and disjointed manner, Gunnar Ambjörnsson told the officer on duty about the horse's head in his shed. The officer then contacted Anders Knutas, who in turned called Jacobsson. Since she lived within walking distance of Norra Murgatan, they agreed to meet there.

When Knutas arrived, she was already waiting outside the fence. They found Ambjörnsson, with whom Knutas was slightly acquainted, wrapped in a blanket and sitting on a chair in the yard. He was speaking agitatedly with a female police officer. When he caught sight of Knutas, he stood up.

"Anders, this is insane. Come see for yourselves."

He led the way to the shed, which stood in a corner of the property.

Jacobsson took out a handkerchief in preparation for what they were about to see and pressed it to her mouth.

Her stomach still turned over when she saw what Ambjörnsson had found an hour earlier. The swollen and bloody head of a horse was affixed to a sturdy wooden pole that was leaning against the door. The pole had been shoved up into the head through the neck. The mouth hung open, and the eyes gave both officers a glassy stare. Several seconds passed before anyone said a word.

"Do you see what I see?" said Knutas in a toneless voice.

Jacobsson slowly nodded from behind her handkerchief. She could hardly bear to look.

"What is it?" Ambjörnsson seemed terrified.

Both the detectives gave him a solemn look.

"Do you know about the horse that was found decapitated recently?"

Ambjörnsson nodded without speaking.

"Well, this head," said Knutas, "doesn't belong to the same horse."

FRIDAY, JULY 9

When Knutas closed the door to his house and set off for work, it was only six thirty in the morning on the day after the discovery in Ambjörnsson's shed. He had lain awake most of the night, and by five he gave up all attempts to sleep. As soon as he got outside, he perked up. The morning air was fresh and clear, and the city was quiet and still.

It was 11:00 P.M. by the time they left the house in Klinten the night before. Ambjörnsson had reluctantly agreed to be taken to the hospital to be examined. He'd had a weak heart for many years and had to take medicine for it. Afterward he was given a police escort over to his girlfriend's place in Stånga. The police refused to allow him to spend the night alone in his house. The horse's head on the pole couldn't be regarded as anything less than a threat.

The conference room had a charged atmosphere when the investigative team took their places. A certain anticipation could be felt in the air. What had happened was definitely out of the ordinary.

"Good morning," Knutas greeted his colleagues. He

then reported on the horrifying scene they had found at the home of the municipal politician Gunnar Ambjörnsson the night before.

When Knutas told them that the horse's head that had been stuck on a pole did not belong to the decapitated horse in Petesviken, everyone was utterly silent.

"What was that you just said?" The words were hesitantly spoken by Martin Kihlgård.

"It's not the same head. The horse's head in Ambjörnsson's shed belonged to a standardbred trotter; the horse in Petesviken was a Gotland pony."

"So that means that somewhere on Gotland there's another decapitated horse."

"Exactly," said Knutas. "We interviewed Ambjörnsson last night, and he says he has no idea what this is all about. He hasn't had any quarrel with anyone, as far as he knows. But I think we still have to assume that this is a threat. What do you think?"

"Politicians are always being threatened in one way or another," said Wittberg with a snort. "It's obvious that Ambjörnsson has reason to be frightened. Methods like this are straight out of the Mafia. It makes me think of drug deals."

"Do you really think the noble Ambjörnsson would be fooling around with drugs? That's going a little too far." Jacobsson looked at her colleague in disbelief.

"I agree." Norrby shook his head. "The Italian Mafia in

Visby? You've been watching too many action films, Thomas. This is real life—and on Gotland."

"The crime is a sophisticated one. That much we can agree on," interjected Sohlman. "Allow me to go over the technical details. The perpetrator shoved the pole up through the horse's neck, under the mandible, and in that way he could affix the head without using rope or anything like that. The pole was placed so that it would fall forward into Ambjörnsson's arms when he opened the shed door. The man suffers from a weak heart; it's incredible that he didn't have a heart attack. The head remained attached, even when the pole fell to the ground, which indicates that the perp knew what he was doing. We called in Åke Tornsjö, the veterinarian, who examined the head last night. According to him, the horse was probably killed in the same way as the one we found decapitated in Petesviken, but he won't be sure until he examines the rest of the body. Unfortunately, we have no idea where to find it. At any rate, this head had been frozen and then thawed before it was fastened to the pole. We know this because it's swollen up, and the flesh is looser than it would normally be. It's impossible to say how long the perp may have preserved the head in a freezer—in principle it could have been for any amount of time. We've found a good deal of evidence on Ambjörnsson's property: footprints, a cigarette butt that doesn't belong to him, and a button that he doesn't recognize. The grass has been trampled in several places, which indicates that the perp first had a look around, presumably to find a suitable place to position the horse's head. By the way, the head has been taken to the veterinarian's office for closer examination."

"How did the perp get into the yard? Don't most people in Klinten keep their places locked up?" asked Wittberg.

"He picked the lock in the gate facing the street. It was easily done. Ambjörnsson didn't even notice any damage to it when he opened the gate." Sohlman pushed his chair back from the table. "If there are no more questions, I'd like to get back there."

"Go ahead," said Knutas.

With a nod to his colleagues, Sohlman hurried out the door.

"The fact that the head belongs to a different horse and not to the one we found out in Petesviken is perplexing, to say the least. We haven't received any reports of a decapitated horse or one that's missing," Knutas went on. "As for Ambjörnsson, he was born in 1942, he's not married, and he doesn't have any children. But he does have a big family, a hell of a lot of siblings and nieces and nephews scattered all over the island. His parents passed away a few years ago. He's not a controversial figure and has never been mixed up in any major political trouble, as far as I can recall, but, of course, that's something we need to look into. At the moment he's staying with his girlfriend in Stånga.

The thing is that he was actually planning a trip abroad, which couldn't come at a better time, if we're supposed to interpret the horse's head as some sort of threat. The day after tomorrow, on Sunday, he's going to Morocco for three weeks."

"With his girlfriend?" asked Kihlgård.

"No, he's traveling alone. Apparently that's what he usually does."

"What does Gunnar Ambjörnsson have in common with Martina Flochten? That's the first question that we need to answer," said Jacobsson. "First Martina was killed, and the murder clearly has ritualistic elements. Then, barely a week later, a horse's head is found stuck on a pole at Gunnar Ambjörnsson's house. That seems extremely odd."

"It would be very strange if there was no connection between these two events," Wittberg agreed. "But the nastiest part about the whole thing is that the head doesn't belong to the horse in Petesviken. Someone is going around decapitating horses and deep-freezing the heads. Someone who might also be a ritual murderer." He nodded toward the window. "Who is he going to strike next?"

Silence settled over the room. The summer greenery outside the window didn't seem as idyllic as it had before.

"All right," said Knutas, as if to break the uncomfortable mood. "We have a statement from the teacher

Aron Bjarke that Staffan Mellgren was romantically interested in Martina. The teacher claims that Mellgren is a real womanizer and that he's constantly getting involved with various young students, even though he's a married man. He even went so far as to describe Mellgren as a sex addict."

"It's just odd that no one else mentioned any infidelities," said Wittberg.

"Yes, especially since they seem to have been so frequent. Is there anyone else who might confirm this information?" asked Kihlgård.

"Not so far. Although you never know. Maybe the other teachers want to protect him. It's a sensitive situation right now, with the murder and all."

"What about the students in the course?"

"Several of them have said that they suspected Martina was secretly meeting someone, but none of them can say who it might be. We haven't talked to the rest of the students at the college. Everyone attending classes right now is a summer student, and they wouldn't know Mellgren."

"What does Mellgren say?"

"He flatly denies it, of course."

"And his wife?"

"The same thing. According to her, they have no marital problems."

Knutas gave his colleagues a solemn look. "Whatever you do, don't let anything get out about the incident at

Ambjörnsson's place," he said emphatically. "The day after tomorrow he's going abroad, which will hopefully give us an opportunity to work in peace and quiet. We also took great pains to be discreet when we were out there yesterday. We've got to keep that up. From now on, all questions regarding the investigation should be referred to either Lars or myself."

After the meeting Knutas went to his office and closed the door. He took out his pipe and began filling it. He needed to be alone to collect his thoughts. The calm that had reigned at the beginning of the summer had now been replaced with a chaos of sensational events, and at the moment he couldn't imagine how everything fit together. The mere fact that somewhere on Gotland there was another decapitated horse was distressing. Why hadn't anyone reported it?

He felt a strong need to light his pipe this time. He went to stand at the window, opened it wide, and struck a match, even though smoking was prohibited indoors. The only exception was in the interview rooms.

Knutas thought about Ambjörnsson: a friendly and unobtrusive politician who lived a quiet life and kept to himself. When it came right down to it, what did he really know about the man? He'd been a politician in the area for thirty years. Knutas had no clue what his private life was like.

Was the threat work-related or personal? They needed to find out quickly what political business Ambjörnsson had on his desk. Maybe that's where the answer would be found.

Knutas puffed on his pipe and slowly let the smoke seep out the corner of his mouth. From somewhere an idea gradually emerged, and all of a sudden it was crystal clear. There *was* a connection between Martina Flochten and Gunnar Ambjörnsson. It was the prestigious hotel project being planned right outside Visby. Martina's father, Patrick Flochten, was one of the architects and financiers of the biggest and most exclusive hotel complex ever to be built on Gotland. The very hotel complex that the building commission had approved just before summer started. Gunnar Ambjörnsson was chairman of the commission. Of course, the city councillors would have to reach a decision, and then the matter would be taken up by the county board, but the fact that the building commission had given the green light was the first step in implementing the plans.

Knutas searched his memory. There had been some protests against the project, although he'd gotten the impression that most Gotland residents took a positive view of it. He thought there was a political consensus in favor of the hotel. Which groups might be opposed? Undoubtedly neighbors who lived at Högklint, conservationists, and ethnogeographers—but surely none of them would be prepared to commit murder over it.

Knutas didn't know if there was anything of archaeological interest at the site. All the groups that had any involvement in the project would have to be checked. Maybe there were political opponents that he didn't know about. He was going to see to it that the matter was investigated at once.

The evening couldn't have been more perfect. They had prepared themselves well. Each of them knew what to do. Everything had been meticulously conceived and planned, down to the smallest detail.

They were going to spend the night out there, at the remote site, near to the gods and under the protection of nature. Every tree trunk, boulder, and bush was blessed with a spirit that would keep them company during the ceremony. They had put up the tent and prepared the food, and within each of them a feeling of excitement was now growing, in anticipation of what was to come.

The crickets were chirping loudly in the thickets that lined the narrow path leading up to the ridge. It was a difficult hike. The slope was steep and not easily accessible. The group of people merged into one by virtue of what they were wearing: ankle-length cloaks with black sashes around their waists. The men's heads were covered with cowls and the women's with kerchiefs. They all walked with their heads bowed, perhaps to avoid stumbling over the tree roots on the ground, or perhaps to pray.

A ceaseless murmuring was mixed with the drumming done by a man leading the way. In one hand he held a flat drum made of animal hide, in the other a leather-covered wooden mallet that he used to strike the drum with an even beat.

When they reached the open clearing that was their destination, one of the men moved away from the group. From his tunic he pulled out an eighteen-inch signal horn made of bone. He raised it to his lips, pointed it toward the sea, and blew. The sound was monotonous and plaintive. A drinking horn was passed around the group. With closed eyes and solemn faces they each drank the wine from the horn, and when everyone had tasted it, they poured the last drops onto the ground. The man with the signal horn appeared to be the leader. He took up a position in front of the participants. He spoke a few words and then turned to face the east as the drumbeats sounded. He shouted into the bright night. With a strong and clear voice he invoked the deities. Then he faced, by turns, the south, the west, and the north as he spoke. Finally he turned toward the center of the circle, where an altar had been erected with idols painted in blood.

One by one the participants stepped forward to place flowers, fruit, and sacks of grain on the holy altar. Stones had been arranged in a circle around the entire site.

The people in the circle stomped their feet on the

ground, and the murmuring started up again, growing louder until everyone was practically screaming. Several of the men lit a fire, which instantly flared up toward the sky.

The drummer struck the drum in time with the people's laments. Someone handed the leader an axe, which he swung in front of him as he uttered incantations. A cage was carried forward, and a well-fed white hen was held up before the participants, who stared at it, enraptured. The hen was placed on the ground in front of the leader, who raised the axe and cut off the bird's head with a precise blow. Blood spattered all around, the lament became even more ecstatic, and the stomping grew more intense.

At last the leader collapsed. The drumming ceased, and the voices stopped. Silence reigned.

One of the participants left the group without drawing attention to himself. No one noticed when he headed back the way they had come. He got into his car and drove off.

SATURDAY, JULY 10

They were going to spend the weekend at the home of Emma's parents on the island of Fårö. Just Emma, Johan, and the baby, Elin. Emma's parents had dropped by the house in Roma to say hello before they set off on the long trip that they usually took each year. She had felt nothing but emptiness during their visit. She didn't sense any sincerity from them, just a superficial babbling about how adorable Elin was. Then they went off to the airport and their travels, which would take them to China this time. That was just as well.

Emma had promised to look after their house, and it would be lovely to have a change of scene. She was already feeling cooped up in the house in Roma. There was so much to remind her of her old life there, and yet there was nothing left of it. The walls breathed Olle and all the bitterness that had emerged over the past six months.

Emma was very fond of the house on Fårö. For the life of her she couldn't understand how her parents could go off traveling when everything was so marvelous right there at home.

The route to the ferry landing at Fårösund passed through a lush farming area. They took the small roads through Barlingbo and Ekeby up to Bäl and the larger village of Slite before they reached Fårösund, where they caught the car ferry over to Fårö. It took only a few minutes to cross the sound. Elin slept the whole way.

When they drove off the ferry on the opposite shore, Emma felt the same sense of contentment that she always felt. Fårö was more barren and windswept than Gotland, and the difference was instantly noticeable. They made the obligatory stop at the Konsum supermarket to buy fresh strawberries and last-minute groceries. They also stopped at the local bakery on the way to Skär to buy some of their amazing sugar buns. Then they drove the last part of the way toward Norsta Auren at the northernmost section of Fårö.

The white limestone house stood all by itself near a low stone wall, with the sea on the other side. Emma felt a slight churning in her stomach; she hadn't been out here in more than six months. The house felt chilly, as it always did when they first arrived. The stone floor was shiny; her parents had done a proper cleaning. She sat down in the armchair by the window to nurse Elin, who was now awake and crying. In the meantime, Johan unpacked the groceries. Through the window Emma could look out at the beach. It was narrow here, where it started, but it got wider the farther out you went. One big advantage was that the sand was packed down so hard that you could push a baby buggy along it.

"Maybe we could take a walk along the beach later," she called to Johan.

"Sure. That would be great. Would you like something to drink?"

"Yes, please. A glass of water."

The next minute he came into the living room, bringing her a big glass of water. Johan looked so happy and relaxed. He seemed glad to be with her and their child. That seemed to be all he wanted. Why couldn't she feel just as happy? Out in the kitchen Johan was humming as he put everything away. She should pull herself together and give him a chance. Elin's cheeks grew rosy as she suckled at her mother's breast. *For your sake,* thought Emma. *And for mine.*

Due to the new situation, the investigative team was holding a meeting, even though it was Saturday.

Knutas was looking forward to hearing what conclusions Agneta Larsvik had reached. She had devoted the past two days to defining what she thought were the distinguishing characteristics of the perpetrator.

Everyone had just sat down when the door opened and Kihlgård came in. He looked happy, his hair was windblown, and he had two big paper sacks in his hands.

"Hi, everybody," he greeted them cheerfully. "I've been to a fantastic party at the Hamra pub, and when I was about to drive away this morning, they insisted on sending some goodies along with me for our coffee. Is there any fresh coffee?"

"No, but I'll put on a pot," Jacobsson offered.

"I'll help you," said Kihlgård, and they left the room together.

Knutas and Norrby exchanged glances. Kihlgård always had to be in the spotlight. On the other hand, he created an atmosphere of well-being, which Knutas appreciated since he wasn't very good at such things himself.

They waited patiently for the coffee to be ready. In the meantime, Thomas Wittberg came sauntering in with a whole liter of Coca-Cola in his hand. Judging by his expression, it had been a late night with plenty to drink for him as well. They chatted a bit about all the partying that had gone on in the city the night before. It had been unusually rowdy. The number of tourists increased every year, especially among the younger crowds who were attracted to Visby's pub life, since the island's summer weather was among the best in the whole country. Unfortunately the young people also brought with them drunkenness, drugs, and fights. Right now everyone gathered around the table had much more serious matters to talk about. As soon as the coffee and Kihlgård's cinnamon rolls appeared, they started going over the status of the investigation. Knutas began by telling everyone that the hotel project represented a link between Martina Flochten and Gunnar Ambjörnsson, just in case anyone had missed the discussions that had been going on in the hallways.

Then he turned to Jacobsson and Wittberg. "What have you come up with?"

"Not much." Wittberg tugged on his blond locks. "Karin and I spent all of yesterday talking to the demonstrators protesting the project and any politicians we could find. It wasn't easy. On a Friday in

July hardly anyone stays at work past lunchtime. We asked about how the protests have been going, about possible threats, and so on. Of course, without mentioning the horse's head that was found at Ambjörnsson's house," Wittberg emphasized when he noticed the nervous expression on Knutas's face.

"In general the opposition seems quite weak and ineffectual," he went on. "There haven't been any threats. Of course, there have been a number of protests, and the authorities have received letters and such, but nothing that seems particularly serious. It seems very unlikely that we're going to find any sort of motive there. Don't you agree?"

He looked at Jacobsson, who nodded.

"Have you gone through the letters of complaint sent to the authorities?"

"Not yet."

"Do that as soon as possible," Knutas urged them. "Is there anything of archaeological interest out at Högklint?"

"Doesn't seem to be. The area has been partially excavated before. There doesn't seem to be any major find, although we still need to talk to more people."

Wittberg took a big gulp of Coke.

"I had an interesting conversation with Susanna Mellgren," said Jacobsson. "She called me this morning to tell me that the report about her husband's infidelities was true."

"Is that right?" said Knutas in surprise. "It was only yesterday that she denied the whole thing."

"I know, but now she claims that it's been going on for several years, with different women. On the other hand, she wasn't sure whether he'd been seeing Martina Flochten or not. She says that she can usually tell whenever he takes up with someone new. She claimed not to mind that he's unfaithful. To be honest, I had the impression that she stays in the marriage because it's the most practical thing to do at the moment, financially speaking. She's in the process of studying to be a massage therapist and wants to start her own business. I'm guessing that she's probably planning to divorce him as soon as she can stand on her own feet."

Knutas frowned. "We're going to have to talk to Mellgren about this again, since he said their marriage was so great," he muttered, making a note on a piece of paper.

Knutas then asked Larsvik to give them a report on how she viewed the perpetrator. She went to stand at the head of the table.

"First and foremost, I want to emphasize that these are preliminary thoughts; nothing can be confirmed for sure at such an early stage. Take what I say as a screening instrument, a working hypothesis, nothing more. Yet there is much to indicate that we're dealing with a perpetrator who is seriously mentally disturbed. He probably carried out these acts alone, which indicates that he possesses great physical strength. The perpetrator most likely had no personal relationship with Martina Flochten. I don't think that they even knew each other. The crime doesn't seem to have been directed at her. On the other hand, I think the way it was carried out indicates that he harbors a hatred toward other people and a contempt for women in particular. There is some sort of symbolism in this, although it's hard to say what it might mean after only one homicide. I think he wanted to humiliate his victim and inject as much powerlessness into the situation as possible. By doing that, he becomes the one with power, and that's something he enjoys. It's possible to imagine that as a child he was abused or in some other way mistreated by one or both of his parents. Now he wants revenge by placing his victim in the same position of powerlessness that he experienced as a child. It wouldn't surprise me if he has a complicated relationship with his mother."

"How the hell do we go looking for a bad mother-son relationship?" Kihlgård threw out his hands, almost knocking over Jacobsson's plastic coffee cup.

Agneta Larsvik smiled. "It might be a good thing to keep in the back of your mind during the interviews, for instance. In case anyone expresses scorn for women or has cut ties with his parents, especially his mother."

"You say that he wanted to put the victim in a position of powerlessness," said Jacobsson, "but why would he keep tormenting her after she was dead? At that point she would no longer be able to feel her powerlessness."

"Keep in mind that the important thing is the feelings of the murderer—it's not a matter of logical or rational thought processes. He's so engrossed in his own emotional state of possessing power, and he's enjoying it so much, that he can't think along logical lines. He reduces his victim to a thing, an object, something that helps him to enter into the state that he's trying to achieve. It's a way for him to ease his own anxiety, at least for the moment."

"Then what do you think about the ritualistic element—the fact that the murder was carried out like some sort of ceremony?" asked Wittberg.

"The one doesn't have to exclude the other. He could be a fanatic who devotes himself to some type of ritual voodoo arts as well."

"What does it mean that she was naked?" asked Knutas.

"Nudity makes us think that the murder has a sexual connotation, of course. Curiosity, perhaps. It might mean that he's sexually inexperienced. We might also ask ourselves what he did with her clothes, and whether there could be some type of fetishism involved."

"The same thing with the blood. What the hell does he want with the blood?"

"For him, collecting the spilled blood might be a way to hold on to the positive feelings the murder has given him. In the same way that a serial killer usually takes with him something belonging to the victim. A lock of hair, a piece of clothing, anything at all."

"A serial killer?" Jacobsson looked shocked.

"Yes, exactly." Larsvik had a serious expression on her face. "Of course it's important not to get locked into one idea, but I think we need to consider the possibility that this murderer may strike again."

SUNDAY, JULY 11

The Antiquities Room, which was the historical section of the Gotland Regional Museum on Strandgatan in Visby, was deserted on this Sunday morning. The entrance hall seemed chilly in contrast to the heat outside on the street, and there wasn't a sound. His footsteps echoed across the stone floor. In the museum reception area, the girl sitting behind the glass window was deeply absorbed in her book. She didn't seem to hear him approach. He was forced to clear his throat twice before she finally looked up. He met her gaze behind the horn-rimmed glasses and paid for a ticket without uttering a word. For appearance's sake he strolled without interest through the rooms with the picture stones, the prehistoric graves, and the reconstructed Stone Age settlements. He seemed to be the only visitor. On a dazzling Sunday during summer vacation, people preferred to spend the day at the beach or in their summer houses rather than in a museum. The weather suited his purposes perfectly.

He climbed the stone stairway that would take him to what really interested him: the treasure chamber.

Whenever he stepped inside he was seized by a feeling of melancholy. Here was only a fraction of all the riches that had been plucked from the Gotland soil since the excavations on the island had started in earnest during the 1960s—caches of silver, jewelry, and coins.

Per square mile, Gotland had produced a larger quantity of Viking Age treasures than anywhere else in the world. No fewer than seven hundred Viking Age silver hoards had been dug up. The most famous was known as the Spillings treasure, the world's largest silver cache from the Viking Age. It was dug up in Spillings in Othem parish on Gotland in 1999. The treasure weighed 148 pounds and contained, among other things: 14,300 coins, almost five hundred armlets, twenty-five rings, and loose silver.

Several of the coins in the Spillings treasure were sensational—in particular, the one called the Moses coin, minted in the Khazarian kingdom, which was eastern Europe's most powerful state during the eighth and ninth centuries. The Moses coin was the first archaeological artifact that tied Judaism to the Khazars, which made it unique in the world.

Sometimes he would spend long periods of time in here, lost in his own fantasies about the coin. It bore the Arabic inscription *Musa rasul Allah*—"Moses is God's messenger." Researchers had interpreted this to be of Jewish origin, alluding to the biblical Moses, who had led the Israelites out of Egypt and received the Ten Commandments from God on Mt. Sinai.

He'd heard talk that the coin might be moved to the Museum of National Antiquities in Stockholm, where it could be viewed by a larger number of visitors. Yet another sacrilege.

He sat down on a bench along the wall in order to run through the plan in his mind one last time. So far no one else had turned up.

Lining the walls were display cases holding silver coins—Arabic, German, Irish, Bohemian, Hungarian, Italian, and even Swedish.

It was not those coins that interested him. He'd been stealing that sort of artifact for years from significantly easier venues than this museum, where any theft from one of the cases would of course be quickly noticed.

This time he had a considerably loftier goal, and it had been carefully planned. The price he had been offered was so high that he couldn't resist the temptation, even though it did involve some risk.

Selling ancient artifacts from Gotland was no problem for him. Since they were going to end up on the mainland anyway, he might as well earn a bit of cash from them. Then he could at least control where they would go. Besides, he used the money for a purpose that would have pleased his Viking Age forefathers. It was a way of completing the circle; that was how he chose to view it. Deep inside he felt that the artifacts belonged to him, at least much more than they belonged to the people in power who made the decisions about removing them from the island. Some of the objects he kept for himself. He had his favorites.

In a glass case in the middle of the room was a gleaming armlet of the purest gold. It was the largest single gold object from the Viking Age on Gotland, and it had been dug up in Sundre parish. The bracelet was made of twenty-four-carat gold and had been dated to approximately A.D. 1000. It was extremely rare to find gold artifacts from the Viking Age, and here lay the largest one, with only a glass wall separating him from it.

He got up and went out to the stairwell. He looked down at the reception area. The girl in the cashier's booth was still reading her book. He glanced at his watch. It was noon. Everyone would be going to lunch except for the cashier. That was what he was waiting for. The risk of being discovered was nonexistent, and his disguise would prevent anyone from pointing him out afterward. He summoned all his powers of concentration, pulled on the thin gloves, and made a quick round of the rooms on the upper floor. Not a soul.

He could hear voices from the ground floor. The employees were on their way out for lunch. The front door slammed. Now he was alone with the cashier.

The museum had no surveillance cameras, but a few years back it had been equipped with an alarm system.

He had found out how it could be disconnected, so that detail had been solved.

He took a small screwdriver out of his pocket and unscrewed the glass case from its pedestal. The whole time he kept his ears open for any sound on the stairs—he didn't want to be caught in the act. Then it was just a matter of lifting off the top part, setting it carefully on the stone floor, and taking out the armlet. He replaced the case and calmly walked down the stairs. The cashier still had her nose in her book. It almost looked as if she were asleep. Unnoticed, he slipped out the door and disappeared down the street.

MONDAY, JULY 12

The theft from the Antiquities Room meant that Johan was forced to leave Emma and Elin on Fårö and hastily return to Visby. He had filed a report on the news story for the Sunday broadcast of *Regional News.*

Now on Monday morning his editor had made it clear that he wanted a follow-up about the shock and dismay, from the angle: How could it have happened? *All ready-packed in his editor's skull,* thought Johan sarcastically, even though he agreed that a follow-up on the story would be natural. He himself wondered most about the fact that the thief had been able to disconnect the alarm system. Did that mean it was an inside job? If so, how many similar thefts might have been committed previously? He had requested news clippings from the press archives pertaining to the theft of artifacts on Gotland, and they had arrived by fax. Most of them had to do with individuals from abroad who had brought in metal detectors and plundered the island's silver treasures.

In a copy of *Gotlands Tidningar* from six months earlier, he found an article that caught his interest: SUSPECTED THEFT AT REGIONAL MUSEUM WAREHOUSE.

None of the people he had interviewed in connection with the current theft had mentioned that objects had disappeared at any previous time. This article dealt with thefts from a warehouse located in a different part of the city, so maybe it wasn't so strange that they hadn't said anything. Naturally they wouldn't want to advertise the thefts any more than necessary.

The article said that several coins were missing from the warehouse in which all artifacts not on display were stored; the Antiquities Room only had space to show a small portion of everything that had been dug up on the island. Interviewed in the article was the person in charge of the warehouse, Eskil Rondahl, who took the matter of the missing coins very seriously.

Johan found the phone number for the warehouse and asked to speak with Rondahl.

He heard a voice, dry as dust, on the other end of the line say, "Hello?"

"Hi. My name is Johan Berg, and I'm calling from Regional News, Swedish TV."

Silence. Johan went on.

"I'm calling about an article in *Gotlands Tidningar* from six months ago. It has to do with the theft of some Arabic coins from the warehouse."

"Yes?"

"Do you know what I'm talking about? You were the one who was interviewed in the article."

"Yes, I know. The theft was solved."

"What happened?"

"It turned out that no theft had actually taken place after all. The missing coins were found. They had just been misplaced. That's all."

"How did that happen?"

"It was a matter of negligence, and I can only blame myself. When coins are received here, they're put in the special security section of the warehouse, where we keep everything that is particularly valuable and might be enticing to steal. In this instance, a box of coins was misplaced, but we found it later. It was quite embarrassing for me, so it's something that I'd prefer to forget."

"I understand. Have you had any other thefts?"

"Nothing that we can pinpoint with certainty, but of course things do disappear sometimes."

"But surely that's a serious matter. People can't very well just walk off with objects that are thousands of years old, can they? What do the police say about it?"

"They don't really care. There's no one on the police force who wants to get involved with the theft of ancient relics. Those kinds of things are way down on their list of priorities," said Rondahl with a snort. "I'm afraid I don't have any more time right now."

Johan thanked him and hung up.

He was puzzled by the conversation. Were thefts occurring and no one cared about the matter?

He called the college and asked to speak with an archaeologist. The only person available was the theory teacher Aron Bjarke.

Johan told him about the article he had read and what Eskil Rondahl had said.

Bjarke partly confirmed what Johan had heard. "It's possible that individual objects have been stolen without anyone noticing, but the worst part isn't that a few things disappear here or there. The big problem is the fortune hunters who come to Gotland to search for silver treasure. Some years ago a new law was instituted to put a stop to the plundering. Nowadays it's illegal to use metal detectors on Gotland without special permission from the county council. Last year the police caught two Englishmen red-handed as they were using metal detectors to search for treasure."

"What happens to the stolen goods?"

"There are collectors all over the world who will pay considerable sums for silver jewelry or coins from the eleventh century, for example. Not to mention all the beautiful jewelry we find from the Viking Age. Naturally there's a big market and plenty of money involved."

"Do thefts still occur?"

"Without a doubt. It's just that the police aren't interested."

"Can you cite a specific theft that you happen to know about?"

Bjarke was silent for a few seconds.

"No, actually I can't. Not at the moment."

FRIDAY, JULY 23

Almost two weeks had passed since the burglary in the Antiquities Room. No arrests had yet been made for the murder of Martina Flochten, for the horse incidents, or for the theft. Knutas didn't actually think that there was a connection between the crimes, but he had asked the officer assigned to the burglary to keep him informed on the progress of the investigation. The crimes did have one thing in common: They were all a long way from being solved.

Knutas hadn't felt that he could join his family in Denmark as long as the murder of Martina Flochten remained unsolved. However, that didn't stop him from longing for a vacation when he could play golf, go fishing, and sit on the porch with a glass of wine and a book. He was tired and worn out and starting to feel truly frustrated. Nothing had turned out as he'd hoped. He thought the investigative work might open up when the severed horse's head was found at the home of Gunnar Ambjörnsson. That hadn't happened. Lina and the children had returned from vacation, suntanned and rested, while he had no good news to tell them when asked about the investigation.

The fact was that the police had made virtually no progress at all. The few neighbors who lived near Ambjörnsson and had been home on the night in question hadn't seen or heard a thing, with the exception of an elderly woman who had noticed an unfamiliar car on the street. She couldn't say what type of car it was or how old it was, only that it was red and big.

It could have been the perpetrator's car—a horse's head was not something that you could carry around on foot—but so far the police hadn't received any reports of a missing horse or a mangled horse's body. Knutas wondered why that was. He knew of only one place where a horse would be able to disappear without anyone quickly taking notice: Lojsta Heath, the refuge for the wild Gotland ponies. The only snag was that the head didn't belong to a pony.

The police hadn't wanted to put out any sort of bulletin because then the incident would become public knowledge. A horse's head stuck on a pole, right on the doorstep of a highly placed politician, would without a doubt cause a stir among both the island residents and the tourists. In the worst-case scenario, it might mean the death knell for the hotel project. The foreign investors might back out, and that wasn't something Gotland could afford. Knutas had met with the police commissioner, the county governor, and the municipal executive board, and they earnestly agreed that the incident had to be kept quiet.

The fact that the media hadn't gotten wind of the matter was just as unexpected as it was fortunate. Maybe it was because the crime had occurred in the middle of the vacation season. Many of the local reporters, who had an extensive network of contacts, were away, and their places had been taken by substitutes. Knutas was extremely impressed that everyone involved had actually kept their promise not to say a word.

On the other hand, he was not nearly as pleased with the work of the police. When it came to the tragic and brutal death of Martina Flochten, they were still fumbling around blindly. They had interviewed the few people she had known on Gotland, including the hotel owner Jacob Dahlén. Unfortunately he could offer no help. He claimed that he hadn't even seen Martina this summer.

Nor had their colleagues from the National Criminal Police contributed anything particularly useful. Agneta Larsvik had gone back to Stockholm for the weekend, and even though Kihlgård was a capable detective, his contribution to the police investigation had so far been limited, to put it mildly. On the other hand, the one thing that he *had* managed to do was to cheer up Karin Jacobsson. She seemed much happier ever since he had arrived on Gotland. Sometimes Knutas even imagined that something was going on between those two, but he was probably just succumbing to his usual touchiness when it came to Karin.

Johan and Pia had done their series of reports on the overheated housing market in Visby, which had been well received by the Regional News editors in Stockholm. At the height of the summer it was hard to come up with good stories that didn't have to do with tourism, pub life, or the quality of the bathing beaches.

Grenfors had left for vacation, and he had been replaced in Stockholm by a reporter who was used to stepping in as editor whenever she was needed. For the most part she let Johan work in peace. He was only able to get a few scattered days off, since he was the summer replacement on Gotland. There was no question of any lengthy vacation time until September. He had cautiously suggested to Emma that it might be fun for them to take a trip somewhere. She seemed doubtful. Elin might be too young to fly.

Sometimes Johan felt genuinely sick of Emma. She could never make up her mind that they were a couple and allow him to move in. Not that he intended to settle for living in the same house where she and Olle had built a life together, but surely it would be all right temporarily. For the sake of Sara and Filip he would put up with the situation. He was ready. He was starting to get annoyed by Emma's constant harping about how complicated her life was. He was fed up. What about him? He had sacrificed everything for her sake. Left his job, his apartment, his friends, and his whole life back in Stockholm in order to move to an island where he hardly knew a soul. He never complained, but it was as if she had no room for him here.

At first he thought it was understandable. Emma had been well along in her pregnancy, and then came the birth with everything that followed. At some point, though, she had to be prepared to go on with her life—and to allow him in. They had argued last night when he brought up the subject, and they hadn't spoken to each other since. Right now what he wanted most was to go out and drink himself senseless.

His thoughts were interrupted by Pia coming into the office.

"Hi."

She put down the camera, the tripod, and the carrying case.

"Where have you been?" Johan asked her.

"Out getting some great summer shots that I think we can use for the closing scenes. That kind of thing is always fun, and I didn't have anything else to do. You haven't exactly come up with any brilliant ideas."

She gave him a teasing smile and sat down at her computer to upload the video.

Johan watched her as she worked. Pia was nice, really nice. Somehow he hadn't noticed that before. It's true that her appearance was a little too punk for his taste, but she was both gentle and feminine, yet at the same time she knew what she wanted. Johan appreciated that. She always had an opinion about things going on in the community. She got involved. When was the last time that he and Emma had discussed anything going on in society? Was she at all interested in what was happening in the world around her? The thought had never occurred to him before. He tried to recall when they'd had a political discussion or talked about some current world problem. The thought gave him pause. Falling in love had overshadowed so much that he wasn't even certain where she stood politically.

"You're sure quiet." Pia turned her head to look at him. "What's up?"

He pulled himself together. He'd gotten lost in his brooding and was probably sitting there staring at her like an idiot without being aware of what he was doing.

"Er, nothing." He shrugged his shoulders. The new thoughts both annoyed and saddened him.

"You look like you could use some cheering up. How about going out for a beer?"

"Great."

They left the editorial office and went out into the

Mediterranean heat of the summer evening. It was a little past seven o'clock, and all the restaurants and bars were starting to fill up with sunburned tourists ready to party. They went to a bar on Stora Torget and chose seats outdoors.

"So what's really going on with you?" asked Pia when they each had a big, ice-cold pilsner.

"I'm okay. I'm fine. It's just that so much has happened lately that I don't know whether I'm coming or going."

"Becoming a father is a big deal, of course." Pia sipped at her beer. "So why aren't you with Emma and Elin tonight?"

"Emma has her other children, Sara and Filip, staying with her. They've been on vacation with their father, so she hasn't seen them in a while. That's why she wanted to spend time alone with them."

"Well, that's understandable."

"Yes, although sometimes I think that all I ever do is worry about getting in the way of her and her other family."

"Jeez, that really must get old," said Pia sympathetically. "As if it's not hard enough trying to keep a so-called normal relationship going." She rolled her eyes.

"So what about you?" asked Johan out of curiosity. Pia had never said anything about a partner, and he hadn't thought to ask. "Are you dating anyone?"

"I wouldn't exactly call it that. You might say that I screw this guy off and on, when it suits me."

"Are we talking about buddy sex?"

"No, I like him a lot, but it's never going to amount to anything, if you know what I mean. We just seem to be treading water. We aren't getting anywhere."

"Rather like me and Emma."

"But good Lord, the two of you just had a baby!"

"Sure. But in a strange way, it seems like that hasn't made much of a difference in our relationship. No matter how odd that sounds. For example, Emma has a thousand arguments for why she doesn't want us to move in together."

"You have to give her time. I'm sure you can see that. She had to split apart her whole family, and she has two other children to take into consideration. Plus the problem of working out everything with her ex. It's not so strange that she can't rush into anything. Elin is only a few weeks old, right?"

"Yes, I can see that," said Johan, disappointed that Pia wasn't taking his side. He could have used a little support right now. He emptied his glass and stood up. "Would you like another?" he asked.

"Sure."

There was a big crowd at the bar, and the volume of the music had been turned up full blast. Johan was enjoying being out on the town. Visby pulsed with life in the summer, and if he hadn't been with Emma, he would have probably gone out every single evening. While he waited to order, he surveyed the bar.

Suddenly he caught sight of someone he thought he recognized. The man was standing with his back to Johan, talking to a cute blonde who couldn't have been more than twenty-five. She was laughing at him as she sipped at her glass, which seemed to contain a sparkling wine or possibly champagne. When the man clinked glasses with his young companion, he turned enough for Johan to see his profile.

It was Staffan Mellgren.

SATURDAY, JULY 24

The next day Staffan Mellgren stayed out at the excavation site for a long time. He had made a late night of it. He was hungover and tired, but he preferred to be at work instead of having to explain to Susanna why he had spent the night in town. Even though he suspected that she knew what he was up to and didn't care in the least whether he saw other women, she still seemed to enjoy pretending just the opposite. She played the role of the gullible and wronged wife, just for the pleasure of seeing him suffer.

In the car on his way home he called her, and, after the obligatory argument, she accepted his explanation that he'd had to work overtime. Sounding hurt, she reminded him that this was the third time in the past week he'd missed dinner. He played along, explaining that there was a lot of work to do during the excavation part of the courses. In fact, that happened to be true. Especially this time, since the excavation work had been delayed by Martina's death and the shock and despondency it had prompted among the students. Some had chosen to leave, but most of them were still there, and he was grateful for that. Three weeks had passed since the murder, and they were still being constantly reminded of it. The fact that the killer hadn't been caught didn't exactly improve the situation. Mellgren tried to explain all this to his wife, but she would have none of it. Instead she accused him of neglecting his family. He couldn't even count how many times he'd heard all this before. He regretted calling her, and he tried to placate her by offering to feed the chickens when he got home.

They lived in Lärbro, about twenty miles north of Visby, so it was a bit of a drive. He turned up the volume on the stereo as loud as it would go, enjoying the music. It helped him to unwind.

He wondered when the love between them had disappeared. He couldn't remember when he'd last seen any warmth in his wife's eyes. He was living in a loveless, phony marriage. The laughter had gotten stuck in his throat long ago. Maybe a divorce was unavoidable, but he was too much of a coward to take the first step.

The children kept him in the marriage. They were still so young; the oldest was only ten. He had neither the energy nor the desire to get out of the marriage right now. It would have to wait. In the meantime he would do whatever he could to make it bearable.

When he drove into the yard, everything was quiet. The kids were probably asleep by now. He might as well go out to the chicken coop right away.

Their farm had a view of the pastures and fields. He

looked at the whitewashed limestone house, the blue-painted trim around the windows with their curtains and potted plants, and the porch with its ornate gingerbread carvings. On one side was the studio where his wife made her pots; she even had her own kiln. How he used to admire her work. When was the last time they had talked about her pottery?

The dilapidated barn that they had planned to paint this summer looked the same as always. So far nothing had come of their plans. Why bother to paint it? Why should they fix up anything? No reason.

A sudden feeling of melancholy came over him, and he sat down on the bench outside the potter's studio and buried his head in his hands. He would feed the chickens in a minute; he just needed to gather his forces first. They had turned half of the barn into a chicken coop. Whatever good that would do. When they were newly in love and had moved out of Visby to live in the country, they both thought it seemed romantic to have chickens. Since then the years had passed and the romance had disappeared, but the chickens were still here.

He had a feeling that life was slipping away from him as he stood on the sidelines and watched. The days came and went, and nothing changed. He and his wife kept up their usual bickering, their sex life was largely non-existent, and one routine followed another in a never-ending stream.

It had been a good long time since they'd had a real

fight. Neither of them seemed to have enough commitment even to argue. Nothing but surliness and a steadily growing distance. Not that he wanted any closeness with her. Not anymore.

He stood up and sauntered across the yard toward the chicken coop. It was a lovely, quiet night. The scent of jasmine from the bushes in front of the house mixed with the smell of chicken manure.

The chickens were strutting around the yard, pecking here and there, and clucking softly. They were unusually quiet this evening.

Suddenly he caught sight of something sticking out above the open barn door. He was too far away to make out what it was, but something was definitely there, he was sure of that. He kept catching a glimpse of it from behind the maple tree's swaying branches that stretched over the building on this side.

He hesitated without knowing why and then stopped abruptly. He glanced around uncertainly but couldn't see anyone. All of a sudden an ominous feeling had settled over the yard.

When he got close enough, he was seized with horror. At first glance he had a hard time taking in what he saw. Slowly it became clearer, and the thoughts swirling around in his head gradually formed a coherent image.

The sight of the bloody horse's head shocked him at first, but it didn't take long before he understood exactly what the whole thing was about.

SUNDAY, JULY 25

The summer heat made people slow their pace, and Knutas was forced to change shirts several times a day. His thoughts flowed like sluggish syrup, often straying far away. The chances of the investigative team finding a solution to this unusual case seemed more remote than ever.

Lina and the kids had gone out to the country, but he couldn't stand the idea of sitting there twiddling his thumbs.

It hadn't rained a single day since early June, but that didn't make him any less irritable. He was in a wretched mood, and when the phone rang he barked an angry hello.

"Hello, my name is Susanna Mellgren," said the voice on the line.

"Yes?"

"My husband, Staffan Mellgren, is in charge of the excavation in Fröjel," the woman explained.

"Oh, right," Knutas hurried to say. He hadn't immediately made the connection.

"He didn't want me to call, but I felt that I had to."

"Yes?"

"The thing is that yesterday evening we found a very odd thing outside our chicken coop."

"Is that right?"

"It was a horse's head stuck on a pole."

Knutas snapped to attention.

"Someone put it there during the evening. Staffan found it when he came home from work."

"What did it look like?"

"It was stuck on a really heavy wooden broomstick. Actually I don't know what kind of pole it was, but on the very end someone had wedged a severed horse's head. It was from a real horse."

"Where was this pole?"

"We have an old barn that is partially used as a chicken coop. It was standing outside the door, leaning against the wall—in full view."

"When did this happen?"

"Last night."

"And you didn't call until now?"

Knutas looked at his watch. It was two fifteen in the afternoon.

"I'm sorry, but Staffan didn't want to tell anyone. He said it would just upset the children for no reason. He didn't want to make a big deal about the matter. In fact, it doesn't seem to have bothered him at all. As if it wasn't important. But I happen to think that it's awfully disgusting, so I felt that I had to contact the police, regardless of what he said."

"It's good that you called. Is the horse's head still in the same place?"

"No. Staffan drove a short distance away and threw it into a ditch. He didn't want the children to see it. They don't even know that anything happened."

"Do you know where?"

"Yes, I actually went out there to have a look. I covered it with some grass and branches so no animals would destroy any evidence."

"We need to drive out there and look at it, of course. Right away."

"Okay. Staffan left this morning and said that he was going to be gone all day. He refused to tell me where he was going. I'd prefer it if he doesn't find out that I called you."

"I'm afraid that's probably impossible," said Knutas. "We're in the midst of investigating an earlier crime against a horse, as well as the case of the young woman who was murdered—the one who was a student in your husband's course. There seem to be too many points of connection for us not to link these cases together. I hope you'll understand."

"I guess so," said Susanna Mellgren, sounding resigned. "But what does Staffan have to do with all this?"

Knutas didn't answer the question.

Knutas, Erik Sohlman, and Karin Jacobsson all rode in the same car up to Lärbro.

The farm was located a mile or two outside town. It consisted of a farmhouse, a smaller wooden building that appeared to be some kind of workshop, and a barn. About two dozen hens were strutting around, pecking at the yellowed summer grass.

Susanna Mellgren opened the door at the first ring of the doorbell. A big woman with short black hair, she was dressed in jeans and a T-shirt. Knutas thought her beautiful with those dark eyes and that olive complexion. *She can't be a hundred percent Swedish,* he had time to think before she held out her hand and greeted him.

"Could you show us where you found the pole with the horse's head?" he asked.

"Sure, it's this way."

She led the way over to the barn. The hens clucked and flocked around her.

"It was right there, next to the door to the chicken coop," she said, pointing at the wall.

"You haven't seen any strangers around here lately?"

"No, and neither has Staffan. I asked the children, a bit cautiously, of course, because they actually have no idea about what happened, but they don't seem to have seen anything unusual, either. Whoever put the horse's head there must have done it sometime between eight and nine o'clock last night. Just before eight I called the kids inside—they'd been out playing—and at that time I didn't see anyone. Then Staffan came home right after nine o'clock."

"Good," said Knutas, offering her encouragement as he took notes. "The narrower the time frame, the easier it will be for us. There's one thing that I want to say right from the start. Don't tell anyone about this. It's important that not a word gets out. Especially for the sake of the children."

"Of course," said Susanna Mellgren hesitantly. "Although my mother . . ."

"That doesn't matter, as long as she keeps it to herself. So where is the horse's head?"

"It's kind of a long walk," she said.

"We'd better drive. We're going to take the head with us," said Sohlman.

"Really?" She looked doubtful, and a new anxiety appeared in her eyes.

"Of course. It has to be properly examined. When we compare samples from the head with the decapitated horse's body, it may help us to solve the case, if things go our way," Sohlman explained pedantically.

"Before we drive over there, I'd just like to have a look inside your house. Would that be all right?" asked Knutas.

"Yes, of course."

Susanna Mellgren showed them in. The house had an old-fashioned feel to it with oiled wood floors, unpainted furniture, and a mostly white decor, which created a bright and cozy impression. The wide window ledges were filled with earthenware pots and wooden and ceramic sculptures of various sizes. Clothes, balls, and toys were strewn everywhere. In the kitchen sat an elderly woman reading from a book of fairy tales to a child sitting on her lap. The woman glanced up and greeted them with a friendly nod when the three detectives appeared in the doorway.

"This is my mother," Susanna explained. "She's here to help me with the kids today."

They took two cars. Jacobsson drove with Susanna Mellgren in the first one, while Sohlman and Knutas followed in the second.

After half a mile on the paved road that took them even farther away from Lärbro, they turned onto a bumpy tractor path. Susanna stopped the car next to a field and a cluster of trees. There was a ditch next to the path. She climbed down in the ditch and started removing grass and branches.

Knutas and Sohlman immediately joined her to

help. Jacobsson chose to stand on the side of the road to watch. She had a hard time coping with the sight of dead bodies, whether animals or people. She had foolishly believed that she would eventually get over it, but instead it had gotten even more difficult over the years. The more bodies she saw, the more unbearable it became.

When the head was uncovered, they climbed out of the ditch and stood on the road to look at it.

"There's no doubt about it. Or what do you think?" said Knutas.

"It's obvious that it's a pony, and it definitely looks like it belongs to the horse's body out at Petesviken," said Sohlman.

"It's extremely well preserved," murmured Jacobsson through the handkerchief she held pressed to her mouth. "And it doesn't smell much, does it?"

"No, it's been frozen, just like the horse's head at Ambjörnsson's house."

MONDAY, JULY 26

On Sunday evening Knutas had tried numerous times to contact Mellgren, but without success. He didn't answer his cell phone, and when Knutas talked to Susanna Mellgren late that night, she still hadn't heard from her husband.

The whole thing was bewildering, to put it mildly. Mellgren had been subjected to the same terrifying experience as Gunnar Ambjörnsson. Yet according to his wife he hadn't seemed particularly upset.

Knutas hadn't bothered with breakfast at home. He was eager to get to work, so instead he got a cup of coffee and bought a sandwich from the vending machine. The only one left was cheese on a rye roll with a few shriveled bits of red pepper. It had been there all weekend, of course.

The phone rang in his office just as he was trying to get the roll out of its tight packaging. As he reached for the receiver, half of his coffee spilled on the floor. He swore, hoping that none of it had splashed onto his pants.

It was Staffan Mellgren.

"I'm sorry that I haven't gotten in touch earlier, but I've been really busy and I forgot my cell phone at home," he apologized.

"Why on earth didn't you tell us about the horse's head?"

"I panicked. I didn't know what to do."

"Do you know anyone who might wish you harm?"

"I don't think so."

"Have you been mixed up in some sort of trouble, or have you made any enemies lately?"

"No."

Mellgren was now claiming that he had panicked. That didn't fit with his wife's version of the story. There was no doubt that the man was holding something back.

"So you have no idea why that horse's head ended up on your property?"

"That's right."

"Can you tell me the real reason why you didn't call the police when you found the horse's head?"

"Good Lord, you heard what I just said," roared Mellgren. "I was so shocked that I didn't know what to do. Then I thought about the fact that one of my students was murdered, and I wondered if there might be some connection."

"What sort of connection, do you think?"

"How the hell should I know?"

"Under no circumstances can this incident with the

horse's head get out to the public. Have you told anyone about it?"

"Of course not."

"Then keep it to yourself, for God's sake. Otherwise you're going to have reporters behind every bush."

"Susanna and I have already talked about that, and the children don't know anything. The only ones who do are her parents, and they won't talk."

"Good. Now to another matter—and I want you to give me an honest answer, once and for all. Did you in fact have a relationship with Martina?"

Mellgren gave a loud sigh. "I've already told you. There was nothing going on between us."

"You've already lied to my face before, when you claimed that everything was just fine between you and your wife," said Knutas impatiently. "She's told us about your infidelities, you see. The fact that you're always going after new women. You seem to have, and pardon my bluntness, a mediocre marriage, to put it mildly. Why should I believe you now?"

Knutas never got an answer. Mellgren had already hung up the phone.

Knutas started off the meeting of the investigative team by telling everyone about the horse's head out at Mellgren's place.

"What is going on here?" growled Kihlgård agitatedly, making the bread crumbs fly. His mouth was full of Gotland rye bread, fresh out of the oven.

"Yes, things do seem to be getting worse and worse," said Knutas with a sigh. "Mellgren found the horse's head stuck on a pole outside his chicken coop on Saturday night. We didn't find out about it until yesterday afternoon when his wife called. He clearly didn't want to tell anyone about the incident."

"Why not?" asked Kihlgård.

"He told me that he panicked and didn't know what to do. At the same time, Susanna Mellgren claims that he seemed entirely unaffected by finding the head. They have completely opposite stories. Something definitely doesn't add up. But I think we should leave that part alone for the time being. The more important thing that I want to discuss is: What does it mean that the same bizarre thing has happened to Mellgren as to Gunnar Ambjörnsson?"

"It must be a similar kind of threat, just like it was with Ambjörnsson," Norrby stated dryly.

"Although Ambjörnsson hasn't received any subsequent threats," interjected Wittberg.

"That's not so strange," said Jacobsson, rolling her eyes. "He's been out of the country ever since."

"He'll be home in a week," snapped Knutas. "So the safety of these two individuals could be at risk. We need to consider giving them some protection."

"Do we have resources for that?" Jacobsson raised her eyebrows.

"Not really."

"But should we actually regard Mellgren as under some sort of threat?" Wittberg objected. "Maybe he's mixed up in this whole thing himself. Why didn't he report the incident at once? And why wasn't he more upset? I, for one, have my suspicions."

"Absolutely," Jacobsson agreed. "Mellgren must have some skeletons in his closet. Pardon the pun."

"He's had a lot of adulterous affairs. Could it be a vengeful lover?" Kihlgård had a look of conspiratorial delight on his face.

"Someone who was also involved with Ambjörnsson?" Jacobsson protested. "An amorous woman who in the heat of passion kills horses and decapitates them, and then puts the heads on poles at the homes of her former lovers? That doesn't sound terribly plausible, does it?" She gave her colleague a friendly poke in the side.

"Never underestimate the power of love," Kihlgård admonished her in a bombastic voice, shaking his finger like some sort of doomsday preacher.

"Let's stop joking around," Knutas interrupted them, sounding annoyed. "This isn't a game. We need to find out more about Mellgren. Who is he really? What sort of things does he do in his spare time? Is he politically active? What links can we find to Ambjörnsson?"

"Yes, that's worth looking into. Maybe they've run into each other in connection with various types of construction. Archaeologists are often brought in on building projects," Kihlgård suggested.

"Here on Gotland that's true with nearly every building," said Jacobsson. "The island is literally overflowing with ancient relics."

"There's something else we should think about, just as Wittberg mentioned. Why did Mellgren seem so unaffected when he discovered the horse's head? At least according to his wife," said Knutas. "Yet he told me that he was panic-stricken, and that was why he didn't contact the police immediately."

"Extremely odd." Kihlgård tugged at a lock of his hair. "The guy is obviously lying."

"He must be a real cold-blooded type," Jacobsson added. "First his wife goes through the shock of seeing a horse's head stuck on a pole near their home. Then what does her husband do? He takes off and leaves her all alone, alarmed and frightened, and with four children. Not only that—he refuses to tell her where he's gone!"

"He doesn't give a shit about her. That much is clear," said Wittberg.

"We've actually already come to that conclusion," said Knutas. "But why was he in such a hurry?"

In his hand he carried an invisible mirror in which he saw his parents. Sometimes their faces disappeared, and he couldn't manage to conjure them up again, no matter how hard he tried. He had been interrupted.

In the early evening, as he stood there painting with even strokes the rough surface of the facade and the air breathed peace and tranquility, the man had appeared from around the corner of the house.

Not that it came as any surprise. The visitor was expected. The meeting could have ended in disaster, but he had managed to restrain his anger. They had talked, and he was indignant that the intruder had succeeded in his intention of upsetting him.

When the man left, he felt shaken, and it had taken a good amount of time to recover his sense of equilibrium. That made him even stronger in his conviction, and in his mind he was able to anticipate enjoying the sweetness of retaliation.

He sat down on the mound that he'd created only a few weeks earlier—yet another holy place that offered him inner peace.

The earth hid its secrets; truth pounded beneath the surface, wanting to get out. It would soon be time. The labyrinth in which he had wandered all his life was about to come unraveled. The angles and corners, the detours and dead ends, the obscure recesses, everything was crawling out into the light, becoming clearer and simpler and filling him with hope for a much better life.

He happened to think of a poem that he'd read in school and had saved ever since. It was by the great nineteenth-century Swedish author Carl Jonas Love Almqvist. *You are not alone. If among a thousand stars only one looks at you, believe in the star's meaning, believe in the gleam in its eye . . .*

Someone was looking at him. Not just one, but many.

Just as Knutas was considering calling it a day and heading for home, someone knocked on the door. It was Agneta Larsvik. She was normally so composed, but right now there was something agitated in her expression, and she moved in an abrupt manner as she sank onto the visitor's chair in Knutas's office.

"I've just come back from the Mellgren place," she explained. "I was in Stockholm over the weekend and didn't get back until around three this afternoon. At any rate, I drove out to their farm in Lärbro, even though no one was home. I couldn't get hold of Staffan Mellgren or his wife, so I took a chance and just drove out there." She leaned forward. "This incident with the horse's head on the pole is a serious matter. Very serious. I think that Mellgren needs immediate protection."

"Why?"

"I interpret this as meaning that the perpetrator feels quite euphoric that he managed to pull off the first murder. It may be his way of announcing his arrival this time. He's sending a warning. At the same time, he's very self-confident, so confident he's going to get away with the crime that it doesn't matter if the individual receives a warning. On the contrary, that makes him all the more elated. I'm prepared to go so far as to say that the horse's head may very well represent a threat of homicide."

"But Martina didn't receive a horse's head before she was murdered."

"No, she didn't. For two reasons. Partly because he's gotten tougher. Partly because Martina lived with a lot of other people. It would have been more difficult to send her a personal warning."

"In that case, your analysis would mean that Ambjörnsson's life is also threatened."

"Of course. Most likely the only reason that nothing has happened to him yet is because he's out of the country."

"It's lucky that nothing about the horses' heads has leaked to the press. At least we're not going to offer the perpetrator that sort of satisfaction. And no one outside this building knows anything about the horse's head found on Mellgren's property."

"Good. Keep it that way. It's important that the news doesn't get out. That would just make him feel even more exhilarated."

"So you seriously think that this man is going to murder more people?"

"I'm afraid that he will. The question is: How long will it take before he does? There's a real risk that another murder is going to be committed soon. Now that he's had a taste of the experience, he's going to want to do it again."

When the workday was over, Mellgren drove home. His wife had left a message on his cell phone, saying that she was taking the children over to her parents' house in Ljugarn. She didn't want to stay at the farm after the incident with the horse's head.

He stopped off at the college to pick up some papers from his office. The green park of Almedalen, which was down by the water, was filled with sunbathers, dogs, baby buggies, and teenagers listening to music. Crowds of youths were on their way to After Beach, near Kallbadhuset, where they had brought in sand from beaches all over Gotland to create a fine-grained sand beach in the middle of town where the shore was otherwise rocky. After Beach was very popular. After listening to a band and drinking a beer, they could move on to the next pub only a stone's throw away. Mellgren almost felt like going over there himself.

Inside the college he found the place deserted and the reception area locked. He picked up the papers and was on his way back to the car when a group of teenagers walked past. They were talking and laughing, and he thought that one of the girls, a cute little blonde, gave him an especially big smile. He stopped to watch them as they went into Kallbadhuset. At the same moment he heard the live band inside start playing. That was enough to make him decide. He hurried back to his office, grabbed a towel and a bar of soap from his closet, and went down to the locker room to take a quick shower. Upstairs again, he splashed on a little aftershave and changed into clean clothes. This was not the first time that he had chosen not to go straight home.

Back out on the street he was in high spirits as he strolled over to Kallbadhuset. It was true that he was over forty, but he looked young for his age. He was tall, slim, and fit. His hair was just as abundant and thick as when he was twenty. Staffan Mellgren was looking forward to the evening.

It was with a growing feeling of uneasiness in his chest that Knutas had listened to the forensic psychologist's opinion that both Gunnar Ambjörnsson and Staffan Mellgren were in danger. Ambjörnsson was expected back on Gotland in a week. As long as he stayed in Morocco he was probably safe. Mellgren, on the other hand, needed immediate protection. Knutas had made numerous calls to the cell phones of the investigative team, but without getting any response.

According to Susanna Mellgren, who was staying with her parents in Ljugarn, her husband was working in Fröjel, as usual. He was then going to drive home. No one answered their home phone, even though the workday should have ended long ago.

"Could he be the murderer?" Jacobsson's voice sounded doubtful as they got into the car to drive out to the excavation site.

"I have a hard time believing that, but we've been surprised before," said Knutas tensely as he zigzagged between cars on the road. In July there was a lot of traffic on the coastal road between Klintehamn and Visby.

Martin Kihlgård, who was sitting in the backseat, leaned forward to offer his two colleagues a bag of onion chips. The car reeked of them. Knutas made a point of declining the offer, then rolled down the window as Jacobsson cheerfully accepted.

"I have a hard time imagining Mellgren as the murderer," muttered Kihlgård as he chewed. "It would be rather stupid to take the life of one of his own students, especially if he was having an affair with her. On top of that, it seems very unlikely that he would use his own pole to stick a horse's head on. And where the hell did he get the first horse's head from, since it wasn't from the same horse? Are there still no reports about any missing horses?"

"Not a single one," replied Knutas curtly. "And no one is saying that Mellgren is the murderer."

"I'd rather bet my money on the wife," Kihlgård went on, unperturbed. "She had both the opportunity and the motive. The guy is notoriously unfaithful, and he could very well have had an affair with Martina Flochten. We know that she was meeting someone in secret, and maybe that proved to be the last drop. Good Lord, the girl was only twenty-one, after all. Afterward, Susanna Mellgren tries staging the whole business with the horse's head in order to warn her husband, to threaten him. If she wanted to kill him, surely she would have done it at once. This is much more sophisticated. She wants him to realize that it's serious this time. If he doesn't stop his adulterous affairs, then he's going to meet the same fate."

Obviously satisfied with his explanation, Kihlgård leaned back and stuck his whole hand in the bag of chips.

"So you think that her intention is to frighten her husband out of his wits to such a degree that he won't look at another woman from now on?" Jacobsson sounded dubious.

"It wouldn't be the first time in the history of the world, at any rate. As I see it, she's the only one with an obvious motive."

"I must admit that I have a hard time seeing why anyone would want to kill Martina Flochten. A jealousy scenario could explain the matter," Knutas agreed. "But why would the wife use such a complicated method?"

"That may be a red herring," said Kihlgård. "Trying to make the whole thing seem mystical and ritualistic even though that has nothing at all to do with it."

They turned off at Fröjel Church and drove all the way down to the excavation site. They bumped along on the last part of the road. It looked disconcertingly quiet and deserted. The carts were all properly locked, and everything seemed to be closed up for the night. Several pits were covered with plastic.

"All right, then," said Kihlgård. "He's not here, at any rate."

Knutas felt his irritation rising. *We need to get hold of him,* he thought, *and quickly.*

"We'll drive over to the college. He might be there."

He had a horrible premonition that they needed to hurry.

It was seven in the evening when Staffan Mellgren left Kallbadhuset to drive home. The band had stopped playing, and the young people were on their way out to join the action in Visby's pubs. He had deliberately chosen to keep a low profile, since he recognized several students from the college. They had greeted him with a nod. That was one thing he detested about living on Gotland—the fact that he could never be anonymous anywhere.

Even though he'd had two strong beers, he got behind the wheel. He drove out of the city as people walked past on their way to the restaurants and evening entertainments. The tourist season was at its peak, Visby was pulsing with life, and it was disappointing to have to leave it all behind and drive home to little Lärbro.

His cell phone was still on the passenger seat, and he saw that he'd received quite a few messages, but he didn't feel like checking to see who they were from. It was probably Susanna, and he didn't have the energy to deal with her nervous carping right now.

The hens were clucking loudly in the yard when he arrived. Of course, they needed food, too; he'd forgotten to feed them in the morning.

In the refrigerator he found several old tomatoes that looked anything but fresh. They were good enough for the chickens. On a shelf Susanna had set a plastic ice cream container filled with eggshells, scraps of food, and stale bread.

He picked up the container and went out to the old barn that was used only as a junkyard and as a garage in the wintertime. At the far end of the barn was the chicken coop. When he opened the door, he was careful where he set his feet so as not to trample to death any of the tiny golden chicks that were peeping around his legs. What a life. He put down the ice cream container with the food scraps and filled a bowl with chicken feed.

Suddenly he heard the door to the barn slam shut. Cautiously he stood up from his squatting position and set down the feed sack. The hens kept up their clucking, making it impossible for him to hear anything. He slipped over to the doorway and peered into the barn.

He let his eyes scan the bare walls, covered with flyspecks and cobwebs. The windows were so filthy that the twilight hardly came through at all. The old stalls, which were lined up with walls separating them, hadn't been used in a long time. *The door must have slammed shut by itself,* he thought. He was just about to go back when he noticed that something was different. The old bathtub, which for years had been upside down among the other rubbish, had been moved and was now right side up.

Puzzled, he moved closer and saw to his surprise that it was filled to the brim with water, but he never managed to wonder who had been there or what the tub was going to be used for.

The college was locked, and they had to phone the security guard to come over and let them in. The place was completely deserted; not a soul around on this hot evening in July. They took the stairs up to the floor where Mellgren had his office. The door was locked. The security guard searched through his big bunch of keys to find the right one.

Mellgren's office was just as deserted as the rest of the rooms they had walked through. The faint scent of aftershave still hovered in his office.

"It's the kind Mellgren usually wears," said Jacobsson. "I recognize the fragrance."

Knutas quickly searched the desk but found nothing of interest. A wet towel was draped over the chair.

"He must have been here recently," said Knutas, "and he took a shower. Why didn't he go home to do that?"

"Because he was going out on the town, of course," said Kihlgård with a grin. "He was going to make a night of it, now that his wife is out in the country."

"Unless he had some other purpose in mind," said Knutas. He tried Mellgren's home phone number. Still no answer. He phoned Susanna Mellgren as well, but she hadn't yet heard from her husband.

"We might as well go and get something to eat," suggested Kihlgård. "I'm starving."

"Can't you ever think about anything but food?" snapped Knutas. "I'm driving out to Lärbro. Are you coming with me, or should I call Wittberg?"

By the time they arrived at the farm, dusk had set in. Lights were on in all the windows, and a car was parked in the yard. The front door of the house wasn't locked, so they went in. The house was well lit but silent. They peeked into all the rooms, and it didn't take them long to realize that no one was there.

They went back out to the yard and saw that the barn door stood open. The only sound was the sporadic clucking of the chickens.

It looked as if the barn hadn't been used in a long time. At the far end a small door was ajar. Light was coming from inside. The three detectives exchanged glances. Surreptitiously they crept closer to the door. The rank smell of urine and ammonia came from what had to be the chicken coop. When they stepped across the threshold, they came face-to-face with a sight that was both unexpected and ghastly.

From a hook in the ceiling above the hens asleep on their perches hung Staffan Mellgren. He was naked, and someone had made a long cut in his abdomen to make the blood run out, but only a small pool had collected on the floor below. Knutas gasped for breath. In his mind he saw a sudden flash of a similar scene. Martina hanging amid the summer greenery. Youth and evil, a sudden death. Here it was red blood against white feathers.

It all had to do with contrasts.

TUESDAY, JULY 27

Everyone was in attendance at the police meeting the following morning. The murmuring faded away as Knutas, looking solemn, sat down at the head of the table. He started by pouring himself a cup of coffee. To his satisfaction he saw that the coffee was nice and black. He gave Kihlgård a grateful look. He was the only one who brewed the coffee as strong as Knutas liked it. Right now he certainly needed it. He hadn't slept much last night.

"As you all know, we have another murder on our hands," Knutas began. "Last night, when Karin and Martin and I went out to Mellgren's place to look for him, we found him dead in the chicken coop. There's no question that it's a homicide, and it appears to be the same MO used to kill Martina Flochten. The farm has been cordoned off, and the body will remain there until the ME arrives later today. Fortunately, the rest of the family wasn't home. They're visiting Susanna Mellgren's parents in Ljugarn, and that's where they'll stay for the time being. The Mellgrens have four children, as you know." He fell silent and turned to Sohlman.

"Without having any specific technical evidence, since none of the tests are ready yet, I still say that all indications are that it's the same perpetrator who murdered Martina," said Sohlman. "The similarities speak very clearly. The marks on the body indicate that Mellgren, just like Martina, was killed before he was hanged with the noose, and the cut in the abdomen was done last of all. Then the blood was presumably collected, since very little was found on the floor. The MO has not been made public, so it can't be a copycat crime. Mellgren was also naked when he was found, and his clothes are missing."

"How was he killed? Was he also drowned?" asked Wittberg.

"It appears so. There was an old bathtub filled with water inside the barn. The water had splashed over the sides, and we found hair and blood in it. Most likely he drowned there when the perpetrator pushed his head underwater."

"That means that the killer must be very strong," said Jacobsson. "Mellgren was not a small man."

"Unless he was drugged first. We don't know that. Or knocked unconscious, but he has no injuries to indicate as much."

"How long had he been dead when his body was found?" asked Smittenberg.

"An hour at most. Our colleagues must have been right on the killer's heels."

"What sort of evidence did you find?"

"Not much. The most interesting traces are footprints that he left after walking around in the blood. The barn has a bare cement floor, so the prints are quite clear. His shoe size is interesting, too. He was wearing wooden clogs, about a size eight."

No one spoke for several seconds.

"So we might also be talking about a woman?" Jacobsson gave Sohlman a look of surprise.

"Yes. We can't rule it out, at any rate. It's rather unusual for a man to wear such a small shoe, don't you think? I'm only five foot nine, but I wear a size nine shoe."

"I know a guy who wears a size seven," said Wittberg.

"What about the wife?" said Kihlgård. "What do you make of Susanna Mellgren? She's quite a big woman, and muscular. She seems very fit. Maybe she would be capable of doing it."

"But why go to so much trouble?" countered Jacobsson. "Why chop off a horse's head and drain out the blood if really all she wanted to do was kill her husband and his lover?"

"It could be a very sophisticated way of misleading us," suggested Wittberg.

"Maybe she wanted to shift suspicion onto someone who might make use of similar methods," suggested Kihlgård.

"What do we actually know about the Mellgren family? To be honest, I don't think we've looked into their background very thoroughly," said Jacobsson. "Especially not the wife's."

"No, we didn't consider her especially interesting, and I have a hard time believing that she would be capable of these crimes," said Knutas. "If she was the one who put the horse's head there, why would she call in the police when her husband refused to do so?"

Jacobsson shrugged her shoulders. "To divert suspicion from herself, of course."

Knutas directed his next question to Agneta Larsvik. "What do you think about all this?"

"From what I've heard, there's much to indicate that we're dealing with the same perpetrator, but I'd like to see the victim and the crime scene before I draw any conclusions. The fact that he's naked and his clothes are missing also points in that direction. Presumably the perpetrator keeps the clothes to hold on to the feeling that he gets from killing. A sort of fetish. Just like the blood. But there's one other question that's important to focus on here."

They all gave their full attention to the forensic psychologist.

"I wonder why Staffan Mellgren didn't call the police himself about the horse's head. There must be some reason for this. Could it be that he knew or at least suspected who had put the head there? Maybe he thought that he could resolve the situation himself by talking to the person in question."

"And just who might that be?" Kihlgård tossed out the question without getting any answer.

Knutas broke the silence.

"Susanna Mellgren has been summoned for questioning. I'm going to meet with her at ten o'clock. I hope that then we'll be able to clear up a thing or two. Of course her alibi for the night of the murder has to be checked also—as well as for the time of Martina Flochten's death."

"This means that we have to take a fresh look at the incident of the horse's head at Gunnar Ambjörnsson's place," said Kihlgård. "His life could very well be in danger, too. Should we contact him?"

"At the very least he's going to need protection the minute he gets back home," said Knutas grimly. "We need to go out and meet him at the airport."

He was interrupted by the ringing of his cell phone. When he finished the conversation he gave his colleagues a solemn look.

"Martina's cell phone was found under the porch at the Warfsholm hotel. She must have dropped it on the night of the murder. Her calls have been checked. The last one was a message that was received by her voice mail on the night of the murder at 11:35 P.M. Guess who called her."

Everyone waited tensely without saying a word.

"It was Staffan Mellgren."

The murder of Staffan Mellgren was the lead story on the television newscasts that morning. The police had sent out a press release about the homicide around midnight, and the night editor at Swedish TV's digital round-the-clock station SVT 24 instantly sent a remote van to catch the next ferry, which left at 3:00 A.M. A little less than three hours later, just before six in the morning, the van rolled onto the Visby dock. In situations like this, it was worth gold to have a news service operating twenty-four hours a day.

The SVT 24 editor had gotten Johan out of bed in the middle of the night. By the time he and Pia met the Stockholm team at the editorial office, Johan had already had the murder confirmed and had been promised an interview with Knutas outside police headquarters. One of the team members who had arrived by van was Robert Wiklander, with whom Johan had worked on Gotland before. Robert worked for the *Aktuellt* and *Rapport* broadcasts, and now they were going to collaborate. A cameraman that Johan vaguely knew had come along, too, as well as an editor who installed himself in the office. He would handle things from there during the morning, which they all realized was going to be anything but calm.

They divided up the work assignments. Pia drove up to the Mellgren farm to take pictures while Johan and Robert took turns reporting for the live newscast, using the cameraman who had come from Stockholm. Whoever was not reporting at the moment spent his time tracking down interview subjects. They got the county police commissioner, the president of the college, and the head of the tourist bureau to come to police headquarters to be interviewed. The entire archaeological community on Gotland was in a state of shock. The excavations at Fröjel were halted, and no one thought they would start up again that summer. The students in the course were forbidden to leave the island for the near future. The excavations at Eksta, where archaeologists were in the process of digging up a gravesite from the Bronze Age, were also stopped. Anyone who had even the slightest connection with archaeology on Gotland was affected by what had now become a double homicide.

The head of the tourist bureau was concerned that this second murder would frighten away the tourists. The media speculated that a serial killer was on the loose on the island—someone who would continue to kill until he was caught. Anders Knutas had called in extra assistance from the NCP in

Stockholm. Thirty or so people were now working on the investigation.

By nine thirty all the morning broadcasts were done, and the editors in Stockholm phoned to praise the reports. In the next breath, they issued new demands. They wanted a piece for the noon show, for all the afternoon programs, and a longer story for the evening newscasts, on both *Aktuellt* and *Rapport*, and the segments should preferably be as different as possible.

Max Grenfors, now back from vacation, wanted to make the Regional News broadcast a priority, of course. That was always a dilemma. Each editor put his own program first, and with so many different newscasts and editors, there was a flood of phone calls. For a reporter, it was easy to feel torn. They agreed that Robert and the Stockholm cameraman would handle the national newscasts while Johan and Pia would concentrate on Regional News. As they gathered material and did interviews over the course of the day, they could always share information with each other. The editor from Stockholm would collate all the material as it came in.

In the afternoon Johan received an unexpected phone call. It was from his friend Niklas Appelqvist, who was studying archaeology at the college.

"Did you know that rumors have been circulating that Martina Flochten was Staffan Mellgren's lover?" Niklas asked.

"Is it true?" Johan retorted.

"So many different people are talking about it, there must be some truth to it."

"Do you know anyone who could confirm it?"

"Maybe. I'll check around. Mellgren was apparently a real Casanova. I heard that he slept with a lot of girls at the college."

"Is that right? But I can't put pure speculation in my report. I need two independent sources who can confirm this for me. Otherwise it's a no-go."

"I'll see what I can do. I'll get back to you."

Susanna Mellgren looked exhausted when she came into Knutas's office that afternoon. She sat down, clasped her hands demurely in her lap, and lowered her gaze, as if she were about to say a prayer.

"I'm sorry for your loss," Knutas began.

She nodded faintly.

"When did you last see your husband?"

"Sunday evening, when I decided to drive over to stay with my parents."

"Why did you do that?"

"I thought the whole business with the horse's head was horrible. I didn't want to put myself or my children in danger."

"Why did you think it would be dangerous to stay in your house?"

"It felt as if someone were threatening us. I've been reading about the whole thing, and I saw the report on TV, too—I mean, that story about the decapitated horse, and then . . ."

"Why would anyone want to threaten you?"

"I have no idea," she replied, shaking her head.

"And your husband?"

"I don't know why anyone would want to harm him, either," she said, looking Knutas in the eye. "He didn't have any enemies, as far as I know."

"How did he seem that evening? What was the mood like between the two of you?"

"As I've told you earlier, he seemed cold and indifferent. He said it wasn't anything to worry about, that whole incident with the horse's head."

"Did you ask him why it didn't bother him?"

"I tried, but he just got annoyed. He said that we shouldn't take it seriously, that we should just forget about it and go on as usual. I'm convinced that he wasn't telling me the truth. Finally I got mad because I was afraid for the children, if nothing else. But he brushed the whole thing off and claimed that it only had to do with him. So that's when he gave himself away: He really did know what it was all about."

"Do you think he knew who was threatening him?"

"I think he knew who put the horse's head there, but he didn't seem to consider it a threat. At any rate, it ended with me packing up our things and taking the children over to stay with my parents. And just look what happened—now he's dead, and the last thing we did was fight. If I hadn't gone away, maybe he'd still be alive."

She burst into tears. Knutas got up and patted her awkwardly on the shoulder. He got some paper napkins and a glass of water and waited for a while so that Susanna Mellgren would have a chance to calm down.

"What time did you and the children leave for your parents' house on Sunday?" he continued cautiously.

"It was after you came out to see us. Staffan came home around seven, and by then we were ready to go. We probably left around eight," she told him, sniffling loudly.

"What did you do when you got there?"

"We unpacked in the guesthouse that they have on their property. Then we watched a little TV and went to bed."

"What about the next day?"

"We went to the beach and spent the whole day there. Me, my mother, and the kids. The weather was so nice."

"And in the evening?"

"We had a barbecue and sat outside, drinking a little wine. The kids and my parents watched a movie after dinner. They didn't want to come with me to the pub. Smaklösa was playing. They're one of my favorite bands. I thought it would be a good distraction after everything that had happened."

"So you went alone?"

"Yes."

"Can anyone vouch for the fact that you were there?"

"I don't know. Maybe the bartender. I've seen him before."

"Do you know his name?"

Susanna Mellgren thought for a few seconds.

"His name is Stefan."

"And his last name?"

She shook her head.

"How long did you stay there?"

"I listened to the band, and they played for at least two hours. Everyone was in a great mood, and people started requesting songs. Then I sat outside for a while and had a glass of wine. It was such a hot evening, and I felt the need to be alone. I probably stayed for about three hours."

"When did you get back?"

"Hm . . . when was it? Maybe ten or eleven."

"And you went home alone?"

"Yes."

"This may seem like a strange question, but what size shoe do you wear?"

Susanna looked at Knutas in surprise.

"Size eight."

WEDNESDAY, JULY 28

When Knutas woke up the next morning, he was so anxious to see what the press had found out about the murder of Staffan Mellgren that he could hardly wait to get to the office. He said a silent prayer that the media hadn't gotten wind of the ritualistic elements this time, either. His cell phone had started ringing right after the story was reported on the evening broadcast of Regional News, when Johan Berg referred to several independent sources who had confirmed that the two murder victims had been having an affair. Out of pure self-preservation Knutas had turned off his cell after the third call. The police spokesman, Lars Norrby, was the only one who had to be available to the media. Knutas had had a long conversation with him last night, and they had agreed on what would be appropriate to reveal. Among other things, the police would not mention anything about a possible relationship between Martina Flochten and Staffan Mellgren. At 6:00 A.M. he listened to the financial news, which fortunately didn't mention anything about a ritual murder or a relationship between Martina and Staffan.

Knutas sat down at his computer and looked up the online editions of the newspapers. When the front page of the evening papers appeared on his screen, he sighed.

At the top of both papers were two big photographs—one of Martina Flochten and one of Staffan Mellgren. On one of the papers a red heart had been drawn around the photos.

This can't be true, thought Knutas, as he clicked to move on. The big headlines worried him: KILLED FOR THEIR LOVE and POLICE SUSPECT JEALOUSY DRAMA. The articles that followed were full of endless speculations. Most of them were based on the Regional News report from the night before. It was disastrous for the investigation, and he silently wondered who had helped Johan Berg to track down this lead. Ignoring the fact that it was only six thirty in the morning, he punched in the reporter's phone number.

"What do you think you're doing?" he asked tersely when he heard Johan's sleepy voice on the other end of the line.

"Who is this?" asked Johan defiantly.

"This is Detective Superintendent Anders Knutas, as if you didn't know. How could you broadcast sensitive information like that in your report last night without talking to me first? Don't you realize that you're sabotaging the whole investigation?"

"I can't very well be responsible for your investigation.

I got the information confirmed, and it's of such great interest that of course we wanted to make it public. Two murders have occurred within a matter of a few weeks, and then it turns out that the victims were having a secret affair. People are terrified because the murderer is still on the loose. So of course the story was too important—it had to be told."

Johan held back his anger as he spoke.

"But don't you understand that it's going to have consequences for our work? How are we going to catch the perpetrator if confidential information comes out in the press every fifteen minutes? This isn't a game—we're talking about a double homicide, and in the worst-case scenario a serial killer who's on the loose!"

Knutas's voice was getting louder on the phone.

"Look, I'm just doing my job," said Johan calmly. "I can't sit on important information out of consideration for your investigative work. You take care of your business, I'll take care of mine. Unfortunately, I don't have time to talk to you any more about this right now."

To Knutas's great annoyance, Johan hung up.

He was shaking all over after the conversation, the phone still in his hand, when Lina came downstairs.

"Who are you talking to on the phone this early?" she asked, ruffling his hair.

"That damned journalist," said Knutas as he slammed down the receiver. He went to get his jacket, even though it was much too warm for it outside.

Lina came out into the hall as he was about to leave.

"Don't you want any breakfast?"

"I'll get some at work," he said, sounding annoyed. "Bye."

He left without giving her a hug. It was a lovely summer morning, but the only thing he noticed was the sun blazing down on his back. He realized that he was going to be sweaty again before he even got to the office, and he slowed his step. He now felt ashamed about his conversation with Johan. He should have behaved in a more professional manner; it was embarrassing. He didn't even recognize himself. Maybe it was being frustrated because they hadn't made any progress that had upset his composure. No, the fact was that he hadn't been himself for the past six months. Last winter's case had taken its toll, and he was having a hard time letting go of what had happened to him back then. His marriage was also suffering negative effects, even though things were basically good between him and Lina. He loved her, and she hadn't given him any reason to doubt her feelings. Knutas was dissatisfied with himself. It felt as if he'd taken a step back in his recovery, and that bothered him. He wasn't seeing his therapist during the summer, but he was thinking of calling her anyway. If she wasn't away on vacation, maybe he could go and see her.

That was at least one concrete step forward he had made. He was no longer afraid to ask for help.

* * *

When he arrived at police headquarters the corridors were already humming with activity. They had received additional reinforcements from Stockholm, and the group was clearly wide awake that morning.

Even Kihlgård was present. He was standing next to the coffee machine having a lively conversation with one of the female officers from Stockholm. He stopped talking when Knutas came walking past in the hallway.

"Good morning to you, Knutie."

Knutas returned the greeting. He had no desire whatsoever to engage in any social chitchat, and he was rescued by the appearance of Karin Jacobsson.

"Hi," he said to her. "I need to talk to you."

He took a firm grip on her arm. Jacobsson looked surprised but let herself be hustled along to Knutas's office.

"What's up?" she asked. "Has something happened?"

"No, nothing. Except that we've got a hell of a problem. Do you know about the information leaking out to the media? About the love affair between Martina Flochten and Staffan Mellgren?"

"It was really only a matter of time before it got out." She shrugged her shoulders.

"How can you take it so lightly?" Knutas had a hard time hiding his irritation.

"But my dear Anders." Karin gave him a sympathetic

look. "What does it matter, *really*? Both of them are dead, and we can't do anything about that. Maybe the solution is a simple matter, and Susanna Mellgren is the murderer. Her alibi for the night of the murder is pretty weak. She was gone for more than four hours, according to her parents, and the only one who can vouch for her being at the pub is that bartender, Stefan Eriksson. Who knows whether he's telling the truth? Maybe they're in it together, or maybe he just wants to protect her. And her shoe size matches the prints at the scene of the murder. We have her under surveillance. Maybe she'll make a mistake all of a sudden, and then the case will be solved."

"What about the horses? How do you explain them?"

"She may have done that to distract our attention, as we said earlier. I've found out a few more things about Susanna Mellgren, you see."

"Okay, let's hear it," said Knutas, who had calmed down.

"When she was younger she worked as a riding instructor. For five summers in a row she worked at the Dalhem Stables during their riding camps, and also with classes that met during the fall. It's been just over ten years since she stopped doing that. Their oldest son is ten, so that fits. Presumably she stopped when she got pregnant."

"What does that prove?" Knutas gave Jacobsson an inquisitive look.

"Nothing. Except that she's used to being around horses, and that's an advantage if you're going to kill one."

"That's not enough."

"Of course not, but there's something else."

"What?"

"Susanna Mellgren has also worked part-time at the ICA supermarket off and on. Guess in which department."

Knutas didn't say a word.

"She worked as a butcher."

"I see. Interesting. I wonder if that's good enough to arrest her."

Jacobsson glanced at her watch. "The meeting starts in five minutes, so we'll soon find out. If I know Birger, he's already here."

THURSDAY, JULY 29

Birger Smittenberg didn't think there was sufficient reason to arrest Susanna Mellgren. Especially not after it became clear from interviewing guests at the pub in Ljugarn that she had been seen there during the entire time when her husband was being murdered. So she had an alibi. Knutas had never really believed that she would turn out to be the murderer. As a woman she didn't have the physical strength to hoist up the victims as had been done in both cases. It was impossible for her to be the perpetrator—unless she hadn't committed the murders alone.

This meant that the investigation was back to square one. The decision was expected, but Knutas still felt disappointed. It would have been too good to be true if the case could have been solved so easily. Especially since then he could have taken his longed-for summer vacation. Now nothing was going to come of it. The hot summer was disappearing outside the window as he sat in his dusty office and racked his brain.

Maybe it was time to turn everything upside down, to

change perspective and point of view, to look at things from a different angle.

The fact that Martina Flochten and Staffan Mellgren were having an affair was undeniable. Susanna Mellgren had previously acknowledged that she realized her husband was once again being unfaithful. Over the years, she had learned all too well to see the signs. On the other hand, she still claimed that she didn't know who the woman was, and Knutas believed her. When it came to the footprints in the chicken house, she explained them by saying that she kept an old pair of wooden clogs out in the barn, but now they were gone. Presumably the perpetrator had put them on to mislead the police.

If it wasn't Mellgren's infidelities that had motivated the murders, then what had? And why the strange way in which they were carried out?

The question was whether the killing was now over. One factor indicated that the perpetrator planned yet another murder, and that was the horse's head at Gunnar Ambjörnsson's house. Ambjörnsson was still out of the country, but he was expected home on Sunday. Knutas decided to call him up to warn him. He found the number and was surprised to see how many digits there were. Ambjörnsson had said that it might be hard to reach him. He had left his cell number. He couldn't provide the name of a hotel because he would be traveling the whole time. Knutas didn't get through;

he got only a strange tone when he punched in the number. After several more attempts he gave up. He'd try again later.

That evening he and Lina made love for the first time in ages. Even though their love life usually blossomed during the summer, his sex drive had been virtually nonexistent lately. He'd been unusually tired, and when Lina asked him what was wrong, he had blamed the investigation for wearing him out. Deep inside, though, he was suffering from a feeling of anxiety that he couldn't get rid of. He had tried to contact his therapist without success, so he would have to wait until his appointment in August. From day to day he functioned more or less normally, but he didn't feel his usual sense of joy. He was thinking and moving like a sleepwalker. It was like being in a dream when you're running but your legs feel heavy and sluggish and you never get anywhere. He had the same feeling in his daily life. He had no energy for anything except what was absolutely necessary. Lina had also pointed out that he had gotten quieter and duller, as she put it. She sometimes asked him why he couldn't be happier. Knutas had no good answer to the question.

FRIDAY, JULY 30

It was Friday night, and Johan and Pia were finished with their evening report. Johan was eager to leave the editorial office. He was going over to Emma's house, and she had asked whether he'd like to stay overnight. As if she even had to ask.

She was going to cook dinner for him since he wouldn't be able to get away until around seven. Sara and Filip were staying with their father, and Johan thought that was just as well. They didn't need to do everything at once.

In the car on his way to Roma, he imagined how it would be to live in that house and drive home like this after work every day.

Home to Emma and the children. He was surprised at how wonderful he thought that would feel. To be part of a family. For someone like him who had lived all these years alone, it was a new feeling. Of course, he'd had some long-term relationships when he had practically lived with a girlfriend for certain periods of time, but it was never the real thing. He'd never shared a home with anyone else. And with the baby it was an even bigger deal. Something entirely different.

The idea of sharing his daily life with Emma in a real way appealed to him more than he ever could have imagined. He heard the clinking sound as the wine bottles in their state liquor store bags rolled back and forth. His stomach was growling. His mouth watered as he thought about the food that would be waiting for him on the table when he arrived. He had been longing so much to spend more time with Emma. To sleep with her and wake up together.

He automatically pressed harder on the gas pedal. Hopefully Elin would be awake so that he could hold her for a while before she went to sleep for the night.

Full of anticipation, he rang the doorbell, hiding behind his back the flowers he had bought.

When the door opened, he felt as if he'd been punched in the face. Emma was not the one standing there; it was her ex-husband. In his arms he held a howling and coughing Filip, whose face was purple with exertion.

"Hi. Come in."

"Hi."

Johan stepped into the hallway, feeling like an idiot.

"Congratulations, by the way. She's beautiful." Olle tipped his head toward the back of the house.

For a moment Johan wasn't sure whether he meant Emma or Elin. "Thanks."

Emma appeared in the doorway. She gave Johan a quick hug and handed the baby to him. He still felt as if he were standing there with his mouth open, a little like a fish gasping for air. He didn't understand a thing.

"Things are kind of a mess. Filip has a terrible attack of the croup, and we have to take him to the ER. I can't take Elin along. One of us has to drive and the other has to hold Filip when he has a coughing fit. You'll have to take care of Elin and Sara. But I've used the breast pump, so there's milk that you can heat up in the microwave. Sara hasn't had any dinner, either. I'll call you from the ER. Bye."

Before Johan had time to react, Emma, Olle, and Filip had disappeared down the gravel path. He stood there at a loss, staring after them as the car roared off.

Consequently, the night turned out a lot different than he had expected. Instead of enjoying a dinner with a bottle of good wine and having a romantic evening with Emma, he was left alone with the children for the first time. *There's no problem with Elin, but what the hell am I going to talk about with an eight-year-old?* he thought a bit desperately as his stomach churned with hunger. He put Elin in the baby buggy, which stood in the hallway, and she promptly started to howl.

"Just for a little while, sweetie," he assured her as he felt the first signs of a headache. In the fridge he found a plastic bag with something he guessed was marinated chicken breasts, but he had no idea what to do with them. There wasn't much else. The same thing with the freezer. What were they going to eat? They had to have food. He took out a little plastic package containing breast milk and put it in the microwave to thaw it out. He called Sara but got no response, so he picked up Elin and started walking through the house to look for her. Johan had met Sara and Filip several times for brief periods, but Emma had always been present. Right now he felt awkward and unprepared, and the fact that Elin was bawling nonstop didn't make the situation or his headache any better. To top it all off, the puppy kept leaping around his feet. Johan was terrified that he might trip over the dog and drop Elin on the floor. At the moment his brain had stopped functioning. He couldn't for the life of him remember the name of the dog.

Finally he found Sara under the table in the living room.

She didn't notice that he had found her, and for several seconds he didn't know what to do. Then he leaned down so that he was almost lying under the table with Elin in his arms. The dog was so delighted that he could hardly restrain his joy. He eagerly licked Johan and Elin all over. Elin started howling again.

"Hi," Johan said to Sara, who made a big show of covering her ears.

What a great start. After a long workday, he didn't have even a drop of energy to deal with a screaming baby, a hysterical puppy, and a recalcitrant eight-year-old—and all on an empty stomach. He was the type of person who couldn't wait too long to eat. If he did, his blood sugar would drop drastically, and he would be in a terrible mood.

But he now realized that he would have to put himself and his own needs last. He tried asking Sara whether there was a pizzeria in Roma. She just kept her hands pressed over her ears. Then he put the screaming Elin on Sara's lap and let go. Instinctively she took down her hands to hold the baby.

"Hi there. I'm hungry," said Johan. "I was thinking of ordering a pizza. Would you like some?"

She didn't answer.

"You're so good at holding Elin," he said. "Do you like having a little sister?"

She gave him a suspicious look but didn't say a word.

Johan started to stand up.

"Well, I'm going to call and order one, at any rate. I want one of those luscious calzones with a big Coke. What do you like? Capricciosa, with ham and mushrooms?"

"No," replied Sara. "Hawaii, the one with pineapple."

"So that's what I'll order for you. Could you hold Elin while I make the call?"

"Okay."

Sara was looking a little happier.

"Then we can take the baby buggy and go get the pizzas," said Johan. "Do you think you could push the buggy?"

"Sure, I can do that."

"Good. Then we'll take the dog along so he can have his walk."

"Her walk. It's a girl dog. Her name is Ester."

"What a cute name," lied Johan. "I can take Elin now. I'll just change her diapers and give her a little milk before we go. Could you set the table in the meantime? I don't know where you keep your plates and things like that. I'm just here as a visitor. Should we watch TV while we eat?"

"Okay." Sara's face lit up. "Mamma never lets us do that," she said. "Pappa doesn't, either."

"Well, I think we can make an exception today," said Johan. "Now that it's just you and me and Elin."

"And Ester."

"Right. And Ester. Has she had her dinner yet?"

"Yes, Mamma fed her before she left."

"That's good. At least one of us has a full stomach."

Except for a faint murmuring from the TV, the house was quiet when Emma came through the door two hours later. At first she was alarmed, but the feeling passed when she peeked into the living room. Johan was sitting on the wide sectional sofa, leaning back and snoring with his mouth open. In his arms sprawled Sara and Ester, sound asleep. Elin was asleep in the crib, which Johan had rolled into place right next to him.

SATURDAY, JULY 31

Knutas had promised to go out to the country on Saturday, but by lunchtime he could already tell that he didn't have the peace of mind to drive off and just do nothing. So far the lead with the hotel project hadn't panned out. Both Jacobsson and Wittberg were going to spend the weekend doing some more digging; they had volunteered to work. Knutas realized that he needed to do the same. He called Lina to explain. Her parents were visiting from Denmark, so they still had a full house. She assured him that they would manage fine without him.

He put on another pot of coffee and petted the cat while he waited for the coffee to finish brewing. He eyed the yellowing lawn with displeasure, thinking that he needed to water it that evening. In terms of the Martina Flochten case, it felt as if they still hadn't made much progress. He was going to talk to Gunnar Ambjörnsson as soon as he arrived home from his trip on the following day. Knutas decided to put aside any consideration of possible connections and just concentrate on Staffan Mellgren. If his wife wasn't the killer, then maybe his relationship with Martina didn't have anything to do with the murders. The police might have gotten too fixated on that particular lead. He decided to completely ignore Mellgren's love affairs as he reconsidered the case.

What else was there in Mellgren's life that might make someone want to kill him? He needed to find out more about the man. He tried calling Mellgren's wife at various phone numbers but didn't manage to get hold of her. She probably wanted to be left in peace after all the upheaval. He would try to phone her again later. Instead he tried calling the college, but no one was there to answer on a Saturday. Knutas leafed through his notes about the excavation leader and found the phone number for Aron Bjarke. Maybe he knew something more. He'd been well aware of Mellgren's love life, after all, and he seemed quite candid and talkative.

It turned out that Bjarke was at home. He lived downtown on Skogränd, inside the city walls, and they agreed to meet there.

"I'll put on some coffee. We can sit outside in the garden," said Bjarke, as if he were planning a social event.

Knutas decided to walk. A fresh breeze was blowing, so it wasn't unbearably hot. He left his jacket at home. He walked through the South Gate and continued along Adelsgatan. It was only a few minutes past ten, and most of the shops had just opened. For the time being the town was deserted. He crossed Stora Torget, where the stall owners were setting out their wares, getting ready for the day's transactions. The contrast with the nearby ruins of St. Karin's Church from the thirteenth century was quite striking.

Aron Bjarke's house was small. Shims had been installed to make the door align properly. The windows were so low that it was only a few inches from the windowsill to the street, where roses had been planted outside the house. The archaeology teacher was apparently a gardener.

Bjarke opened the door after the first knock; there was no doorbell. Knutas had to stoop as he stepped inside in order not to bump his head. The ceiling was low and the interior quite drab.

On his way out to the garden in back of the house, Knutas cast an inquisitive glance at the kitchen. It was bright and old-fashioned, with white wooden cabinets, a small drop-leaf table, and blue-and-white-checked curtains. Various knickknacks were lined up on the windowsill. The living room had the same low ceiling, with rustic beams. All the pieces of furniture were antiques.

"What a nice place," commented Knutas. "Are you interested in antiques?"

"Not especially, as a matter of fact. I inherited most of them."

They sat down in the small garden. A coffee tray was

already on the table, and Bjarke poured without asking Knutas whether he'd like to have any. He had put some little chocolate macaroons on a plate, to serve with the coffee.

"I'm actually here to talk about Staffan Mellgren," Knutas began.

"Is that right? It's certainly terrible, what happened, completely incomprehensible. It's frightening that a student and then a teacher have been murdered. It makes you wonder if you're going to be next. Everyone is probably thinking the same thing. There's a great sense of uneasiness among the teachers and the students at the college."

"I can understand that," said Knutas curtly.

All week long, frightened and angry people had been calling the police—college students' parents who felt their children's lives were in danger, the Business Association, which was worried that the tourists would be scared off, and what seemed like everyone affiliated with the college, all on the verge of collapse when they called to demand that the police find the murderer immediately. Of course it was understandable, but the police had better things to do than function as a crisis call center. He sighed at the thought and met Bjarke's eye.

"How well did you know him?"

"Quite well, you might say. We worked together for years. For the past five years at the college, and before that at Hemse Folk High School, which was previously in charge of the archaeological excavations."

"Did you also meet socially?"

"No. He had his family, after all. Four children and everything. We lived very different lives."

Bjarke smiled and stuffed a macaroon in his mouth.

Knutas studied the middle-aged man sitting on the other side of the table. He was casually dressed in shorts and a polo shirt. Friendly, bordering on ingratiating. Knutas had a feeling that Bjarke, in spite of his amiable and open demeanor, was very lonely. He found himself wondering about the man sitting across from him, even though it was Staffan Mellgren he wanted to ask about.

"Good coffee," he said to break the silence that had settled in. "You told us before about Mellgren's love life, and you seemed very well informed. Was it common knowledge that he was romantically involved with his students?"

"Unfortunately, I'd have to say that there were quite a few people who knew about it, at least among the students that attended Mellgren's classes. These are college students, of course, so we're talking about adults. I know that the head of the college thought it was inappropriate, but there wasn't much she could do. It was also a sensitive issue. Mellgren was very talented and respected, both as a teacher and an archaeologist."

"Didn't anyone ever complain?"

"I think people chose to turn a blind eye. He was

married, and he and Susanna kept having one child after another. I don't think his colleagues really knew how to handle the whole situation."

"How about you?"

"Staffan and I knew each other professionally, but we didn't discuss our personal lives. I never told him what I thought about his behavior. Maybe that was stupid, now that we're sitting here with the facts in hand."

"What do you mean?"

"I think we can assume that his murder has to do with his infidelities. At least that's what my colleagues are saying at the college."

"Do you know of anyone he used to socialize with when he wasn't working?"

"Not really. I don't think he spent much time with any of his work colleagues. Maybe he realized that people were aware of what he was doing and he felt ashamed. I have no idea whether he and Susanna had other friends."

Knutas left Bjarke's home without feeling any wiser.

SUNDAY, AUGUST 1

The call came just as Knutas was nodding off on a deck chair out in the garden. He had spent the whole morning at the office without making any headway. By lunchtime he gave up and went home. He made himself an omelet and then went to sit outdoors, where he dozed off. He had only managed to sleep for five minutes before the phone rang. Startled awake, he picked up the phone.

"Hi, it's Jonsson out here at the airport."

"Yes?"

"We're out here, Ek and I, to meet Gunnar Ambjörnsson. His girlfriend is here too."

"Yes?"

Knutas could hear how impatient he sounded.

"He's not here."

"What?"

"He wasn't on the plane from Stockholm like he was supposed to be."

"Are you sure that you didn't just miss him?"

"All three of us have been standing here the whole time. He couldn't possibly have slipped past us."

"What about the plane from Marrakech? Was he on board?"

"We don't know. We haven't checked yet."

"See that you do. Right away. Call me back as soon as you find out."

Knutas got up and went to the bathroom to splash cold water on his face. Where the hell was Ambjörnsson? Had he decided to stay in Marrakech?

When he came out the phone was ringing. Jonsson had been amazingly fast.

"He was on the plane from Marrakech. He checked in and went to the gate and showed his boarding pass, so we can be absolutely certain that he was on board. He must have disappeared somewhere between the international and domestic terminals at Arlanda airport in Stockholm. He never checked in for the Visby flight."

"Are you sure?"

"Yes, yes, I'm sure. I checked with the airport staff."

"How could he just disappear like that?"

"I suppose he changed his plans. Things like that happen."

Knutas leaned back in his chair to think. Had Gunnar Ambjörnsson suddenly decided to stay in Stockholm?

That was actually quite possible. Maybe he'd met someone on the trip who made him want to stay in the capital. Although, considering everything that had happened, it was disturbing that the man had disappeared.

Knutas punched in the number for the Stockholm police.

MONDAY, AUGUST 2

The weekend had turned out far better than expected, and Johan was feeling happier than he had for a long time when he arrived at the office on Monday morning. He and Emma hadn't done anything special. They had taken long walks, cooked good food, and relaxed in front of the TV. Just like a normal family. What he had enjoyed most was being able to spend time with Elin, both day and night. Waking up with her in the morning, feeding her, dressing and undressing her, changing her diapers. He realized how much he missed taking care of his daughter. Even though he had enjoyed the weekend, it also meant that he was going to make new demands. He was no longer going to agree to be shut out. If Emma didn't want him to move into her house, she would have to accept that he occasionally took Elin home with him.

One reason he felt so good after the weekend was that the first evening with Sara had gone rather well. He felt renewed hope that he might be able to function as a stepfather. He was looking forward to seeing both Sara and Filip again.

As usual, he started the day by talking to Grenfors in Stockholm. For a change the editor thought that Johan could take things easy if nothing special was going on.

Johan started by cleaning up his cluttered desk.

Pia drove off to get the car washed and serviced. In the meantime he went through all the piles of papers, throwing out most of them and putting the important ones in file folders. Dust flew everywhere. The place needed a good cleaning.

His attention was caught by a newspaper clipping from *Gotlands Allehanda* that had to do with the bold burglary at the Antiquities Room a few weeks earlier. Because of the two homicides, what would otherwise have been a big story had been virtually overlooked.

He called the police and asked to speak with the officer in charge of the case. He was put through to Erik Larsson. Johan told him what he was interested in.

"We're working on the burglary, but I'm sorry to say that we haven't made much progress," said the officer, sounding worried.

"Do you have any suspects?"

"I can't say that we do."

"Any leads?"

"Nothing that has made it possible for us to catch the thief."

"This type of burglary—has it happened before?"

"Not from the Antiquities Room, no."

"What can the perpetrator do with that gold armlet

he stole? It must be hard to fence something like that."

"Either he'll keep it for himself, which is not very likely, or he'll sell it. We think this was a commissioned job, meaning that he already had a buyer. It could be a collector, maybe somewhere abroad. We know that Gotland's relics are often sold on the international market."

"What would that sort of armlet be worth?"

"Impossible to say. A collector could pay practically any amount. When it comes to coins, we usually say that an unusual silver coin in good condition from the Viking Age is worth around ten thousand kronor. So you can imagine what someone could get for a whole treasure trove with hundreds of coins. We know that there are hoards of silver that haven't been excavated yet. On average, one cache is still being found on Gotland every year."

"But why is so little being done about these thefts?" asked Johan in surprise. "It's not right that so many artifacts should keep disappearing from here without anyone reacting!"

"Of course we try to find the individuals who are stealing relics, but it's not easy. To be quite honest, I think one reason for the passivity of the police is that the perpetrators—if, contrary to all expectations, the case even gets to court—are given sentences that have virtually no impact. They're judged under the laws having to do with cultural relics. The sentences are so light that the police don't think it's worth spending a lot of energy on catching felons who will be back on the street after only a few months."

"Do you feel the same way?"

"I didn't say that, but it's difficult to track down these sorts of thieves unless you catch them in the act."

Johan thanked the officer and ended the conversation. He had been promised an interview within the next few days. He wanted to do some more checking on the thefts before he did a story. He called the switchboard at police headquarters and asked for a copy of all the police reports that dealt with ancient relics or archaeological finds during the past few years. The records clerk promised to fax over the reports as soon as possible. She didn't think there were more than ten at most.

While he waited, Johan made coffee. He was puzzled by the nonchalance displayed by the police regarding the thefts. He happened to think it was terrible that cultural treasures were being offered on a lucrative market and disappearing—not just from the island of Gotland but from Sweden as a whole.

He rushed over to the fax machine when it started whirring. There were only seven reports. One had to do with the most recent burglary at the Antiquities Room. The rest concerned similar thefts from the antiquities warehouse and from various excavations.

One report caught his interest. A necklace had

disappeared from the excavation at Fröjel. The police report was dated Tuesday, June 29. The stolen item was an amber necklace with silver settings. It had been found in the earth on the previous day by the person who filed the report. She had put the necklace in a bag that was placed inside a box in one of the carts that stood lined up a short distance away from the excavation site. That was where the archaeologists stored their finds along with a computer and various tools and implements. When the person who filed the report went to look at her discovery the next day, it was gone. No one could explain how it had happened. The cart had been locked up for the night, and the lock was undamaged.

The person filing the report was named Katja Rönngren. Johan thought he recognized the name and began searching through his notes. He found the list of people who had participated in the same excavation course as Martina. Sure enough, there was the name.

Katja Rönngren was one of the students who had left the course after Martina's death.

She lived in Göteborg. Johan tried different information services until he tracked down her phone number. He called her up at once. He introduced himself and explained what he wanted to know.

"This is Katja's mother," the woman said. "Katja's not here."

"This is very important. How can I get hold of her?"

"Katja's on Gotland."

"But she left the course several weeks ago, didn't she?"

"She was only home for a couple of days. Then she went back to try to finish it after all."

"Have you heard from her since then?"

"Several times. She said that she couldn't stay at the youth hostel because it was booked up. So she's staying with some friends in Visby. You can call her on her cell. Do you want the number?"

They had checked the passenger lists from Destination Gotland without result. Ambjörnsson had apparently not changed his mind and taken the boat instead of the domestic flight.

A large number of people had been questioned, but it had given them no leads. Knutas's colleagues from the NCP were extremely capable, but they hadn't come up with anything new, either. And Agneta Larsvik had been forced to take on another case back in Stockholm.

After the eight o'clock meeting, Knutas decided to leave police headquarters and follow in the footsteps of the murderer on his own. He told the switchboard that he'd be gone for several hours. Then he got into his old Benz and chugged off. The weather kept changing. It had rained during the night, and clouds were gathering in the sky in dark, threatening clusters as he drove south along the coast road. Right before Klintehamn he turned off at Warfsholm and parked outside the hotel. The place was deserted. The tourists had no doubt gone into Visby since the weather was bad.

He went up to the hotel porch and sat down at the

same table where Martina and her friends had sat just over a month earlier. A chill wind was blowing, and it had started to drizzle. The water was gray, and from the harbor he could hear the machines roaring. It was far from the vacation paradise that he had encountered when he was last here with Karin Jacobsson. He stood up and looked toward the path that led to the youth hostel. That was where young Martina Flochten had presumably met her killer. Why in that particular spot?

He strolled along the pathway, heading in the same direction that Martina had taken, and then stopped in the middle, where the willows on either side formed a tunnel. They sheltered him from both the wind and the rain. Somewhere along here she had been attacked. Then the perpetrator must have dragged her across the parking lot to the lawn with the juniper bushes and finally down to the water where her ring was found. Knutas continued on, taking the route that he imagined the killer had taken. On this side of the shore he would have been well hidden from view, so no one would have bothered him. After he drowned her, he must have stuffed the body into his car and driven away. Knutas stood still and looked around for a moment. Had they arranged to meet? Did Martina have a secret that was not linked to any romantic involvement? During her stay in Sweden, had she gotten to know someone without anyone else finding out about it?

The investigative team had exhausted all possibilities

with regard to the excavation course and the college. There had to be something else, something hidden.

Knutas's next stop was Vivesholm, where he walked through the wooded area over to the birdwatching tower. That was the place where Martina's body had been hung from a tree. He would never forget the sight he had encountered on that morning.

He walked all the way out to the end of the promontory. The landscape was wild and barren. It reminded him of the heaths of Northern Ireland where he and his family had taken a driving vacation several years earlier. The wind forced him to squint, and the drizzling rain ran down his face when he looked up at the sky. The chilly gray weather made it feel like fall. He looked in the direction of the boathouses at Kovik. In the rainy mist he could hardly distinguish the outline of the solitary little chapel that he knew stood there. The funeral for one of his best friends had been held in that chapel barely six months ago. It was a small limestone building that stood all alone, with narrow windows facing the sea. Many a seaman had been buried out there over the years.

Deep in his subconscious something awoke as he stood there in the wind and the rain. He thought about what Agneta Larsvik had said about the murderer's modus operandi. Suddenly Knutas knew exactly what he needed to do.

Katja Rönngren didn't answer the phone. Johan left a message, asking her to call him as soon as possible.

He leaned back in his chair and clasped his hands behind his head. What did it mean that Katja had reported a theft, and that she had dropped out of the course but later returned? Maybe nothing, but the thefts were making him uneasy.

He sat down at his computer and logged on to the Internet. He plugged in various words and searched at random for things that might have to do with relics found on Gotland. He got a lot of hits, but most of them he could screen out as uninteresting. Then he gave a start. An American Web site purported to be selling ancient artifacts from Gotland. Objects such as tools, implements, coins, and jewelry were offered for sale, quite openly. There was also a contact address. Johan had an idea. He typed in a pseudonym and wrote that he was interested in buying some of the objects. He asked for a reply ASAP.

The phone rang. It was Katja Rönngren. She confirmed that she had filed a report with the police but that subsequently nothing had happened. She had no idea who might be behind the thefts. She couldn't even venture a guess. On the other hand, she told Johan that Martina had also discovered that an object they had excavated was missing, and she had talked about filing a report. Katja didn't know whether anything had ever come of it. She had the feeling that Martina suspected someone, although she wasn't willing to admit it.

The phone call gave Johan pause. So Martina had been about to file a police report but had never gotten that far. Maybe if she had, she wouldn't have been killed. Were the thefts the motive? Someone who wanted at all costs to continue to steal but had felt his activities threatened by the girls who were on his trail? If that was the case, then Katja should have been threatened, too. It would have been logical for her to be killed first, since she had actually taken steps to file a report with the police. How did Staffan Mellgren come into the picture? Was he mixed up in the plundering? Johan sensed that the identity of the murderer might be found by looking closer into how the whole theft operation had been set up. It must all fit together somehow: the burglary at the Antiquities Room and the thefts from the warehouse and the excavation site. Now it turned out that goods were even being sold on the Internet. As far as the police were concerned, this should clearly be considered a crime. How were the Americans getting hold of ancient Nordic relics unless they had been stolen?

Suddenly his computer beeped. He had received an e-mail. It was from the United States.

He sat down at his computer again to reply.

Back at police headquarters, Knutas phoned Agneta Larsvik in Stockholm. He was lucky enough to catch her between meetings.

"The part about the modus operandi," he began, "could it have something to do with a religion?"

"In what way?"

"Both Martina Flochten and Staffan Mellgren were interested in the Viking Age. They were excavating a Viking Age port area when they were murdered. The religion at that time had to do with a belief in the Æsir gods—you know, Thor and Odin and all the others. The Vikings made offerings and sacrifices and the like. That's fairly common knowledge. You said that the modus operandi was ritualistic. Could it have something to do with a belief in the Æsir gods? I mean, the way in which sacrifices were made to them?"

"I don't really know," she said hesitantly. "Unfortunately, I don't know much about the subject, but it's not out of the question. Could you hold on for a moment?"

"Of course."

Knutas heard her put down the phone and leaf through some papers in the background. A few minutes later she was back.

"Are you still there? I know someone at Stockholm University who teaches the history of religion. He specializes in ancient Nordic religion and mythology. His name is Malte Moberg, and I'm sure he could help you."

Knutas jotted down the number, and less than a minute later he had the historian on the line. He explained what he wanted to know and briefly described how the victims had been killed.

Malte Moberg spoke slowly, in a gruff, dry voice. "There's something known as the 'threefold death,' meaning that a victim's life is taken in three different ways. This way of killing has its origin in the religion of Celtic and Germanic tribes, and it was utilized for a period from 300 B.C. to A.D. 300. When the victim suffered a threefold death by hanging, stabbing, and drowning, it was thought that each was dedicated to one of three different gods."

The most important piece in the puzzle had now fallen into place. It was that simple. Knutas felt so elated that he could hardly sit still.

"What does this have to do with the ancient Nordic religion?" he asked eagerly.

"In the pre-Christian North, the offering of sacrifices was central to the religion. The creation myth of the

Æsir gods begins when Ymer the giant is sacrificed to give the world a body. Odin sacrificed one of his eyes in exchange for wisdom, and himself to achieve insight into the secrets of the runes. People most often offered food and drink to the gods, but animals were also sacrificed and, in rare cases, human beings. The type of death that you're describing in these murder cases also occurred in the ancient Scandinavian religion. The threefold death was dedicated to the gods Odin, Thor, and Frey—meaning the three most powerful gods in the ancient Nordic pantheon, which was prevalent during the Viking Age. In Nordic mythology, there are three families of gods: the Æsir, the Vanir, and the Elves. The Æsir, who included Odin and Thor, were most closely associated with power and warfare; the Vanir, who included Frey, were linked to fertility. How familiar are you with ancient Nordic mythology?"

"We studied it in school, of course, but that's a hundred years ago. Refresh my memory."

"Odin is the original deity, the Almighty according to many—the most powerful of the gods, who ruled over all the other Æsir. He was also the supreme deity of the human world. He is the oldest and the wisest and lives in the fortress Valhalla. He's the god of war, but also the god of poetry, and he's the one who created the runes. Thor is Odin's son, and he's also the god of war, although he's best known as the god of thunder. Thor has a hammer called Mjölnir, and when he uses it, he produces thunder and lightning. I'm sure you know all about that. Finally, Frey is the foremost god of fertility. People worshipped him in order to obtain a good harvest, peace, sensual pleasure, and bountiful livestock."

"What about the idea that the perpetrator may have drained his victims of their blood? Does that fit in with ancient Nordic mythology?"

"Absolutely. The blood itself was an important part of the sacrificial rite. They would kill the animals, such as pigs, horses, and bulls, and then collect the blood in bowls. One feature of Æsir worship was that they used blood to paint idols."

Knutas let out a long breath.

"It all fits," he said. "The modus operandi, the emptying of the blood, all of it."

There was just one more question he needed to ask. So far no mention of the horse's heads had reached the public, so Knutas told Malte Moberg about the two heads stuck on poles that had been left at the homes of Mellgren and Ambjörnsson.

There was silence on the phone. It lasted so long that Knutas wondered if they'd been cut off. Then Moberg was back, and his voice had taken on a new tone.

"What you're describing is called a *nidstång*—a horse's head is stuck on a pole, often made of hazel-wood, and positioned outside someone's house as a threat. It has to do with a tremendously powerful magic rite, a curse that is leveled at someone. To place a *nidstång* constitutes a serious threat against an individual."

"The excavation leader Staffan Mellgren was murdered a couple of days ago, after he found the *nidstång* at his house."

"And the other man who received a *nidstång*?"

"It's not entirely clear where he is right now," said Knutas cryptically.

"Really? If I were you, I'd try to get hold of him as soon as possible. In addition, I'd advise you to find out quickly who among the victims' circle of acquaintances is interested in Æsir worship."

As soon as he was through talking to Malte Moberg, Knutas called Susanna Mellgren to find out if her husband had ever shown any interest in the Æsir cult. The answer was negative. She'd never heard about anything like that. She admitted that he'd often been gone in the evenings and even on weekends without her finding out what he was doing; she'd taken it for granted that he was meeting with other women.

Knutas received the same answer to his question about Æsir worship from Ambjörnsson's girlfriend. According to her, Ambjörnsson was an atheist.

Knutas summoned the investigative team and reported on his phone conversation with the Stockholm historian who specialized in religion.

"Who the hell would have thought that this had anything to do with religion?" said Kihlgård. "Although who would worship the Æsir gods in this day and age? That seems really odd."

"Surely it's not any odder than believing in Jesus or Muhammad or anything else," objected Jacobsson. "I think it's rather cool to believe in the Æsir gods. I like the thought that there are multiple gods, and that the female deities seem to be just as important as the male ones."

"Now is not the time to be discussing our opinions on various types of religion. We need to talk about this hot new lead that we've got. Hopefully it will help us solve this case," said Knutas impatiently. "The perp is most likely here on the island, and I'd be surprised if he's acting alone. He probably has at least one accomplice."

"Since he seems to have experience in butchering animals or at least in handling their bodies, we've checked out all employees of the Gotland butcher shops. Unfortunately we didn't turn up anything especially interesting," Jacobsson interjected. "Or from the veterinarians or their assistants, either."

Knutas looked discouraged. "Well, at least we know that the modus operandi of these murders was derived from something called the threefold death, and that it was part of ancient Nordic tradition. Who might conceivably have an interest in something like that?"

"Someone who's interested in the Æsir religion and ancient Nordic mythology. The type who's a member of a group dedicated to such things," Kihlgård suggested.

"Do we have anything like that here on Gotland? Does anyone know?" Knutas tossed out the questions. They all shook their heads.

"I suppose this is something different from the

medievalists?" Jacobsson queried. "There are lots of people who are busy putting together the medieval festival for next week, but they wouldn't be interested in the Æsir religion, would they?"

"The Middle Ages came after the Viking Age, at the same time that the North became Christian. I think that was around 1100," said Knutas. "Still, it's possible that the two could be linked. We need to start by looking at the groups that are focused on the Æsir religion. After that somebody should also talk to the people involved with the medieval festival. Surely they have some kind of formal organization, don't they?"

"I can look into it," Jacobsson offered.

"I'd be happy to help," said Kihlgård. "It sounds incredibly exciting."

"Fine. Get some others to help you, too. This has to be regarded as a major lead. We need to give it top priority. This whole story started with the decapitated horse out at Petesviken in June. We're going to have to start back there and make a list of all the people who've come into the picture in some way during the investigation. Then we need to find out which of them has ties to the Æsir religion or to ancient Nordic mythology."

WEDNESDAY, AUGUST 4

His cover name was Viking Venture, but Johan quickly realized that the contact he'd found via the American Web site was Swedish and presumably lived on Gotland. Though it seemed very unlikely that a Gotlander would be selling ancient relics on the American market. He had been e-mailing back and forth with Viking Venture, presenting himself as an interested buyer who was prepared to pay well for Viking Age artifacts from Gotland. The contact said that he could offer quite a number of rarities that might be of interest. Johan pretended to be a collector from Skåne, and after they had exchanged e-mails a number of times, he managed to get the man who called himself Viking Venture to agree to a meeting. They decided to meet on the following Saturday at the indoor ice-skating rink, right outside Visby.

Johan was going to try to get this seller of stolen goods on videotape, using a little camera that they had at the office. On Wednesday Pia had carefully explained to him how to use it. They agreed not to say anything to the police or to the home office back in Stockholm.

This was their own project. Johan felt quite excited.

Emma had called him at work, suggesting that they could have dinner together at her house on Saturday and invite Pia Lilja and Niklas Appelqvist. It would be their first dinner party. He interpreted this as yet another sign that Emma was starting to relent. Maybe they were finally on their way to having a real relationship. The management at Swedish TV had decided to keep the team on Gotland for a trial period in the fall, and Pia had been given the camera job. Johan was the obvious choice for reporter, since he wanted the position and had so far done a good job. He was grateful to be able to stay on the island; at least he could stop worrying about that. Besides, he had the legal right to see his child, and it was a right that he wanted to safeguard.

One thing he was sure of. No matter what happened between him and Emma, he would never budge an inch when it came to his relationship with his daughter.

To his great joy, he had noticed a change in Emma's attitude toward him since Elin was born. She was more loving and tended to cling to him more, daring to show her weaknesses. It was as if he had become more important now that he was the father of her child. She would always be dependent on him, in one way or another. The thought appealed to him.

THURSDAY, AUGUST 5

The cruise liner *Nordic Star* arrived from Riga, Latvia, and majestically slid into berth number eleven in Visby harbor on this Thursday morning. The city couldn't have presented a more beautiful image. The sun colored the facades with a warm, golden sheen, and the temperature had already reached sixty-eight degrees. The American tourists, who had only one day at their disposal to explore Gotland before they continued their journey to Stockholm, were delighted before even stepping off the gangway. The cathedral tower, the ring wall, and the medieval buildings looked fascinating, and a mood of enthusiastic anticipation hovered over the harbor. Ten shiny, air-conditioned tourist buses were parked in a row, ready to swallow up the hundreds of chattering tourists who came streaming off the boat. They wore shorts, T-shirts, and caps, and every single one had a camera around his or her neck. The average age was somewhere between fifty and sixty, although there were a few younger couples. Waiting on the dock, the local guides were clearly visible in their blue vests from the guide association. The buses quickly filled, and one by one they rolled out of the harbor, ready to explore the island.

Matilda Drakenberg's bus was one of the first to leave. The guides had divided up the sightseeing tour so as not to overlap with each other. Matilda's bus was supposed to start outside the city and then proceed inward from there. First stop was the nature preserve of Högklint, just south of Visby. From there they would have a wonderful view of the city and the sea. Next would be the Botanical Gardens and a stroll inside the wall. The tour would end at the East Gate, when the tourists would be free to have lunch and go shopping on their own.

She welcomed the visitors, and before the bus had even reached the coast road heading for Högklint, she had already started telling them about Visby's history. The tourist groups were all strangely similar. Americans were positive, full of questions, and fascinated by anything that was more than a hundred years old. When she told them that the ring wall had been built in the thirteenth century, they all looked amazed.

The bus stopped as close to Högklint as possible. Americans were not known to be a people fond of walking, and several in the group were seriously overweight. An older man used a cane, and he seemed to have a great deal of trouble getting around.

Mathilda was already dreading the walk through Visby's cobblestone streets. She waited until everyone was off the bus and then led the way up the little hill toward the overlook.

When Matilda later had to recount what she saw on that morning, she had a hard time remembering the order in which everything occurred. She had a strong memory of the cheerful chatter of the group and of the man from Wisconsin who ended up walking beside her, asking a hundred questions about everything from the average income in Sweden to where Ingmar Bergman had lived on Gotland. He also wanted to know who the Swedes thought had murdered Olof Palme. There was always one of those in each group, someone who showed up and asked tons of questions in private, draining her energy. Afterward she recalled how she had tried to evade his questions, explaining to him that she would answer them later in front of the whole group, so that everyone could hear. The man didn't seem to get the message. He kept on asking questions.

The group gathered at the top of the slope and enjoyed the magnificent view of Visby and the dramatic coastline.

The plateau was 165 feet above the sea, and the cliffs dropped straight down to the foaming waves far below. Here the wind almost never stopped blowing. Matilda told the tourists about the ledge a short distance below the precipice that was called the Starving Goat Ledge.

Goats that managed to climb down to eat the succulent grass down there were never able to get back up. Eventually they starved to death. Some of the tourists braved the steep stairs and made their way, with varying degrees of success, down to the place where the goats met their grim fate. Others chose a more comfortable alternative and made their way over to the grove of trees a short distance inland. From there they could enjoy the view in the shelter of the trees.

Suddenly a hair-raising scream was heard. For a few seconds Matilda was afraid that someone had fallen from the precipice, but the cry had come from the grove of trees. She rushed over there—and she would never forget the sight that met her eyes.

The naked body of a man was hanging from a tree, dangling lifelessly from a noose. Someone had used a knife to slice open his belly, and the blood had run down his legs and onto the ground. When Matilda saw his face and his wide-open eyes staring down at her, she recognized him at once.

Twenty minutes after the call came in to police headquarters, Knutas and Jacobsson climbed out of their car at Högklint. Without uttering a word, they made their way through the crowd of agitated tourists, who had been given a sightseeing tour far beyond the usual fare. Police officers were cordoning off the area. More tourist buses had arrived, only to be stopped in the parking lot by officers who ordered them to turn around and drive off. No explanation was given. The astonished guides and their drivers did as they were told without getting any answers to their questions. Knutas heard in passing how some people were murmuring about suicide; it was not an unlikely theory. Högklint was a place that was regularly used by people wanting to kill themselves.

As they reached the plateau, Sohlman, Wittberg, and Kihlgård came up to join them. From a distance they could see the body as it swung freely in the air with the glittering sea and the cornflower-blue sky in the background. Knutas slowly shook his head as he recognized every single sign from the previous victims.

Gunnar Ambjörnsson had returned to Gotland.

The murder of the Visby Social Democratic politician was the lead story all over Sweden on that Thursday. At the press conference the police held in the afternoon, reporters from the Norwegian, Finnish, and Danish press were also present. Given the large number of witnesses this time, it was impossible even to try to keep secret the macabre circumstances surrounding the murder. The air was buzzing with speculations about sects, ritual killers, and occultism, and the police were bombarded with questions about the way in which the previous murders had been committed. They had to admit that there were certain similarities, but they declined to be specific.

Knutas felt drained after the press conference, which was the longest one he had ever attended—and it was going to get worse.

During the afternoon, word had leaked out that Gunnar Ambjörnsson had received a horse's head stuck on a pole. Then the news that Staffan Mellgren had been subjected to the same thing before he was killed spread like a wave through the media services in Sweden.

Journalists from all the national media organizations caught the first available plane to Gotland.

After the press conference Knutas and the other members of the investigative team became unavailable—except for the much put-upon Lars Norrby, that is. In his position as police spokesperson, he had to take them on all by himself. The police realized that the intensive media attention was going to make it even harder to catch the killer.

The investigative team, along with the NCP, began the huge task of interviewing demonstrators who were opposed to the construction project, groups interested in the Æsir religion with ties to Gotland, Ambjörnsson's political colleagues, and anyone else who in any conceivable way might have something to do with the case.

Knutas sensed that the perpetrator was somewhere close by, partly because the places where the victims and horses' heads had been found testified to a good knowledge of the local area. He didn't think that someone from the mainland would have chosen the sites that had been used.

The police had completely given up any thought that the murderer might be a woman. Dragging Gunnar Ambjörnsson's body up the hill at Högklint and then managing to hoist it up into a tree required a physical strength that far exceeded a normal woman's ability. If their assumption that the perpetrator was a Gotlander was right, it meant that he would have had to leave the island for Stockholm late Saturday night or early Sunday morning in order to meet Ambjörnsson when he arrived on his connecting flight from Paris. Somehow they must have met in Stockholm, maybe even out at the airport. There were no indications that the meeting had been planned earlier, since Ambjörnsson arrived from Paris at 12:45 P.M., and the plane he had booked to Visby was supposed to leave an hour later. He would barely have had time to get his luggage, go through customs, and head over to the domestic terminal to check in.

Someone had gone to Stockholm and most likely met Ambjörnsson when he disembarked from the plane. Would he have gone voluntarily with a stranger when he knew that he had been threatened? Hardly. So it had to be someone that he knew and trusted. This person had persuaded him to leave the airport instead of flying home. Why would he do that?

Later Ambjörnsson had returned to Gotland, either dead or alive. They didn't yet know whether he was killed on the mainland and then transported to the island, or whether he had lost his life on Gotland. From what he could tell, Erik Sohlman thought that Ambjörnsson had been dead for at least several days. The ME was on his way by plane, so it wouldn't be long before they knew more.

The police had contacted Ambjörnsson's relatives in Stockholm, but none of them had spoken to him in a long time. His girlfriend in Stånga was beside herself with grief, and she had no idea where he had gone after he got off the plane at Arlanda airport. He hadn't been in touch with her since he returned to Sweden.

After the ME had examined the body at the scene, it would be taken to the forensic medicine lab in Solna for autopsy. Knutas already had some idea what the autopsy report would contain. All indications were that Ambjörnsson had met the same fate as the previous victims. Knutas had now received confirmation from many different angles that the theory about the threefold death was correct. No doubt everyone would be discussing that very topic on the morning talk shows the next day.

Even so, he almost choked on his coffee when heard *Dagens Eko* on the radio at 4:45 P.M. Both the symbolism of the *nidstång* and the threefold death were mentioned. Knutas was even more surprised when he heard Susanna Mellgren being interviewed. There seemed to be no limit to what was reported. It remained to be seen how all the media attention would affect the murderer. Maybe he would crawl into the nearest hole and bide his time until the storm blew over.

Earlier in the day the police had received a call from an Estonian by the name of Igors Bleidelis who worked aboard a freighter that frequently called at Visby. He'd heard talk of the ritual murders, and he said that he'd noticed something mysterious at Högklint almost six months ago. He'd seen a fire and people with blazing torches moving around on top of the cliff in a ritual dance. He thought they were conducting some type of ceremony. He remembered the date: March 20. That's all he could tell them. He had thought it was odd. That's why he had called, because there might be some connection with the murder of the politician who was found at the very same place.

Jacobsson came into Knutas's office. He asked her if she knew whether there was anything special about March 20. She leafed through her calendar.

"Nothing really special, except that it's the vernal equinox."

Knutas leaned back in his chair. "Would that have any significance? A form of ritual that takes place on the vernal equinox? Who celebrates that day?"

"I have no idea, but it shouldn't be so hard to find out. Couldn't you ask your expert on the Æsir religion whether that particular day has some special meaning for people who worship the Æsir?"

Five minutes later he had his answer from Malte Moberg in Stockholm. The vernal equinox turned out to be one of the most important days in the year for Æsir worshippers.

"All the puzzle pieces are falling into place," said Knutas. "This has to do with some religious fanatics who believe in the Æsir gods and who have gone too far. But

I just can't figure out what their motive could be for murdering those individuals."

"This Estonian may have seen the very sect that the killer belongs to, a sect that has managed to remain so secret that no one even knows it exists. It sounds like something occult, with the fire and the dancing people. We already have a connection between Martina Flochten and Gunnar Ambjörnsson through the hotel project at Högklint. The fact that his body was found there just confirms that the connection has significance."

"So then we have Staffan Mellgren. There has to be something else besides the fact that he was having an affair with Martina."

"Could he have been a member of this Æsir sect?"

"I think it's likely, and that's exactly where we're going to find the killer."

SATURDAY, AUGUST 7

When Johan woke up, he didn't know where he was at first. Then he felt a tiny body next to his and realized that he was home with Emma and Elin. His little daughter was sleeping right next to him, breathing calmly. Emma was asleep, too. Each of them lay on her side, facing him, and he was struck by how alike they looked. The work he'd done the past few days reporting on the murder of Gunnar Ambjörnsson had been intense. It had taken its toll on him. He was annoyed that he hadn't managed to find out the part about the decapitated horse heads, but all the other journalists were in the same boat. The police had really succeeded in keeping that information to themselves. It was actually quite impressive.

Fortunately more Swedish TV reporters had come over to Gotland to help cover the story. Johan had asked to have the weekend off to work on his report on the thefts of ancient artifacts, even though it was regarded as a sidetrack. Grenfors hadn't been unreasonable. It might turn out to have something to do with the murders.

His meeting with the fence had been arranged the day before Ambjörnsson was found, and Johan didn't want to miss the opportunity to meet him in person.

He put on some coffee, took a shower, and then went to get the morning newspaper before he woke Emma with a kiss.

"Good morning. I can change Elin," he offered.

"Thanks," she mumbled, turning over and crawling farther under the covers.

On his way to the bathroom he kissed his daughter's soft cheeks, which were still warm with sleep, and blew on the back of her neck. Johan thought that the moments he spent at the changing table were so cozy. He would talk to Elin and cuddle her as he allowed her bottom to air out for a moment.

When he had finished changing her diaper, he picked the tiny baby up and carried her close to his chest, humming softly in her ear.

Before he'd had a child, he never would have imagined how nice it could be. Most of what he heard from the parents of small children was how trying and difficult everything was. Late hours and dirty diapers, crying and colic. Of course, he knew it was different if you had to take care of a baby full-time, but Emma actually said the same thing—that Elin was an unusually happy baby who was easy to care for.

They ate breakfast and read the paper in peace and quiet. Nothing new had come out about the murder of

Ambjörnsson. According to the police spokesperson, they were working on a broad front, conducting a thorough investigation, but so far there was no suspect in the murder. On the other hand, the police admitted that they were working on the theory that the same perpetrator was behind all three murders, although they still refused to confirm that a horse's head was found at the homes of two of the victims shortly before their deaths. Instead the spokesperson stated that the investigation had reached a sensitive stage.

A sensitive stage, thought Johan. *I wonder what that means.*

After breakfast he put Elin to bed; she had fallen asleep again after her second feeding. She had a crib next to their bed, and she usually slept soundly, without any fuss. Johan went over to Emma, who had on only her bathrobe, and pulled her close. He looked into her warm eyes. There was something vulnerable about them that he found fiercely attractive. That's how it had been from the very first time he saw her.

Now he held her in his arms, and she pressed herself against him. Without her doing anything else, he knew what she wanted. Her response was passionate when he kissed her. Johan felt instantly dizzy and wildly excited. They tumbled onto the bed, kissing more intensely than he ever remembered doing before. Maybe the force of their kisses was part of his feeling of desire.

She reached for him, fumbling her hands over his

body, pressing against him as if he were saving her life. The intensity surprised him, and he lost all sense of space and time. All of a sudden he heard himself moaning loudly, and he tore off her bathrobe. Her body was soft and warm with sleep. She was plumper than usual, and her breasts were heavy with milk. He burrowed into her, digging his fingers into her flesh and tasting her breasts with his lips. As if it were the first time, he found his way inside of her, and he nearly lost consciousness when they both came at once.

He had thought that she would feel less like herself than she did. In fact, it wasn't her body that was so different. It was something else entirely.

Knutas had never before encountered such rushing about in the corridors on a Saturday. The investigation had expanded, and the work was taking up everyone's time.

This was the most miserable summer he'd experienced in years. He'd hardly had a chance to enjoy it at all. He'd gone swimming in the sea only a couple of times, and he could count on one hand those occasions when he'd had a barbecue outdoors with his family, even though it had been the most beautiful summer in a long time.

Now it seemed as if the investigative work was finally making headway. There was definitely a new energy in the air.

When Knutas came back from lunch, someone had placed the Destination Gotland passenger lists on his desk, as he'd requested. Officers had already checked the lists on Friday without finding Ambjörnsson's name or the name of anyone connected to him, but Knutas wanted to go through them personally, just to make sure. He had the names of the passengers from all the departures starting with Sunday, August 1, which was the day when Ambjörnsson was expected to return from his travels abroad.

Knutas got a cup of coffee from the machine and sat down at his desk to read.

He went over the lists of names of everyone who had traveled from Nynäshamn to Visby on the same day that Ambjörnsson was supposed to come home. Knutas didn't discover any name that might give him a lead.

Of course, Ambjörnsson could have traveled under another identity, but why would he do that? Had he been forced to do so? Had someone threatened him? One reason he might not have come back to the island alive was that it would have exposed the perpetrator to risk, both by arousing attention and because someone might have caught sight of Ambjörnsson and recognized him. No, that wasn't what had happened. Knutas sighed and put the papers aside.

The body had been transported to the forensic medicine lab in Solna. The preliminary autopsy report should arrive on Monday.

Knutas decided to take a walk in order to clear his head. It was a beautiful afternoon. A new high-pressure ridge had moved in from the east, promising a warm week for the medieval festival. The events had already started in town. From Strandgärdet he could hear the announcer's voice and applause from the tournament that was held in classic chivalric style. A juggler group was performing at the East Gate, and at Hästgatan Knutas was practically run over by a group of people moving through the lanes dressed in medieval garb.

He crossed Stora Torget and decided to take a stroll down to the sea. On the way he passed by Skogränd, where Aron Bjarke lived. As he neared the teacher's house, Knutas slowed down. He had a sudden impulse to visit Bjarke. He rang the bell several times, but no one came to the door. Bjarke was apparently not at home. As he stood there on the porch, Knutas's eye was caught by one of the objects on the windowsill. Among the pots and old jars stood a wooden figure that was only a hand's breadth tall. He went over to the window for a closer look and was struck by how risqué it was. It was a male figure with a disproportionately large, erect penis. Knutas was sure that he'd seen it before, and he frantically searched his memory. He had the feeling that it might be important. Something fluttered past in the back of his mind, but it vanished just as quickly.

He rang the bell one last time, then waited a moment, but the house looked dark and silent inside. Again his gaze fell on the figure in the window. Somewhere he had seen that figure before.

Johan had agreed to meet the unknown seller at four in the afternoon. He felt tense all day, and he talked to Pia several times on the phone to make sure that they had everything under control. He had explained to the seller that he wasn't going to bring any money to their first meeting. It was a precautionary measure. First he wanted to see some samples of the sort of Gotland artifacts that were being offered for sale.

The camera was in the editorial office. Pia was going to get it and then bring it out to Johan in Roma so that he could practice using it. He had hardly ever filmed anything before, and he needed all the help he could get to make sure everything functioned properly. The agreement was that if Johan was satisfied with the goods, he would pay cash on Monday.

He counted on being checked out, so he had given a phony name and address. Fortunately he had a wealthy friend, who happened to be a nobleman, in Skåne. This was not the first time that Johan had used his friend's identity for his job. Having his name in the Peerage Book and belonging to one of the richest families in

Sweden had its advantages. Now it was just a matter of Johan playing his role well when he met with the fence.

Knutas wanted to read through the passenger lists one more time before leaving the office for the day. It was possible that, in spite of everything, he had missed Ambjörnsson's name. So far he had just looked for the first syllable of his last name, but now he read through the whole list, running his index finger carefully over the names so as not to miss anything.

Suddenly he caught sight of a name he recognized. It was Aron Bjarke. The archaeology teacher had traveled from Nynäshamn to Visby on Monday, August 2. That meant that Bjarke had been in Stockholm at the same time that Ambjörnsson was expected home from Morocco.

With his pulse racing, Knutas looked through the names of passengers from Visby to Nynäshamn. He had the lists from Sunday, August 1, but he couldn't find Bjarke's name. He phoned his contact at Destination Gotland, who had sent over the information, and asked for the lists from Saturday, July 31. That was the same day that he'd had coffee with Bjarke in his garden, which meant that he couldn't have left any earlier.

The lists were going to show up within half an hour. Knutas leaned back in his chair to wait as thoughts whirled through his mind. Aron Bjarke was an archaeologist and a teacher at the college. That gave him a connection to both Martina and Staffan. The question still remained: What was his link to Ambjörnsson? The e-mail from Destination Gotland appeared after only a few minutes, and he immediately found the name he was looking for. Bjarke had left the island by car on Saturday afternoon, July 31. Knutas raised his eyes from his computer and looked out the window. Once again he had a vague feeling that he was missing something. That annoyed him.

He wondered what Aron Bjarke could have in common with Gunnar Ambjörnsson. With Staffan Mellgren there was a natural connection. Both taught archaeology, and each had been Martina Flochten's teacher.

The instant he had that thought, he realized what he had overlooked: the figure in Aron Bjarke's kitchen window. He now realized what it represented: Frey, the god of fertility in the Æsir pantheon. Hence the penis. Knutas had noticed a similar idol at Mellgren's house. He picked up the phone and ordered that the figure be brought in to headquarters at once.

He didn't have time to do it himself. He was extremely anxious to get hold of Aron Bjarke.

Johan left in good time for his meeting with the seller. He had practiced using the camera all afternoon, and it was now attached to a belt around his waist. One problem was that he risked being recognized. He was pretending to be a nobleman from Skåne, but the seller might have seen him on TV. Occasionally Johan's face appeared on the screen when he did live reports or stand-ups.

He decided to disguise himself behind a big pair of sunglasses and a cap to hide his dark curly hair. In the mirror he looked like a whole different person.

Traffic was heavy on the road to Visby. Lots of people were headed for the city to take part in or to watch some of the countless events that had been organized for the first day of Medieval Week. He had borrowed Emma's car and reached the indoor ice-skating rink twenty minutes before the appointed time. He felt like a regular gangster, one half of a criminal transaction. The mere thought made him feel guilty.

Johan managed to work up a good case of nerves as he waited. He gave a start when a red pickup drove up in front of him soon afterward. He discreetly slipped his hand inside his jacket to turn on the camera. The man driving the truck was also wearing dark glasses. He had gray stubble on his face and was slightly overweight. About fifty years old.

Without saying a word, he reached over and opened the passenger-side door of his vehicle. With some hesitation Johan got into the pickup.

They greeted each other briefly.

"If we're careful, we can take a look at the artifacts here, but it'll have to be quick," said the man, speaking with a marked Gotland accent. He cast a glance out the truck windows and then looked in the rearview mirror. Maybe he was new at this game.

The seller lifted up a toolbox that was wedged between the seats. He opened the box and took out a cloth-wrapped bundle. Inside were a number of objects: a chisel, a few axe blades, several silver coins, spear points, and a circular clasp.

Johan assumed an expression that he hoped would give him the look of an expert and slowly picked up each and every artifact.

Niklas had given him some tips about the types of remarks he could make. The seller was watching him attentively.

"As I said on the phone, these are just a few samples. I have many more, but I don't know how much you're interested in."

"Now that I see what you have, and that the goods are genuine, I could be interested in a large number of items," said Johan.

"How much are we talking about?"

"I'd rather not go into that right now. One thing at a time. What do you want for these?"

"All of them?"

"Yes."

"A hundred thousand kronor."

"That's too much. I'll give you fifty."

Niklas had warned him that he would undoubtedly be quoted too high a price, if for no other reason than to check him out.

"Ninety."

"I can go as high as seventy-five thousand. Just to show you my goodwill on the first deal. But next time I'd appreciate it if you'd ask a reasonable price right from the start."

"When can I get the money?"

"On Monday."

"In cash?"

"That's what we agreed, wasn't it?"

Aron Bjarke didn't answer his home phone or his cell.

Knutas switched on his computer and looked up the personal data on Bjarke. He was born in 1961 at Visby Hospital. He went to Säve High School in Visby and then studied archaeology at the University of Stockholm. For a long time he lived in Hägerstan, a suburb south of the city. Knutas confirmed that Bjarke had never married or registered as living with anyone. Nor did he have any children. A few years ago he had moved back to Gotland, and he now lived on Skogränd.

Aron Bjarke had one sibling, an older brother named Eskil Rondahl. Their parents had died in a fire only a year ago. Knutas remembered that fire in Hall quite well. It was quickly put out, yet two people had died. So they were Bjarke's parents. Knutas frowned at the strange coincidence. The police techs had done a thorough investigation, but the cause of the fire had never been determined.

It turned out that Bjarke's brother still lived at the family farm in Hall.

Maybe he would find Aron there.

The tension that Johan had felt before meeting the seller dissipated as he sat in his own vehicle. He felt sick to his stomach and weak in the knees. Not because the man had made a particularly frightening impression; in fact, he seemed quite timid.

For the time being, Johan pushed aside any thought of possible consequences. He turned off the camera, hoping that he'd gotten it all on film. Then he took off his dark glasses and cap.

In Gråbo he picked up Niklas Appelqvist, who was carrying two bottles of good wine and a bouquet of flowers for Emma. Johan was impressed. He hadn't thought his friend would be so considerate.

When they reached the house they were met with loud music. Pia and Emma were sitting on the sofa, each of them holding a glass of wine and rocking out to Ebba Grön. It had been a long time since Johan had seen Emma looking so lively. She needed a break. Maybe her uncertainty about their relationship had a lot to do with simple fatigue.

At that instant he decided to take her on a trip,

whether she wanted to go or not. It would be a surprise that he would book in advance. They would have to take Elin along, of course, but he would make all the arrangements. Emma wouldn't have to do anything except nurse the baby.

When Emma caught sight of Johan, she came dancing toward him with a mischievous smile to give him a kiss. He had a feeling that she had read his mind.

After dinner they sat down on the sofa group in the living room to look at the video. The visual quality left a lot to be desired, and the images were shaky, but they could clearly hear what was said.

Johan breathed a sigh of relief when he saw that the material was good enough for him to put together a TV report. Suddenly the face of the seller appeared, at first blurred, then clearer. Niklas gave a shout.

"What the hell! That's the guy from the warehouse. Eskil. Eskil something or other."

Everyone looked at Niklas in surprise.

"I remember now. His name is Eskil Rondahl. He works at the antiquities warehouse. He's been there for ages. I'm not surprised that he could get his hands on artifacts."

"I know who you mean!" exclaimed Johan excitedly. "I've interviewed him about the thefts on the phone. Good Lord. That dried up, sad old man. Are you sure it's him?"

"Of course I'm sure. Everyone who studies

archaeology has to take a few classes from him. He demonstrates how to handle ancient relics and archive them."

"So that means it's an inside job. If he's selling artifacts, maybe there are others doing the same thing."

"This is fucking insane," Niklas said, shaking his head. "I wonder how long he's been doing this."

"What do you know about him?"

"Not much. He seems like an anonymous type of guy. Incredibly reserved and uptight. Hardly says a word. A real oddball, to put it bluntly."

"Do you know whether he has a family? Or where he lives?"

"I have no idea. Although I have a hard time imagining that he'd have a family."

"I'll check."

Johan got up and switched on the computer in Emma's study. He searched for Eskil Rondahl in the municipal records and found his address.

"He lives in Hall. That's north of here, isn't it?"

"What's the address?" asked Niklas, who had followed Johan into the study. He was standing behind him, looking at the screen.

"It just says Sigvards, Hall."

"I wonder where that is. Large sections of Hall are a nature preserve up along the rocky coast. There's hardly anything out there. It's desolate and barren."

Johan glanced at his watch. It was nine fifteen.

"I'm going to drive out there."

"Right now?"

Johan printed out the information about Eskil Rondahl.

"I'll go with you," said Niklas resolutely.

"No, it's better if Pia comes along, so she can film things if we need it," said Johan. "You can stay here with Emma while we're gone."

Pia was in high spirits as she drove, and she greatly exceeded the speed limit. She had cut back on the amount of wine she drank because she had to get up early the next day, and now she was glad that she had. They drove via Visby and then north past Lickershamn. It was still light out, and when they passed Ireviken the landscape started to change. The area looked more barren; the vegetation got scruffier. Here and there dead trees stretched their bare branches toward the sky. They searched for the place for a long time. They had to ask for directions to the farm, which they finally found at the end of the road. Darkness had begun to set in, and they didn't dare drive all the way up to the farm. As soon as it appeared from behind a hill, Pia stepped on the brakes and backed up. She parked the car a short distance away in the woods.

The farm was impressive in size but clearly in need of repair. To their surprise, they saw five or six cars parked in the yard. Eskil Rondahl apparently had visitors. Farther away a red pickup was visible, along with an old, rusty horse trailer. Pia took the small camera along, although it would have to be used indoors; it was too dark outside. Cautiously they approached the house. They had it in view when they suddenly heard the sound of a car engine behind them. Johan flinched—was there another visitor?

He was dumbfounded when he saw who got out of the car. It was Anders Knutas. He was alone, and he wasn't driving a police vehicle. Was he on the track of the thefts, too? Johan cast a quick glance at his watch. It was almost ten o'clock.

Knutas didn't seem to have noticed Johan and Pia, who were standing in the shelter of several tall bushes. When Johan stepped forward, Knutas gave a start.

"What the hell are you doing here?" he snarled. What an absurd situation. Here they stood in the dark, in the middle of a nature preserve, close to a remote farm, stupidly glaring at each other.

"I might ask you the same question," said Johan.

"That's none of your business," snapped Knutas. "What's going on here?" he then asked with a nod at the parked cars.

"No idea. We just got here."

Pia stepped into view, and Knutas greeted her.

"Now you're going to have to explain what brings the two of you out here."

Johan briefly told Knutas how he had found the

American Web site and about his meeting with the seller. When he said that the fence was Eskil Rondahl, Knutas's eyes widened.

"Not bad," he said. He actually sounded impressed.

"But you're here for some other reason?" said Johan.

Knutas hesitated for a moment. Maybe it was the intimacy of standing there in the dark, maybe it was because he was so tired, completely worn out after everything that had happened lately—but something made him decide to tell them why he had come.

"Aron Bjarke, who's a teacher at the college, was in Stockholm when Gunnar Ambjörnsson was expected home from his trip abroad. We didn't know this before, but Aron Bjarke and Eskil Rondahl are brothers. Bjarke changed his name twenty years ago when he was studying in Stockholm. Before that his name was Aron Rondahl."

"Do the police think that Aron might be the murderer?"

"Yes. And now you've turned up a whole new aspect of the case—the thefts. We just may have the solution to the burglary at the Antiquities Room, too."

Pia gave Johan a poke in the side.

"Look," she said. "Something's happening."

Inside the house they could see people walking back and forth. Johan heard someone bolt the door from the inside. *Strange,* he thought. *Out here in the country no one locks their doors.*

Cautiously they crept forward and peeked through a window. They were looking at the kitchen, which was old-fashioned and seemed very poorly outfitted. A decrepit electric stove and a small refrigerator and freezer were the only appliances. A considerable number of dirty dishes were littered about, along with glasses and bottles. Johan crept along the wall of the house, crouching down so as not to be seen. He went around the corner, summoned his courage, and then straightened up enough so that he could peer inside.

It was a big room, almost like a hall, but sparsely furnished. About ten people were inside, men and women of various ages. Everyone was dressed in identical, long, cloaklike attire. Johan's first thought was that they were performing some sort of ceremony in connection with Medieval Week, but he quickly realized that something else was going on. A man came in, clad only in a pair of shorts. He was carrying a flat drum with an animal skin stretched across it. It looked like a tambourine. He was beating the drum with a wooden stick that had one end wrapped in leather. At the same time, he was droning a song that lacked any sort of melody. It consisted mostly of a monotone chanting. Johan couldn't understand a single word, but he had the feeling that the drummer was pronouncing incantations or invoking some higher powers.

Another man stood in the center of the group, his face hidden from view. As if at a signal, a circle formed around him. He turned in different directions as he spoke, and the others in the group seemed to answer him.

Knutas had come to stand beside Johan.

"Who's the guy with the drum?" whispered Johan. "He looks like a shaman."

"Yes, he does, though I don't know who he is. Take a look at the man in the middle, the one who seems to be the leader. That's Aron Bjarke."

At that instant Bjarke turned in their direction, and for a moment Johan thought they had been discovered. But Bjarke continued on, undisturbed.

Then Johan caught sight of Eskil Rondahl. He was standing off to one side with his eyes closed, murmuring just like everyone else. He looked totally different from when Johan had met him earlier in the day. Like a different person. He seemed to be in a trance, and Johan had the feeling that the drummer was transporting the others and even himself into some sort of ecstatic state.

Suddenly a scantily clad woman came dancing into the room. She had curly red hair that reached down to her waist. Like the shaman, she was almost naked. Around her hips she wore a short piece of cloth, and above, a simple top. She danced around the drummer, tossing her hair. In her hands she carried something that looked like a horn, and she offered it to the others, who drank from it.

After that, a bowl was brought in. The woman carried it carefully in her hands, and Johan and Knutas instinctively leaned closer to see better. She moved the bowl back and forth, and a look of ecstasy appeared in the eyes of the participants. Everyone was staring at the bowl. Then she held it out in front of her while the man with the drum pounded his club even harder and raised his voice. Now the sound bellowed out, but Johan and Knutas still couldn't distinguish any words. They'd never seen anything like this. Then the woman drank from whatever was in the bowl as the shaman shouted. A dark red liquid ran down the sides.

Knutas and Johan exchanged looks of disgust.

"What do you think they're drinking?" whispered Johan. "I bet you anything it's blood."

"That wouldn't surprise me," said Knutas, taking his cell phone out of the inside pocket of his jacket. These people looked capable of just about anything. He called the officer on duty in Visby without taking his eyes off the spectacle.

All of a sudden Johan noticed that Pia had disappeared. He took a step back and looked around. He didn't see her anywhere. He was both annoyed and worried. These people didn't look sane. What would they do if they found Pia sneaking around with a camera outside the window?

Knutas also called Karin Jacobsson, who happened to be visiting her parents in Tingstäde, which wasn't far away. Martin Kihlgård was with her, and they said they would drive over immediately.

Johan wondered what Knutas was planning to do. Was he going to arrest Aron Bjarke? If so, on what grounds? The fact that he'd been in Stockholm at the same time as Ambjörnsson was hardly a good enough reason.

Now the other people inside the house had started drinking from the bowl, too. After they drank, they began rhythmically stomping on the floor. They were all stomping to the same beat.

One of the members of the sect moved away from the group and dipped what looked like a small sculpture of a god in the bowl. Then the person held it up for the others to see. Johan thought the sculpture reminded him of an ancient Nordic god, maybe Thor or Odin. The idol was passed from hand to hand, and the participants became daubed with the red liquid, which they rubbed on their faces. It looked quite macabre.

Johan leaned toward Knutas.

"It looks like they'll be at it for a while. I'm going to find out where Pia has gone. Just whistle if anything happens."

He walked around the house. There were lights in all the windows on the ground floor, but the second floor was dark. He crossed the yard and opened the barn door. It was pitch-black and smelled damp and musty. The light switch was inside the door. It took a few minutes of fumbling around in the dark before he found it. After some hesitant flickering, the fluorescent tube in the ceiling went on, producing a faint light. A pile of boards and a couple of bundles of insulating material lay in a corner.

Along one wall stood a large freezer. Johan noticed that it was plugged in, and out of curiosity he went over and opened it. The lid was big and hard to lift, and the handle was slightly broken. Cold air rose up toward him as he peered down inside the freezer. All he could see was several rectangular plastic packages, completely frozen. He picked up one of the boxes and scraped the frost off the lid. A label was stuck to it. He had trouble making out what it said. Part of the text, which had been written with black ink, was smeared. All of a sudden the letters became clear enough to be legible. It was a name that he recognized. MELLGREN. Instinctively he looked up to check that no one was around to see what he was holding. He twisted and turned the small package. It seemed to contain a brown liquid that had solidified. His stomach lurched when he realized that what he was probably holding in his hands was Mellgren's blood. He picked up another package and began scraping off the frost, but he was interrupted by a noise from outside.

He glanced toward the barn door and watched as the handle slowly moved downward.

Jacobsson and Kihlgård drove toward Hall in the August darkness. The road got narrower the farther they went, and they met only a few other cars. They passed the exits to Lickershamn and Ireviken, and they almost missed the turnoff for the farm. Jacobsson braked hard and then turned onto the small road. It was now pitch-dark all around them; there were no streetlights or houses. The scruffy woods got thicker, and here and there they caught a glimpse of dead trees with bare, gnarled branches.

"Are you sure this is the right road?" asked Kihlgård, sounding worried.

"Absolutely. I checked the map. This has to be the right way. But I have to admit that even though I've lived my whole life on Gotland, I've never been out here before."

"It's damned desolate. Like some kind of ghostly landscape."

"Yes, it is," Jacobsson agreed. "It feels like this is as far away from civilization as we can get."

The car jolted along as the terrain became more and

more rugged. Jacobsson wondered if they'd be able to keep going without getting stuck somewhere. Just as she was starting to look for a place to turn around, they saw a car parked up ahead in the woods. Farther along was another car. She recognized it as Knutas's old Benz.

Jacobsson parked next to it. Then they made their way up to the farm, moving as quietly as possible.

The expression on Eskil Rondahl's face hardly changed at all when he found Johan holding a package in his hands. Only his eyes revealed a flash of surprise. For the second time that day, they met.

"What the hell are you doing here?"

"I was just going to ask you the same thing."

Johan held out the packages toward him.

Rondahl didn't reply. His arms hung clumsily at his sides, as if he didn't know what to do. They stood there for a moment, staring at each other.

"Who are you?"

"My name is Johan Berg, and I'm a journalist."

"For a newspaper?"

"For TV. Swedish TV, Regional News."

"Did you follow me?"

As Eskil talked, he slowly came closer. Johan took a step back and cast a surreptitious glance to either side. Where the hell was Knutas? And Pia?

Rondahl was now circling around him like a wild animal about to attack its prey.

Johan didn't know what to do. The door was closed, and he hadn't noticed any other exit. Outside everything was quiet. He suddenly found himself in a situation over which he had no control whatsoever. He hadn't counted on ending up in the danger zone himself. Images of his daughter flickered past. He cursed his stupidity. How could he have landed in this situation without thinking about the consequences? This had to do with a triple homicide. Emma's face appeared in his mind.

He saw the white walls of the barn with the peeling plaster, the old stalls where the cows must have stood, chained and lined up in a row, shackled and unable to escape, just like him. He noted how Rondahl's eyes darkened, and he realized that the man who had seemed so timid was actually deadly dangerous. He was standing face-to-face with the killer.

The windows gleamed black; the darkness from outside came in, squeezing around his heart and blocking his brain. Then he saw the glint of a knife blade in the man's hand. At first he thought he was imagining it, but then it glittered again. Ice-cold terror settled like a tight band around his neck. He stood perfectly still. Incoherent thoughts were racing through his mind, giving him no guidance. He didn't know how many seconds or minutes passed as he stood there as if frozen to the spot. Then he woke from his momentary, fear-induced torpor and made a lunge for the door in a hopeless attempt to escape. The next second the man was on him. Johan felt a burning pain in his stomach.

He sank to the floor.

Jacobsson and Kihlgård hurried toward the farm and caught sight of Knutas, who was pressed up against the side of the house.

"What's going on?" whispered Jacobsson as she inquisitively peeked through the window.

"They're performing some kind of ritual. Both Eskil Rondahl and Aron Bjarke are inside, and Bjarke seems to be the leader, as you can see. I don't know what it means, but it looks as if they're drinking blood."

"Are you serious?"

Kihlgård made himself as small as possible, considering the bulk of his body.

Knutas was starting to get very worried. The reinforcements that he'd called for hadn't arrived, and he wondered where Johan and Pia had gone.

"Where's Rondahl?" asked Jacobsson.

Knutas crouched down and let his eyes survey the mysterious figures inside the hall. He couldn't see Rondahl anywhere. Apparently he had left the room without Knutas noticing.

"Both Johan and Pia have disappeared, too," said Knutas tensely. "And that was quite a while ago."

Pia was lying in the most uncomfortable position imaginable. She had found a stairway at one end of the house, on the outside. She'd gone up to the attic and discovered a hatch that she was able to lift up so she had a full view of the living room below.

Up there she could stretch out and film what was happening undisturbed, as long as none of the participants decided to look up and peer through the crystal chandelier hanging from the ceiling.

She would not have dreamed that what was playing out in the room below would ever occur in reality.

Several of the participants were holding figures, which they dipped into the bowls containing something that actually did look like blood. She tried to zoom in on the sculptures to make out what they were supposed to symbolize. One woman was kissing her sculpture, and to Pia's horror, she then carefully began licking off the blood.

Pia recognized Aron Bjarke, although he was behaving in a totally unexpected manner. His face was contorted and his eyes rigid as he stretched his arms overhead and intoned incantations that she couldn't understand.

She let the camera roll, hoping that the images would be clear enough.

Suddenly something happened. The door opened, and the man who had left the room a while ago came back. He looked agitated. Now Pia recognized him. It was the man from the film, Eskil Rondahl. She noticed that he had blood on his clothes and his hands, although she didn't recall seeing any on him when he left the room. But it could have come from one of the bowls that were being passed around.

He went over to Aron and whispered in his ear. Aron's expression instantly changed. He turned toward Eskil to talk to him, but what they said was inaudible. Pia silently cursed. Now she could see only his back.

Suddenly she saw through the camera's viewfinder that Aron was saying something to the man with the drum, and the rhythmic pounding abruptly stopped. One by one the participants noticed that the drumming had ceased, and they, too, stopped moving as they looked around the room in confusion. Aron raised his hand and started speaking. Pia heard him order those present to go home now, but to return on the following night to complete the ritual when the moon was full. If they came back, they would all experience something extraordinary.

Some tried to ask Aron what he meant, but he merely raised his hand and gave them a faint smile.

At the very moment when they discovered that Eskil Rondahl was gone, he came back. They watched him go over to his brother, they watched Aron speak to all the people gathered in the room, and they watched as a certain amount of confusion arose when the ritual was interrupted. One by one the participants left the house. The moonlight forced the three police officers to back so far away from the house that they had a hard time hearing what was said or seeing who came out. Neither Knutas nor Jacobsson recognized any of the individuals in the mysterious sect, except for Aron and Eskild. Since everyone's face was painted, it was hard to make out their features.

Knutas was getting more and more worried about Johan and Pia. Where had they gone? He was afraid that something had happened to them.

Where the hell were the police cars?

They decided to wait to launch an assault until the guests had driven off. As soon as the last car disappeared beyond the hill, the door to the house opened and the two brothers came out. They walked briskly across the yard toward the dark barn. With tense and serious expressions, they went in, carefully closing the door behind them. A light went on inside.

Knutas had an ice-cold feeling in the pit of his stomach, and he urged his colleagues to hurry. The three of them raced across the barnyard. When Knutas peered through the window, his fears were confirmed. Both brothers were bending over someone lying on the ground, and Aron was holding a knife.

The man on the ground was Johan. It took only a few seconds before Knutas, followed by his colleagues, stormed through the door with their pistols drawn.

"Police!" shouted Knutas. "Drop your weapon and put your hands up!"

Aron and Eskil were leaning down, with their backs to the door. For a second they froze.

"Drop the knife!" Knutas shouted again.

He tried to see whether Johan was still alive, but the reporter's body was hidden from view. Slowly the two men straightened up and turned around. Even though Knutas had met Aron several times before, he hardly recognized him. His face had changed, but Knutas couldn't figure out what was different about it. His expression was not the same; his mask had fallen away. Knutas was struck by how similar the brothers looked.

So far Aron had made no sign of letting go of the knife. He stared at Knutas with a remote look in his eye, as if he weren't really present in the room.

"Drop the weapon!" Knutas shouted for the third time.

He sensed Jacobsson and Kihlgård on either side of him, standing a couple of paces back. They had their guns aimed at the brothers.

Knutas had to summon all his forces to make himself stand still. Precious time was being wasted while the life was possibly running out of Johan as he lay motionless on the floor. *We have to call for an ambulance,* thought Knutas. *He could be dying.*

Slowly Aron released his grip on the knife, and with a hollow clang it fell to the floor. The officers immediately rushed forward and seized the men.

Johan lay on the floor, his face white and his eyes closed. His shirt was dark red with blood that had soaked through and run out onto the floor.

"He has a pulse, but it's faint," said Jacobsson.

The door opened, and Pia came in, holding the camera in her hand. When she caught sight of Johan, she screamed and ran over to him.

"He's alive," said Jacobsson, "but just barely."

SUNDAY, AUGUST 8

The walls were painted with soothing colors, and all the sounds were muted. She sat with the baby in her arms, as the chair she was sitting in rocked back and forth. It might have been a day like any other. She was nursing Elin. The baby greedily sucked in life, letting it flow through her little body. Emma had no tears. She wished that she could cry, but her anguish and despair were dry. Something became petrified inside her when she received word that Johan had been seriously wounded and was hovering between life and death. Inside she felt frozen solid, and she didn't know whether she would ever thaw out again.

She looked down at Elin. It was quiet in the waiting room. By now it was undoubtedly all over the news: the story about the local reporter from Swedish TV who had been stabbed by one of the arrested perpetrators and who was now undergoing surgery at Visby Hospital.

She thought that this was her punishment for not accepting Johan and his love. She had shut him out. She now regretted doing that, but it was too late. The doctors had told her that he had internal bleeding as a result of multiple stab wounds to the abdomen. A team of doctors was working to save his life.

When the door to the intensive care unit opened, she gave such a start that Elin let go of her nipple.

A doctor came out. She recognized him. He was one of the doctors who had spoken to her earlier. He was a tall man, with a sympathetic air, maybe ten years older than she was. It was a long way to the door, which gave her time to study him. She realized that he was coming to talk to her. He had a loping gait; he was wearing white wooden clogs, and some of the polish had scuffed off the toes. She noticed that he was wearing a wedding ring. A ballpoint pen was sticking out of his breast pocket. Did doctors always have pens in their breast pockets? She couldn't remember ever seeing a doctor without one. He was suntanned, and he had those white rings around his eyes that people got from going sailing.

He looked at her. He came closer. He was only a few yards away. Should she fall over now? She ventured a glance up at his face. He was very close.

The sun was shining, Elin was sleeping, it was summer outside the window.

The doctor looked kind, but she couldn't read anything at all from his expression.

She felt him take her hand.

FRIDAY, AUGUST 13

Not that Knutas was superstitious, but the day's date hadn't gone unnoticed. Feeling rather despondent, he noted that his vacation was starting on Friday, the thirteenth of August. Rain was pouring down outside the windows of police headquarters. He had four weeks' vacation ahead of him. All that remained was for him to clear off his desk and compile his last report before he could put the shocking investigation behind him.

The court proceedings for charging Aron Bjarke and Eskil Rondahl had been held on Thursday and resulted in both of them being arrested for the murders of Martina Flochten, Staffan Mellgren, and Gunnar Ambjörnsson. The charges also included attempted murder, theft, breach of the laws regarding national cultural treasures, illegal threats, fencing of stolen goods, and animal abuse.

It was Aron who was thought to have carried out the actual murders. He was the stronger of the two brothers and the one more inclined to violence. Eskil handled the stolen goods operation, but he had also helped his brother with the homicides.

Both of them denied any crime, which made no real difference. There was strong evidence against them—both the testimony of witnesses and the technical evidence, including the plastic packages containing blood that were in Eskil Rondahl's freezer. Aron Bjarke's fingerprints had been found on both the packages and the freezer itself. The stolen gold armlet that had disappeared from the Antiquities Room was discovered among Eskil Rondahl's possessions at the farm in Hall, along with a large quantity of other artifacts that had gone missing from various excavation sites on Gotland. His computer, which contained information about the sale of relics, had been confiscated. In addition, there was the film that Pia Lilja had given to the police. At the farm in Hall the body of a standardbred stallion was found buried under a mound of dirt. The horse had been sent out to graze in the summer pastures at Sudret along with sixty other horses, and that was why it hadn't been missed. It had been transported alive to the farm and decapitated there. The clothing of the victims was found in a locked chest in the burned-out bedroom belonging to the brothers' parents.

After the arrest of the brothers at the farm in Hall, a whole new series of facts had emerged. It turned out that Staffan Mellgren belonged to a small group led by Aron Bjarke that practiced an extreme form of Æsir worship and shamanism. During the past week the police had succeeded in locating every single one of the twelve members. The little Æsir group existed solely in the minds of its members—there were no Web sites, no documents, and no group roster. Maybe that was how they had managed to keep it so secret. They had devoted themselves to an occult form of idol worship in which the blood sacrifice of various animals was a common practice. On the other hand, none of the other participants was aware that it had included human blood. Many were horribly shocked when they realized that they had drunk the blood of a former member, Staffan Mellgren.

During the interrogation, it emerged that the murder of Martina Flochten was apparently provoked by the controversy surrounding the plans for a hotel at Högklint, which was the group's most sacred site. When the plans became known, a conflict arose between the leader, Aron Bjarke, and Staffan Mellgren, who was regarded as the second in command of the group.

Bjarke wanted to take drastic measures to stop the construction, but Mellgren was opposed to the idea, and he persuaded the rest of the members to support his view. This schism then became a determining factor. Apparently Bjarke couldn't let go of his own ideas, which got stronger and stronger. When Patrick Flochten's daughter, Martina, started having a love affair with Mellgren, Bjarke saw an opportunity to administer a double blow.

Knutas had spoken with Agneta Larsvik, who was

convinced that the impending forensic psychiatric examination would show that both brothers were seriously unbalanced. According to her, Aron had manipulated Eskil into taking part in the murders. Eskil wouldn't have been capable of carrying them out alone. In terms of guilt, however, both had to be considered perpetrators of the crimes.

During the interrogation, which went on all week, an image of the brothers' childhood had emerged. Both had endured a difficult upbringing. They'd had trouble fitting in and were frequently bullied. Their parents had been devout Christians who had strict rules for everything in their home. If either of the boys broke a rule or did anything wrong, he was harshly punished. Physical violence was just as common as psychological abuse.

They had both managed to make it through school. It had gone better for Aron than for Eskil, because things came easier to him, and he was also more outgoing. The fact that he was a handsome boy helped him more than he realized. Aron had gone on to continue his education. He studied in Stockholm, and it was then that he came into contact with Æsir worshippers. His interest in ancient Nordic mythology went hand in hand with his interest in archaeology. His belief grew stronger over the years, and while in Stockholm he changed his last name to one that had more of an Æsir sound to it. When he returned to Gotland, he found some like-minded people through the college, and eventually they started the small extremist organization that shunned any other Æsir groups.

Aron awakened an interest in Æsir worship in his elder brother, who was still living with their parents, even though he was over fifty. The brothers were strongly influenced by their parents and remained utterly devoted to them when Aron moved back home. By taking part in the group meetings, Eskil began the process of liberating himself. All his life he had taken refuge in the artifacts that he worked with, and through them he had made contact with spiritual beings. He started having trouble distinguishing between what was real and what wasn't. He began regarding the artifacts as his own. He spent a lot of his free time sitting in front of the computer when he wasn't helping his parents on the farm, and after a while he discovered a market for ancient relics. He gradually started selling objects, and it went extremely well. Now and then he would go to Stockholm to meet a contact person. He made a lot of money on the thefts, and he used most of it for the farm.

Each of them had his own way of filling in the holes from his childhood—the lack of care and parental support and solace. Yet something more was needed to fill in the painful void. That was how the whole thing got started. Presumably the fire in which their parents had perished was the deciding factor. That was Knutas's theory, at any rate.

Prosecutor Birger Smittenberg thought there was

sufficient cause to reopen the investigation. In light of the summer's violent crimes, there was reason to suspect that the brothers had also set the fire that brought about the death of their parents.

Knutas put aside the last report.

He left police headquarters and walked out into the rain. He now had a week ahead of him out in the country with his family before the fall semester started for his children. Then he would be alone in the summer house and could spend his time doing woodwork and going fishing, which was his favorite pastime. When he was halfway home, the sky darkened and he heard thunder rumbling in the distance, over the sea.

Somehow that seemed just as it should be.

THE END

ACKNOWLEDGMENTS

Occasionally I have taken artistic liberties to change things for the benefit of the narrative. This includes Swedish TV's coverage of Gotland, which in the book has been moved to Stockholm. I have nothing but respect for Swedish TV's regional news program *Östnytt*, which covers Gotland with a permanent team stationed in Visby.

The settings in the book are almost all described as they actually appear in reality, although there are a few exceptions.

Any errors that may have slipped in are entirely my own.

First and foremost, I wish to thank my husband, journalist Cenneth Niklasson, for his loving support, tough criticism, and good ideas.

Thanks also to:

Gösta Svensson, former detective superintendent with the Visby police, for his invaluable help with all the police work.

Olle Hoffman, archaeologist, for his willingness to

share his expertise and information about his fascinating work.

Mikaela Säfvenberg, archaeologist and authorized guide.

Martin Cstalos, the Forensic Medicine Laboratory in Solna

Johan Gardelius and Bo Ekedahl, crime technicians, Visby police.

Håkan Onsjö, veterinarian

Ulf Åsgård, psychiatrist

Marie and Göthe Modin, managers of the Warfsholm hotel

My first readers for their valuable opinions:

Lena Allerstam, journalist, Swedish TV

Bosse Jungstedt, my brother, and Kerstin Jungstedt, my sister-in-law

Lilian Andersson, editor at Bonnier Educational Books

Anna-Maja Persson, journalist, Swedish TV

My publisher Jonas Axelsson and my editor Ulrika Åkerlund

Last, but not least, thanks to my wonderful children, Rebecka and Sebastian, for their great patience with their mother's writing.

Älta, June 2005
Mari Jungstedt